WESTERN GHOSTS

Haunting, Spine-Chilling Stories from the
American West

Edited by
Frank D. McSherry, Jr., Charles G. Waugh,
and Martin H. Greenberg

D1445614

Rutledge Hill Press
Nashville, Tennessee

Published in Nashville, Tennessee, by Rutledge Hill Press, Inc., 211 Seventh Avenue North, Nashville, Tennessee 37219.

Typography by Bailey Typography, Nashville, Tennessee
Cover design by Harriette Bateman

Library of Congress Cataloging-in-Publication Data

Western ghosts : haunting, spine-chilling stories from the American
    West / edited by Frank D. McSherry Jr., Charles G. Waugh, and Martin
    H. Greenberg.
        p.   cm.
    ISBN 1-55853-069-X
    1. Ghost stories, American — West (U.S.)   2. Western stories,
I. McSherry, Frank D. II. Waugh, Charles. III. Greenberg, Martin
Harry.
PS648.G48W4   1990   90-8072
813'.087408 — dc20   CIP

Manufactured in the United States of America
2 3 4 5 6 7 8 — 96 95 94 93

Table of Contents

Gone West

The frontier—the great American West—lived, had its days of glory, and died.

But its spirit—its ghost, you might say—still lives.

Its many ghosts.

The vast West is haunted by the great adventures, dramas, and conflicts said to create ghosts . . . or be shadowed by them.

Gen. Custer and the tattered remnants of his Seventh Cavalry are pinned down on a rounded hilltop in Montana while the surrounding Indian horde below forms for the last, overwhelming charge . . .

Four men stride steadily through the streets of Tombstone, Arizona, the icy, dusty wind making their yellow slickers flap. That's Marshall Wyatt Earp in the middle, star on his shirt and pistol in his hand, and Doc Holliday beside him, the skull-faced man carrying the sawed-off shotgun. Earp's brothers Virge and Morg flank them, striding toward another line of armed, silent men at the O. K. Corral . . .

The Donner Party, trapped by blizzards in the high passes of the Nevada Mountains, running out of food and thinking of the dead men outside the shelter, each more than a hundred pounds of frozen meat . . .

And the immigrants, coming in a never-ending wave, arrive pulling handcarts piled with their pitifully few belongings, more than a thousand miles from the Missouri River to the sea because they could not afford mules. They cross borders into the unknown, finding fulfillment of their dreams. Or their nightmares . . .

These themes of the great frontier—the search for a better life, greed for riches, combat to the death—pervade these tales of those eerie beings called ghosts.

In "Custer's Ghosts," an aging Indian who believes himself to be the last survivor of the Battle of the Little Bighorn, learns in 1926 that there is one more, a cavalryman who will be honored at a ceremony at the Custer Battlefield Memorial. And the ghosts of his ancestors speak to John-Walks-Across-the-Prairies: *The battle is not over yet. Kill!*

A love story is provided by Paul Gallico, author of the novel and film *The Poseidon Adventure.* An airliner is down, lost in the snow-covered mountains of Utah. The man Judith Shorell loves is aboard that plane, and she's convinced that the thin, ghostly voice she hears at night trying to reveal the plane's location is him. But she can't hear him clearly; there are too many ghostly voices, too much *interference.* Perhaps if she flew up, higher, higher, to where there is less static . . .

Harlan Ellison tells how the ghost of playgirl "Pretty Maggie Moneyeyes" comes to haunt a slot machine in Las Vegas and captures the neon-lit frenzy of modern-day gold hunting with accuracy and skill.

Pulitzer prize winner Oliver La Farge gives a gentle tale of an aging archeologist whose important discoveries in New Mexico's Navajo villages are made by means unusual indeed.

And more.

It is not surprising that the themes of the western frontier should blend so well with the ghost story. For what does a ghost symbolize but a frontier, into a dark and unknown land filled with dangers and hopes where travelers may find the fulfillment of their dreams.

Or their nightmares.

The spirit, at least, of the great American West—the drive to build a better life—is with us yet. It lives on, ghost-like and undying.

—Frank D. McSherry, Jr.
McAlester, Oklahoma

WESTERN GHOSTS

Most people don't want ghosts in their homes, but Miss Annie would do anything to keep hers. Anything.

ONE

Harry's Ghost
Talmage Powell

Harry's ghostly visitations became the focus of Miss Annie's unhappy life. She anticipated his ectoplasm with the breathlessness of a schoolgirl, and if several evenings passed without a sign from him, she was more miserably lonely than before.

Now that she was in the twilight of her life, she'd had nothing but memories bleak and barren of all the years BH (Before Harry).

It could have been so different, she would think bitterly. Certainly no spot on earth should have been more conducive to happiness than the southern California, Pasadena to be precise, into which she had been born.

It was the Eden in those days, the irresistible lure that had drawn, like flies to the honey pot, the despoiling millions who had cut the flower-quilted hillsides, smothered the orange groves in concrete, piled the spaghetti-tangled morass of freeways for the insane rushing multitudes, and blanketed the friendliest sun on earth with a poisonous curtain of smog.

Those days . . . a lazy interurban between Pasadena and downtown Los Angeles, strollers window shopping on Colorado Avenue, where the bus station was furnished with over-stuffed couches and chairs like a friendly living room, radishes two cents a bunch, avocados for a nickle, families dining on the front porch of a house that had been converted into a neighborhood cafe, a war between oil companies reducing gasoline prices to nothing for the guzzling Stutz or Dusenberg or Cadillac, a morning tobogganing on

1

pristine snow in the mountains and driving past olive and date groves on your way home that evening to the perfume of flowers and the welcoming nod of palm trees.

But only in retrospect was Miss Annie aware . . . the shadow of papa, from her first squalling breath to the end of his days, had been her reality.

Why couldn't he have died early-on, that martinet she called papa, when she still had time to realize that she, too, was a person? But he hadn't, and she hadn't. And she couldn't at last explain how it had all happened, this process she called her life. The years had somehow simply crept away, in his shadow, in the sound of his voice, cautioning, warning of the evils of the world, opening her eyes to the filth of the young males, claiming her time and attention, making her aware of how much she owed him, how dutiful she must be, how he was poor, dear papa.

And when he had finally died, it had been too late. And her reward had been endless hours of days in which to dwell on the past, her only security three small houses in an old section.

Life had certainly changed for Miss Annie after the advent of Harry. It was no longer a dull gray abyss. Nothing in this three-dimensional realm could equal the experience of having a real live ghost for one's own, especially one as nice as Harry. And only the confirmed addict of an hallucinatory drug might have comprehended Miss Annie's wracking anxieties during those periods when Harry refused to appear.

Then, just as Miss Annie was about to succumb to despair, the first swirl of ectoplasm would glimmer in the narrow, dark hallway or in a corner of the kitchen.

Miss Annie would rise from her inner ashes, blood stirring in her old, stiff veins, the most delicious fright and fascination searing through her brittle bones and wrinkled-parchment tissues.

Neither her reaction nor Harry's existence perturbed her in the least. It was inconceivable that anyone could fail to respond to such a dear as Harry. And on the second point, Harry's existence, to Miss Annie's way of thinking, was no more surprising than this year's rebirth of the tiger lily that had died last autumn.

"Harry?" she would say through the pulse beating in her

thin, bony neck. Then her dentures would click as her soft, chiding smile belied her sternly wagging finger: "You've been a very naughty young man, Harry, staying away so long. I was on the point of moving out, like the others. How would you like that?"

The quick shimmering of ectoplasm hinted that he wouldn't like it at all. He partially succeeded in materializing there in the dim hallway, a quivering, uncertain image of a tall, thin, clean cut young man with dark hair and the imprint of deep sorrow on his gaunt face.

He was trying to tell her something. He was always trying to tell her.

She stood with eyes enrapt, her heart beating in wild excitement. From crown to toe she came to tingling life. Emotions, long banked like embers of half-forgotten fires, sputtered and flamed. She ached with the desire to know his secret, but she was in the same moment torn with the fear that if he ever managed to reveal it he would go away forever.

"Harry. . . ." She could barely whisper above her shortness of breath. "What is it like? Is there day and night? Cold and hot? Harry, please!"

But his grip weakened on forces beyond her own space-time continuum, and his already-fuzzy image melted and slipped away, until there was just a wisp of ectoplasm coiling and writhing a dozen feet from her face.

"Oh, Harry . . . Harry . . ." she sobbed faintly, and then the hallway was quite empty.

Miss Annie returned to limp awareness of her surroundings. With a petulant little sigh, she turned toward the living room. It hadn't been a good visitation, not at all. If Harry would only try as hard to get here as she expended the effort to bring him—

She started slightly as the front door chimes sounded. Frowning at the unexpected event of someone calling on her, she crossed the living room.

She opened the door on a tall, lean young man who was dressed in dark denim slacks and a blue peajacket.

"Miss Annie Loxton?"

She nodded, struck by the strange sense of familiarity aroused by his gaunt face and shock of dark hair.

"I'm Horace Grimshaw," he said. "Harry's brother."

That explained it. She expelled a tiny breath. Peered at closely, he wasn't Harry at all. Though similar on the surface, the cast of Horace's features, the charisma, contrasted with Harry. Horace was tougher, that was the word. Harder bitten. More capable of meeting the world's cruelty head-on.

"If you don't mind, Miss Annie," he was saying, "I'd like to talk to you."

"Of course," she said quickly. "Do come in."

He surveyed the modest living room with a glance as he entered. This was the first time he'd been in the house where Harry had died, and a tightness tugged the corner of his mouth.

"Please sit down, Mr. Grimshaw. Would you like some coffee?"

"No, thanks. Just some talk about Harry, if it's okay."

She nodded, watching him sit down in the barrel-backed chair near the window. He was bigger boned than Harry. Big knuckles. Big wrists thrusting a half-inch from the sleeves of the worn seaman's jacket as he bent his arms and rested his elbows on the chair arms.

"I didn't know that Harry had a brother," she said.

"We haven't seen each other in a long while. I was working on a scabby island freighter in the Celebes and Banda Seas when news of his death finally reached me."

She slipped into a chair opposite him, blue-veined, chicken-claw old hands folded tightly in her lap. She saw the grief-darkness in his face, and she felt she should say something. But she didn't know what would be entirely appropriate. The dull gray years, devoid of human fellowship and communication, had hardly trained her in the art of consoling a saddened stranger.

He pushed aside his remote moment, lifting his eyes. "They say that Harry killed himself."

"Yes," she murmured.

"Here in this house. In the basement. They say he hanged himself in the basement."

"Please, Mr. Grimshaw. It happened weeks ago. It's all over and done."

His weather-tanned young face studied her a moment.

His lips had the look of being chiseled from ice. For an instant, he was just a little frightening.

"I knew my brother, Miss Annie. I don't believe he would have done such a thing. I don't honestly think he had the guts."

Her watery blue eyes glanced away. She was beginning to dislike Harry's brother. To talk of Harry in such terms, as if it was Horace who possessed all the intestinal fortitude in the family.

"You rented the house to him," Horace said.

"Yes," Miss Annie nodded. "To him and his wife. She left him shortly afterward, for another man, I think. He continued on in a bachelor existence, with a cleaning woman in twice a week. It was she who found him—the cleaning woman, I mean. Later, Harry's ex-wife came and claimed their things."

"Do you know where she is now?"

"No, Mr. Grimshaw. Such affairs are not my business. She had a legal paper. She took their belongings. That's the last I've seen of her."

He'd assessed Miss Annie's tone.

"Good riddance?" he suggested.

She refolded her hands.

"If you wish to put it that way," she said stiffly. "I think your brother was a far finer person than his wife was."

"Were you here when she took the things away?"

"Naturally, and so was a detective. I rented the house partially furnished, and I had to watch after my own things. Later. . . ."

"Yes, Miss Annie?"

She straightened her thin shoulders an inch. "Well, the next two tenants didn't stay long. They—they claimed Harry was still here, making little noises in the plaster and sometimes glowing in the dark. Well, not glowing exactly. Kind of a shower of sparks. Like those childrens' toys, sparklers."

He waited, and she felt the need to break the sudden silence.

She stifled her sense of aggravation with him and forced herself to speak calmly. "I didn't believe it myself, Mr. Grimshaw. But the tenants kept running, so to speak, and I had to have my rents. My father left me three little cottages like this one. It's all I have. So, if I could not keep this one rented, I decided to move in myself and rent out the one in which I'd lived. It worked out nicely. Good tenants in the other places, and I like it here, very much."

"Even with Harry around?"

She bristled inwardly at the faint scorn in his voice, but before she could tell him how much she liked having Harry around, he was on a new tack.

"My brother worked for an outfit called Happy Havens, I believe."

"An executive director," Miss Annie said proudly. "And a wonderful organization it is, too. They build and support nursing homes, for helpless senior citizens without kin or money."

"They'd conducted a big fund drive just before Harry's death," Horace said. "Is that correct?"

"Yes, that is true."

"And forty thousand dollars showed up short when all the collections were in and the kitty totaled up."

Miss Annie looked at the pulsing blue veins on her tight knuckles and wished Horace would go away.

Remorse over the forty thousand in embezzled funds was what had killed Harry. Too nice. Too fine. Too decent and honest to go against his own conscience, no matter what had been his reasons in his once-in-a-lifetime moment of weakness and temptation.

"The police tell me, Miss Annie, that they never did recover the forty thousand. Could Harry have reconciled with his wife? She's quite a beauty, I hear. Could she have talked to him, coaxed him, worn him down, conned him into taking the money?"

"A Jezebel," Miss Annie whispered. "Filthy creature of her sex!"

"What was that, Miss Annie?"

"I think," she said, lifting her eyes, "that Harry was deeply infatuated with her at one time, but I think he got over her when she left."

"You saw him often?"

"Whenever I collected the rents."

"But you noticed a change in him?"

"Yes. He seemed harried, absent-minded when I first rented them the house. After she left he seemed to find a sense of relief. His color was better. He gained a little weight."

He cut a side glance. "You seem to have noticed a lot, Miss Annie."

"I was fond of your brother, Mr. Grimshaw. He didn't treat me like a prune-faced landlady. In all my life—"

Again he waited. And she pinked, wondering how she could be so open to a perfect stranger.

"I won't trouble you with the details of my life, Mr. Grimshaw. Sufficient to say that I was a shy, sickly, ugly little girl. My mother died, and I never escaped the shadow of my father, who rather despised me and felt that I was incapable of coping with the world. To sum up, it hasn't been much of a life, and your brother was one of the rare people who looked at me and saw a person, who seemed to understand—"

She broke off. Horace, unlike his brother, lacked that particular empathy. Horace's eyes held a nearly hidden chill, as if he found her soft voice repugnant.

"If there's nothing more, Mr. Grimshaw—"

But before she could rise and dismiss him, he said, "There is more. A lot more. In seaman's language, I'm not—but I'd better not use any seaman's language, Miss Annie. Let's just say that I'm not satisfied with a lot of things."

"As?"

"The note my brother was supposed to have left, for one thing. The suicide note, saying he had stolen the money, realized later that he was bound to get caught, and simply couldn't stand the prospect of scandal, shame, and prison." The chair creaked slightly under his shifting weight. "The note was typewritten, Miss Annie. Anyone can type a note."

"But it had his signature."

"Which gets us to the nitty-gritty," he said. "If Harry didn't take the money or write the note, then it had to be someone who had both access to the money and to Harry's signature so it could be copied."

"You're dismissing his wife?"

"For the moment. The other angle narrows down the suspects to people within or close to Happy Havens. How many people were there in executive directorships or posts above that?"

"Three at the time, I think. Harry, and a Mr. Philbin, and Mr. James Fellows who lives third house down the street," Miss Annie said. "Harry and Mr. Fellows used to take turns driving their cars and riding to work together."

"And while they're riding along," Horace said, "this guy Fellows, sick to death with the boring details and fawning over contributors and the low pay that goes with every charity job, this guy decides to grab a big fat plum while he's got the chance to use the trusting, dumb cluck on the car seat beside him for a fall guy."

"But the police—"

"Do their routine and are promptly swamped with a dozen, a hundred, a million other crimes. Sure, they look for the missing money. They figure every place Harry might have put it. They go over every crack here in the house he occupied. But he is hanging by the neck in his own basement and a note with his signature says he did it and the missing money is another unanswered detail in an already cluttered file."

"But they questioned the others!"

"For hours," Horace agreed. "Probably searched their premises, too. And no doubt really put the ex-wife over the coals. But the question of the money remains, and if I knew that soft-sister Harry he would have gone crawling back with it instead of killing himself."

Miss Annie thought: Philbin? She knew him only through Happy Havens publicity releases that had appeared in the newspapers. A frail little man, very old, very gray. Far too weak to have hanged Harry.

Fellows? James Fellows? A far different case, indeed! He had been here a time or two when she'd dropped by for the rent. Big, jovial. Too hearty, that was Fellows. The back-slapper. The glad-hander.

Oh, by all means, now that she came to think of it. Fellows. A big, broad smile for big contributors whose wealth he secretly envied. An ogling phony and four flusher, her instincts had told her that the first time she'd met him.

"A penny, Miss Annie?" Horace's words nudged into her thoughts.

"For my thoughts?" She arose stiffly, and crossed to the window. She slipped back the drape and looked at the Fellows house down the street. Modest, like the rest of them on the block. But the lawn needed cutting, and there was Mrs. Fellows coming out the front door. Sexpot blonde in those dreadful hotpants. Cheap and vulgar. Crossing to the Fellows car, which was too flashy for Mr. Fellows's salary.

Miss Annie recognized her suspicion as just that. A suspicion. But it was possible. Fellows was cunning enough and strong enough to have pulled it off. Fellows could have taken the money and before the theft was discovered he could have strolled over for a chat with Harry that unspeakable evening.

Fellows could easily have overpowered an unsuspecting Harry, knocked him out, carried him unconscious to the basement. When he departed, Fellows could have left the forged suicide note which he'd prepared in advance. And Harry, slowly turning left and slowly turning right, his neck secured by the rope to the overhead waterpipe . . . .

Then Fellows simply waits, bides his time until the "heat was off" as the late movies put it. In due time Fellows manages to get himself fired at Happy Havens and, quite naturally, fades from sight—with his blonde and the forty thousand dollars bought with Harry's life.

Miss Annie didn't know she was biting her knuckles until Horace tapped her shoulder and said sharply, "Miss Annie, what is this you're mumbling? About Harry being here, about Harry trying to tell you—?"

She turned, tears in irregular course on the bleached crocodile leather of her face. "He is here, Mr. Grimshaw. Harry really is here. If you don't believe me, ask the previous tenants, the ones who rented the house after he was hanged."

Horace was stilled for a moment. He crept a glance over his shoulder.

"I don't see him, Miss Annie."

"Oh, for heaven's sake," she shrilled, jerking away from his touch. "You're like so many other people. To you, I'm

9

just an old prune-face. Pixillated now. Old, you know. A little cracked. Imagining things. Well, I don't imagine a blessed thing, you foolish and cruel young man. I don't see Harry, either, when he isn't there. Only when he is able to materialize. But not with creakings in the walls, not as a dime store sparkler in the dark. Not with me, young fellow! Harry and I understand each other, something that you would never comprehend. With understanding, Harry and I have almost bridged the gap."

She hobbled over to a chair, feeling suddenly weak.

"Miss Annie—"

"No! Just go. You don't believe and—"

"But maybe I do, Miss Annie." His shadow fell across her chair. "I've seen some kookie things in the Celebes. Things I can't account for. Things science can't explain. Miss Annie, let me come back. If my brother is present, you owe me the privilege of coming back."

She didn't want him to come back. She didn't want him around. She was content to be alone in the house, with Harry's ghost.

She drew her head to one side, looking up at him from the corners of her eyes. He seemed quite serious, not making fun of her at all.

"Harry was all the kin I had, Miss Annie. Parents dead. No wife. No real friends. Just some guys and chicks I knew knocking around in the south seas. Nobody but Harry, Miss Annie."

"Very well," she relented reluctantly. "You may come and see him—if he appears."

"Does he favor certain times?"

"Not precisely. He doesn't call by appointment."

"Certain places here in the house?"

"The hallway, the kitchen, and the basement, where he was hanged."

"Murdered, Miss Annie."

"Murdered," she said.

They sat quietly in the confines of the basement with its earthen smell and feel of dusty cobwebs. It was the second evening in a row that they'd sat here for two-hour stretches. Eight o'clock to ten o'clock each night. Thinking back over the visitations, Miss Annie had concluded that Harry favored the hour of nine. It was the hour, the coroner had officially reported, when Harry's life had been surrendered to the length of rope and water pipe.

They sat on two old kitchen chairs that had been stored in the basement, just the two of them. Miss Annie near the foot of the narrow, steep stairs and Horace a few feet away. There was no sign of Harry, and nothing broke the silence, until Horace remarked, "Not like a regular seance, Miss Annie. No tilting table. No joining of hands and calling up the spirits."

"I don't believe in such humbug, Horace."

"Neither do I."

"Now and then a being such as Harry is forced to return. That's what I believe. And dishes fly off the shelves to make a poltergeist's presence known."

"It's happened in some well-authenticated instances," Horace agreed, "with even hard-headed cops and newspaper reporters on hand to witness the knockings."

Miss Annie's silence dropped the subject. In a moment, she stirred, watching the brief emergence of Horace's hard-bitten young face in the glow of his cigarette.

"Horace?"

"Yes, Miss Annie?"

"Was there bad blood between you and Harry?"

"Why do you ask, Miss Annie?"

"I'm not sure, except that he doesn't seem inclined to appear while you're present."

"No, Miss Annie. Nothing like that. Frankly, I used to make him out a sissy sometimes, but I think that deep down he knew that I did admire other qualities he had."

"Then we shall wait."

"Right on, Miss Annie."

He finished his cigarette and ground it under his heel.

"It's after nine, Miss Annie. I don't think—"

"Shhhh!" It was a softly barked expletive, cutting him short, freezing him in his chair. "I feel that strange warmth, Horace, that tingling of life, that sensation quite unlike any

11

other I've ever known . . . There, Horace! Near the water heater!"

Horace stumbled to his feet, toppling his chair. In the dim corner at which Miss Annie was pointing the first thin tendril of ectoplasm threshed like the body of a headless, silvery glowing snake.

The manifestation eeled and crawled its way through the space-time warp. It grew, eddied, steadied. It strained itself into shape, shimmering unsteadily.

"Harry," Miss Annie said to the image, "your brother Horace has come all the way from the south seas to see you."

The image quivered a greeting to Horace, and Horace, supporting himself with one hand against a brick pillar, got his sea legs under him.

"Hello, Harry," Horace said. "I'm sorry it has to be like this, under these circumstances."

Harry darkened, sharing Horace's sentiment.

Horace had strength to push away from the basement support.

"I want to help you, Harry. I know it must be hell, trapped the way you are," Horace said.

Harry brightened perceptibly.

"Okay," Horace said on a deep breath, "I know you can't stick around long at a time, so let's hit the point. You can move up and down, and you can move side to side. I've got some questions. Move up and down for a yes answer, side to side for a no. Can do?"

Harry moved up and down fitfully.

"Swell," Horce said. "First off, were you murdered?"

Yes, Harry replied.

"By your wife?"

No.

"By someone at Happy Havens who wanted to steal money safely, using you for a patsy?"

Yes, Harry answered with a quick up-down bob of his disembodied reflection.

"Was it James Fellows?"

Yes, yes, yes!

Miss Annie was drawing to her feet, breathless spectator, her gaze dashing from brother to brother.

"Fellows is now just waiting his chance to leave without suspicion," Horace pressed on, "taking the forty thousand dollars with him?"

Yes, Harry replied.

"You must get around in a brand new way nowadays," Horace said. "Walls can't stop you. Have you looked in on the Fellowses?"

Yes.

"Do you know where he's got the money hidden?"

Yes.

Horace paused, taking breath. Harry could signal only positive or negative responses, and Horace spent a moment framing his questions.

"Is the money stashed in a safety deposit box?"

No.

"Bus station locker, maybe?" Horace said.

No.

"In his house?"

Yes, yes!

"None of the usual hiding places," Horace mused to himself, "or the cops would have found it."

"Horace," Miss Annie remarked, "Harry is slipping away. He's barely hanging on. I can tell."

"Harry, stick with us," Horace pleaded. "If all the furniture were taken out of the house, would the money still be in there?"

Yes.

"In the attic?"

No.

"Basement?"

No.

"In the walls?"

No.

Horace looked a bit helplessly at Miss Annie. "What other parts of a house—" He suddenly bit the words off, snapped his fingers. Then asked, "The floor, Harry?"

Yes.

"He spread the money and hid it with an inlay of fresh tile?"

No. And again No, as if Horace were the biggest dummy on the high seas.

"Then the carpet . . ." Horace said. "Sure! Fellows just loosened the edge of the carpet, rolled it back, spread the money, and then refastened the wall-to-wall carpeting!"

Yes. In capitals. A bob from floor to partially through the ceiling. Then the movement became a swirl, and the swirl a vortex, and the vortex was sucked into empty space. Harry was gone, and a silence came to the basement.

Miss Annie felt Horace's touch on her arm. They looked at each other in the dimness filtering down the narrow stairs. Then, silently, they started up, Miss Annie in the lead.

When they were halfway up, Horace remarked, "Somehow we've got to figure a way to get the police to roll back every inch of floor covering in the Fellows house. Can't very well tell them a ghost told us to do so."

"No, we can't," Miss Annie agreed. She struggled to the top of the stairs, reaching for the door jamb.

"We'll figure a way," Horace said confidently, "even if I have to sneak into the Fellows house when they're away and call the cops from there, after I've uncovered the money. And the money will put the guilt where it belongs."

"It surely will, Horace," said Miss Annie.

"And that will certainly balance whatever cosmic forces we're dealing with. Don't you see? Harry is trapped where he is, but when we restore the cosmic balance, it should release Harry, forever."

Framed in the doorway at the top of the stairs, Miss Annie stopped and turned.

"What is this you're saying, Horace?"

A couple of stair treads below her, he looked up at her wiry figure.

"I'm an amateur at this sort of thing, exorcising ghosts, getting messages from the great beyond," he admitted. "But we can be sure of one thing, Harry is stuck. And Harry is tormented with the need to see his murderer brought to justice. And while he was visible to us, he gave me the strongest impression that justice for his murderer would complete the equation, put things in balance. He was trying to let me, his brother, know that it was the one way I could help him get unstuck. I'm certain of that."

"Justice for his murderer," Miss Annie murmured, "and Harry is chased away for good."

"Released, Miss Annie," Horace corrected. "He'll never bother you again or chase away another tenant."

"I'm sorry, Horace," Miss Annie said in that instant that she put out her hands and pushed him with all her wiry old strength.

She saw the look of surprise on his face as Horace went over backward and fell all the way to the bottom, bumping and banging. She flinched when his head struck the bottom step and he came to rest in an awkward pile of outflung arms and twisted legs.

She slipped down the stairs quickly. She'd expected, at the very least, that the fall would stun him, give her the advantage, offer her time enough to grab the handaxe from the tool cabinet and finish the job. But as she knelt beside him, she saw that the most, not the least, had happened. He was dead. His skull had cracked and was seeping red.

Now all that remained was the burial of Horace, here in the basement. He had no relatives, no friends. He was a stranger in the city for whom no one would come asking. No one would ever know.

Then, still in her kneeling position beside Horace, she sensed a presence. She turned her head a few inches and in the further corner of the basement, she saw the first spark, a little burst of stardust against the darkness.

"Harry," she said, rising slowly and reaching out entreating hands, "I simply had to do it. I couldn't take a chance that Horace was right, that you'd go away if Fellows was brought to justice. I'd die, Harry, before I'd risk the destruction of the only relationship I ever had . . . ."

Her words faltered. The nice, strange warmth had failed to come. Instead, a breath of inter-spacial zero oozed through the basement.

And she knew. As the form before her materialized, the full truth flowed suddenly through her mind. This wasn't Harry. This was Horace, trapped hellishly in cosmic imbalance. This was a Horace transformed to raw wrath and a dark, boundless thirst for revenge.

And Miss Annie started screaming.

A former reporter, Talmage Powell was born in North Carolina in 1920. A graduate of the University of North Carolina, he sold his first story, a mystery, in 1943; he has since sold more than six hundred short stories, as well as television and film scripts, children's books, and more than twenty novels. *The author of* Written for Hitchcock *(1989), his stories are tightly told, suspenseful, and filled with surprises.*

With a last desperate act any gambler could understand, Kostner won a fortune—and paid the ultimate price.

TWO

Pretty Maggie Moneyeyes

Harlan Ellison

With an eight hold-card and a queen showing, with the dealer showing a four up, Kostner decided to let the house do the work. So he stood, and the dealer turned up. Six.

The dealer looked like something out of a 1935 George Raft film: Arctic diamond-chip eyes, manicured fingers long as a brain surgeon's, straight black hair slicked flat away from the forehead. He did not look up as he peeled them off. A three. Another three. A five. Twenty-one, and Kostner saw his last thirty dollars—six five-dollar chips—scraped on the edge of the cards, into the dealer's chip racks. Busted. Flat. Down and out in Las Vegas, Nevada. Playground of the Western World.

He slid off the comfortable stool-chair and turned his back on the blackjack table. The action was already starting again, like waves closing over a drowned man. He had been there, was gone, and no one had noticed. No one had seen a man blow the last tie with salvation. Kostner now had his choice: he could bum his way into Los Angeles and try to find something that resembled a new life . . . or he could go blow his brains out through the back of his head.

Neither choice showed much light or sense.

He thrust his hands deep into the pockets of his worn and dirty chinos and started away down the line of slot machines clanging and rattling on the other side of the aisle between blackjack tables.

He stopped. He felt something in his pocket. Beside him,

but all-engrossed, a fiftyish matron in electric lavender ca-
pris, high heels and Ship'n'Shore blouse was working two
slots, loading and pulling one while waiting for the other to
clock down. She was dumping quarters from a seemingly
inexhaustible supply from a Dixie cup held in her left hand.
There was a surrealistic presence to the woman. She was
almost automated, not a flicker of expression on her face,
the eyes fixed and unwavering. Only when the gong rang,
someone down the line had pulled a jackpot, did she look
up. And at that moment Kostner knew what was wrong and
immoral and deadly about Vegas, about legalized gambling,
about setting the traps all baited and open in front of the
average human. The woman's face was gray with hatred,
envy, lust and dedication to the game—in that timeless instant when she heard another drugged soul down the line
winning a minuscule jackpot. A jackpot that would only lull
the player with words like *luck* and *ahead of the game*. The
jackpot lure; the sparkling, bobbling, many-colored wiggler
in a sea of poor fish.

The thing in Kostner's pocket was a silver dollar.

He brought it out and looked at it.

The eagle was hysterical.

But Kostner pulled to an abrupt halt, only one half-
footstep from the sign indicating the limits of Tap City. He
was still with it. What the high-rollers called the edge, the
vigorish, the fine hole-card. One buck. One cartwheel.
Pulled out of the pocket not half as deep as the pit into
which Kostner had just been about to plunge.

What the hell, he thought, and turned to the row of slot
machines.

He had thought they'd all been pulled out of service, the
silver-dollar slots. A shortage of coinage, said the United
States Mint. But right there, side-by-side with the nickel
and quarter bandits, was one cartwheel machine. Two-
thousand-dollar jackpot. Kostner grinned foolishly. If you're
gonna go out, go out like a champ.

He thumbed the silver dollar into the coin slot and
grabbed the heavy, oiled handle. Shining cast aluminum
and pressed steel. Big black plastic ball. Angled for arm-
ease, pull it all day and you won't get weary.

Without a prayer in the universe, Kostner pulled the handle.

She had been born in Tucson, mother full-blooded Cherokee, father a bindlestiff on his way through. Mother had been working a truckers' stop, father had popped for spencer steak and sides. Mother had just gotten over a bad scene, indeterminate origins, unsatisfactory culminations. Mother had popped for bed. And sides. Margaret Annie Jessie had come nine months later; black of hair, fair of face, and born into a life of poverty. Twenty-three years later, a determined product of Miss Clairol and Berlitz, a dream-image formed by Vogue and intimate association with the rat race, Margaret Annie Jessie had become a contraction.
Maggie.

Long legs, trim and coltish; hips a trifle large, the kind that promote that specific thought in men, about getting their hands around it; belly flat, isometrics; waist cut to the bone, waist that works in any style from dirndl to disco-slacks; no breasts—all nipple, but no breast, like an expensive whore (the way O'Hara pinned it)—and no padding . . . forget the cans, baby, there's other, more important action; smooth, Michelangelo-sculpted neck, a pillar, proud; and all that face:

Outthrust chin, perhaps a tot too much belligerence, but if you'd walloped as many gropers, you too, honey: narrow mouth, petulant lower lip, nice to chew on, a lower lip as though filled with honey, bursting, ready for things to happen; a nose that threw the right sort of shadow, flaring nostrils, the acceptable words—aquiline, Patrician, classic, allathat; cheekbones as stark and promontory as a spit of land after ten years of open ocean; cheekbones holding darkness like narrow shadows, sooty beneath the taut-fleshed bone structure, amazing cheekbones, the whole face, really; simple uptilted eyes, the touch of the Cherokee, eyes that looked out at you, as you looked in at them, like someone peering out of the keyhole as you peered in; actually, dirty eyes, they said: you can get it.

Blonde hair, a great deal of it, wound and rolled and smoothed and flowing, in the old style, the page-boy thing

19

men always admire; no tight little cap of slicked plastic; no ratted and teased Everest of bizarre coiffure; no ironed-flat discothèque hair like number 3 flat noodles. Hair, the way a man wants it, so he can dig his hands in at the base of the neck and pull all that face very close.

An operable woman, a working mechanism, a rigged and sudden machinery of softness and motivation.

Twenty-three, and determined as hell never to abide in that vale of poverty her mother had called purgatory for her entire life; snuffed out in a grease fire in the last trailer, somewhere in Arizona, thank God no more pleas for a little money from babygirl Maggie hustling drinks in a Los Angeles topless joint. (There ought to be some remorse in there somewhere, for a Mommy gone where all the good grease-fire victims go. Look around, you'll find it.)

Maggie.

Genetic freak. Mommy's Cherokee uptilted eyeshape, and Polack quickscrewing Daddy Withouta-Name's blue-as-innocence color.

Blue-eyed Maggie, dyed blonde, alla that face, alla that leg, fifty bucks a night can get it and it sounds like it's having a climax.

Irish-innocent blue-eyed French-legged innocent Maggie. Polack. Cherokee. Irish. All-woman and going on the market for this month's rent on the stucco pad, eighty bucks' worth of groceries, a couple of months' worth for a Mustang, three appointments with the specialist in Beverly Hills about that shortness of breath after a night on the hustle-bump the sticky thigh the disco lurch the gotcha sweat: woman minutes. Increments under the meat; perspiration purchases, yeah it does.

Maggie, Maggie, Maggie, pretty Maggie Moneyeyes, who came from Tucson and trailers and rheumatic fever and a surge to live that was all kaleidoscope frenzy of clawing scrabbling no-nonsense. If it took lying on one's back and making sounds like a panther in the desert, then one did it, because nothing, but nothing, was as bad as being dirt poor, itchy-skinned, soiled-underwear, scuff-toed, hairy and ashamed lousy with the no-gots. Nothing!

Maggie. Hooker. Hustler. Grabber. Swinger. If there's a

buck in it, there's rhythm and the onomatopoeia is Maggie Maggie Maggie.

She who puts out. For a price, whatever.

Maggie was dating Nuncio. He was Sicilian. He had dark eyes and an alligator-grain wallet with slip-in pockets for credit cards. He was a spender, a sport, a high-roller. They went to Vegas.

Maggie and the Sicilian. Her blue eyes and his slip-in pockets. But mostly her blue eyes.

The spinning reels behind the three long glass windows blurred, and Kostner knew there wasn't a chance. Two-thousand-dollar jackpot. Round and round, whirring. Three bells or two bells and a jackpot bar, get 18; three plums or two plums and a jackpot bar, get 14; three oranges or two oranges and a jac—

Ten, five, two bucks for a single cherry cluster in first position. Something . . . I'm drowning. . . . Something . . .

The whirring . . .

Round and round. . . .

As something happened that was not considered in the pit-boss manual.

The reels whipped and snapped to a stop, clank clank clank, tight in place.

Three bars looked up at Kostner. But they did not say JACKPOT. They were three bars on which stared three blue eyes. Very blue, very immediate, very JACKPOT!!

Twenty silver dollars clattered into the payoff trough at the bottom of the machine. An orange light flicked on in the Casino Cashier's cage, bright orange on the jackpot board. And the gong began clanging overhead.

The Slot Machine Floor Manager nodded once to the Pit Boss, who pursed his lips and started toward the seedy-looking man still standing with his hand on the slot's handle.

The token payment—twenty silver dollars—lay untouched in the payoff trough. The balance of the jackpot—one thousand nine hundred and eighty dollars—would be paid manually, by the Casino Cashier. And Kostner stood, dumbly, as the three blue eyes stared up at him.

There was a moment of idiotic disorientation, as Kostner

stared back at the three blue eyes: a moment in which the slot machine's mechanisms registered to themselves; and the gong was clanging furiously.

All through the hotel casino people turned from their games to stare. At the roulette tables the white-on-white players from Detroit and Cleveland pulled their watery eyes away from the clattering ball, and stared down the line for a second, at the ratty-looking guy in front of the slot machine. From where they sat, they could not tell it was a two grand pot, and their rheumy eyes went back into billows of cigar smoke, and that little ball.

The blackjack hustlers turned momentarily, screwing around in their seats, and smiled. They were closer to the slot-players in temperament, but they knew the slots were a dodge to keep the old ladies busy, while the players worked toward their endless twenty-ones.

And the old dealer, who could no longer cut it at the fast-action boards, who had been put out to pasture by a grateful management, standing at the Wheel of Fortune near the entrance to the casino, even he paused in his zombie-murmuring ("Annnnother winner onna Wheel of For-chun!") to no one at all, and looked toward Kostner and that incredible gong-clanging. Then, in a moment, still with no players, he called *another* nonexistent winner.

Kostner heard the gong from far away. It had to mean he had won two thousand dollars, but that was impossible. He checked the payoff chart on the face of the machine. Three bars labeled JACKPOT meant JACKPOT. Two thousand dollars.

But these three bars did not say JACKPOT. They were three gray bars, rectangular in shape, with a blue eye directly in the center of each bar.

Blue eyes?

Somewhere, a connection was made, and electricity, a billion volts of electricity, was shot through Kostner. His hair stood on end, his fingertips bled raw, his eyes turned to jelly, and every fiber in his musculature became radioactive. Somewhere, out there, in a place that was not this place, Kostner had been inextricably bound to—to someone. Blue eyes?

The gong had faded out of his head, the constant noise level of the casino, chips chittering, people mumbling, dealers calling plays, it had all gone, and he was imbedded in silence.

Tied to that someone else, out there somewhere, through those three blue eyes.

Then in an instant, it had passed, and he was alone again, as though released by a giant hand, the breath crushed out of him. He staggered up against the slot machine.

"You all right, fellah?"

A hand gripped him by the arm, steadied him. The gong was still clanging overhead somewhere, and he was breathless from a journey he had just taken. His eyes focused and he found himself looking at the stocky pit boss who had been on duty while he had been playing blackjack.

"Yeah . . . I'm okay, just a little dizzy is all."

"Sounds like you got yourself a big jackpot, fellah," the pit boss grinned. It was a leathery grin; something composed of stretched muscles and conditioned reflexes, totally mirthless.

"Yeah . . . great. . . ." Kostner tried to grin back. But he was still shaking from that electrical absorption that had kidnapped him.

"Let me check it out," the pit boss was saying, edging around Kostner, and staring at the face of the slot machine. "Yeah, three jackpot bars, all right. You're a winner."

Then it dawned on Kostner! Two thousand dollars! He looked down at the slot machine and saw—

Three bars, each with the word JACKPOT on it. No blue eyes, just words that meant money. Kostner looked around frantically, was he losing his mind? *From somewhere, not in the casino room, he heard a tinkle of rhodium-plated laughter.*

He scooped up the twenty silver dollars, and the pit boss walked him to the rear of the casino, talking to him in a muted, extremely polite tone of voice. At the cashier's window, the pit boss nodded to a weary-looking man at a huge Rolodex card file, checking credit ratings.

"Barney, jackpot on the cartwheel Chief; slot five oh oh one five." He grinned at Kostner, who tried to smile back. It was difficult. He felt stunned.

The Cashier checked a payoff book for the correct

amount to be drawn and leaned across the counter toward Kostner. "Check or cash, sir?"

Kostner felt buoyancy coming back to him. "Is the casino's check good?" They all three laughed at that. "A check's fine," Kostner said. The check was drawn, and the Check-Riter punched out the little bumps that said two thousand. "The twenty cartwheels are a gift," the cashier said, sliding the check through to Kostner.

He held it, looked at it, and still found it difficult to believe. Two grand, back on the golden road.

As he walked through the casino with the pit boss, the stocky man asked pleasantly, "Well, what are you going to do with it?" Kostner had to think a moment. He didn't really have any plans. But then the sudden realization came to him: "I'm going to play that slot machine again." The pit boss smiled: a congenital sucker. He would put all twenty of those silver dollars back into the Chief, and then turn to the other games. Blackjack, roulette, faro, baccarrat . . . in a few hours he would have redeposited the two grand with the hotel casino. It always happened.

He walked Kostner back to the slot machine, and patted him on the shoulder. "Lotsa luck, fella."

As he turned away, Kostner slipped a silver dollar into the machine, and pulled the handle.

The pit boss had only taken five steps when he heard the incredible sound of the reels clicking to a stop, the clash of twenty token silver dollars hitting the payoff trough, and that goddammed gong went out of its mind again.

She had known that sonofabitch Nuncio was a perverted swine. A walking filth. A dungheap between his ears. Some kind of monster in nylon undershorts. There weren't many kinds of games Maggie hadn't played, but what that Sicilian De Sade wanted to do was outright vomity!

She nearly fainted when he suggested it. Her heart— which the Beverly Hills specialist had said she should not tax—began whumping frantically. "You pig!" she screamed. "You filthy dirty ugly pig you, Nuncio you pig!" She had bounded out of the bed and started to throw on clothes. She didn't even bother with a brassiere, pulling the poorboy sweater on over breasts still crimson with the touches and love-bites Nuncio had showered on them.

He sat up in the bed, a pathetic-looking little man, gray hair at the temples and no hair at all on top, and his eyes were moist. He was porcine, was indeed the swine she had called him, but he was helpless before her. He was in love with his hooker, with the tart that he was supporting. It had been the first time for the swine Nuncio and he was helpless. Back in Detroit, had it been a floozy, a chippy broad, he would have gotten out of the double bed and rapped her around pretty good. But this Maggie, she tied him in knots. He had suggested . . . that, what they should do together . . . because he was so consumed with her. But she was furious with him. It wasn't that bizarre an idea!

"Gimme a chanct'a talk t'ya, honey . . . Maggie . . ."

"You filthy pig, Nuncio! Give me some money, I'm going down to the casino, and I don't want to see your filthy pig face for the rest of the day, remember that!"

And she had gone in his wallet and pants, and taken eight hundred and sixteen dollars, while he watched. He was helpless before her. She was something stolen from a world he knew only as "class" and she could do what she wanted with him.

Genetic freak Maggie, blue-eyed posing mannequin Maggie, pretty Maggie Moneyeyes, who was one-half Cherokee and one-half a buncha other things, had absorbed her lessons well. She was the very model of a "class broad."

"Not for the rest of the day, do you understand?" she snapped at him, and went downstairs, furious, to fret and gamble and wonder about nothing but years of herself.

Men stared after her as she walked. She carried herself like a challenge, the way a squire carried a pennant, the way a prize bitch carried herself in the judge's ring. Born to the blue. The wonders of mimicry and desire.

Maggie had no desire for gambling, none whatever. She merely wanted to taste the fury of her relationship with the swine Sicilian, her need for solidity in a life built on the edge of the slide area, the senselessness of being here in Las Vegas when she could be back in Beverly Hills. She grew angrier and more ill at the thought of Nuncio upstairs in the room, taking another shower. She bathed three times a day. But it was different with him. He knew she resented his smell; he had the soft odor of wet fur sometimes, and she had told him about it. Now he bathed constantly, and hated it. He was a foreigner to the bath. His life had been marked by various kinds of filths, and baths for him now were more of an obscenity than dirt could ever have been. For her, bathing was different. It was a necessity. She had to keep the patina of the world off her, had to remain clean and smooth and white. A presentation, not an object of flesh and hair. A chromium instrument, something never pitted by rust and corrosion.

When she was touched by them, by any one of them, by the men, by all the Nuncios, they left little pitholes of bloody rust on her white, permanent flesh; cobwebs, sooty stains. She had to bathe. Often.

She strolled down between the tables and the slots, carrying eight hundred and sixteen dollars. Eight one-hundred-dollar bills and sixteen dollars in ones.

At the change booth she got cartwheels for the sixteen ones. The Chief waited. It was her baby. She played it to infuriate the Sicilian. He told her to play the nickel slots, the quarter or dime slots, but she always infuriated him by blowing fifty or a hundred dollars in ten minutes, one after another, in the big Chief.

She faced the machine, and put in the first silver dollar. She pulled the handle that swine Nuncio. Another dollar, pulled the handle how long does this go on? The reels cycled and spun and whirled and whipped in a blurringspinning metallichumming overandoverandover as Maggie blued-eyed Maggie hated and hated and thought of hate and all the days and nights of swine behind her and ahead of her and if she only had all the money in this room in this casino in this hotel in this town right now this very instant just an instant thisinstant it would be enough to whirring and humming and spinning and overandoverandover and she would be free free free and all the world would never touch her body again the swine would never touch her white flesh again and then suddenly as dollarafterdollarafterdollar went aroundaroundaround hummming in reels of cherries and bells and bars and plums and oranges *there was painpainpain a* SHARP *painpainpain in her chest, her heart, her center, a needle, a lancet, a burning, a pillar of flame that was purest pure purer* PAIN!

Maggie, pretty Maggie Moneyeyes, who wanted all that money in that cartwheel Chief slot machine, Maggie who had come from filth and rheumatic fever, who had come all the way to three baths a day and a specialist in Very Expensive Beverly Hills, that Maggie suddenly had a seizure, a flutter, a slam of a coronary thrombosis and fell to the floor of the casino. Dead.

One instant she had been holding the handle of the slot machine, willing her entire being into that machine, wanting to suck out every silver vapor within its belly, and the next instant her heart exploded and killed her and she slipped to the floor still touching the machine.

> *On the floor.*
> *Dead.*
> *Struck dead.*
> *Liar. All the lies that were her life.*
> *Dead on a floor.*

[A moment out of time ■ lights whirling and spinning in a cotton candy universe ■ endless nights that pealed ebony funeral bells ■ out of fog ■ out of weightlessness ■ memory running backward ■ gibbering spastic blindness ■ a soundless owl of frenzy trapped in a cave of prisms ■ sand endlessly dripping ■ billows of forever ■ edges of the world as they crumbled ■ the smell of rust ■ rough green edges that burn ■ memory the gibbering spastic blind memory ■ seven rushing vacuums of nothing ■ chill fevers ■ this is the stopover before hell or heaven ■ this is limbo ■ trapped and doomed alone in a mist-eaten nowhere ■ a soundless screaming a soundless whirring a soundless spinning spinning spinning spinning ■ spinning spinning ■ spinning ■ spinning ■ spinning ■ spinning ■ spinninnnnnggggggggggg]

Maggie had wanted all the silver in
the machine. She had died, willing
herself into the machine. Now
looking out from within, from inside
the limbo that had become her own
purgatory, Maggie was trapped, the
soul of Maggie was trapped, in the
oiled and anodized interior of the
silver-dollar slot machine. The prison
of her final desires, where she had
wanted to be, completely trapped in
that last instant of life between life/
death. Maggie, all soul now, trapped
for all eternity in the cage soul of the
machine. Trapped.

"I hope you don't mind if I call over one of the slot men,"
the Slot Machine Floor Manager was saying, from a far distance. He was in his late fifties, a velvet-voiced man whose
eyes held nothing of light and certainly nothing of kindness.
He had stopped the pit boss as the stocky man had turned
to return to Kostner and the jackpotted machine; he had
taken the walk himself. "We have to make sure, you know
how it is, somebody didn't fool with the slot, you know,
maybe it's outta whack or something, you know."

He lifted his left hand and there was a clicker in it, the
kind children use at Halloween. He clicked half a dozen
times, like a rabid cricket, and there was a scurry in the pit
between the tables.

Kostner was only faintly aware of what was happening.
Instead of being totally awake, feeling the surge of adrena-
line through his veins, the feeling any gambler gets when he
is ahead of the game, when he has hit it for a boodle, he
was numb, partaking of the action around him only as a
drinking glass involves itself with an alcoholic's drunken
binge.

A tired-looking, resigned-weary man wearing a gray
porter's jacket, as gray as his hair, as gray as his indoor skin,
came to them, carrying a leather wrap-up of tools. The slot
repairman studied the machine, turning the pressed steel

body around on its stand, studying the back. He used a key on the back door and for an instant Kostner had a view of gears, springs, armatures and the clock that ran the slot mechanism. The repairman nodded silently over it, closed and relocked it, turned it around again and studied the face of the machine.

"Nobody's been spooning it," he said, and went away.

Kostner stared at the Floor Manager.

"Gaffing. That's what he meant. Spooning's another word for it. Some guys use a little piece of plastic, or a wire, shove it down through the escalator, it kicks the machine. Nobody thought that's what happened here, but you know, we have to make sure, two grand is a big payoff, and twice . . . well, you know, I'm sure you'll understand. If a guy was doing it with a boomerang—"

Kostner raised an eyebrow.

"—uh, yeah, a boomerang, it's another way to spoon the machine. But we just wanted to make a little check, and now everybody's satisfied, so if you'll just come back to the Casino cashier with me—"

And they paid him off again.

So he went back to the slot machine, and stood before it for a long time, staring at it: The change girls and the dealers going off-duty, the little old ladies with their canvas work gloves worn to avoid callouses when pulling the slot handles, the men's room attendant on his way up front to get more matchbooks, the tourists, the observers, the hard drinkers, the sweepers, the busboys, the gamblers with poached-egg eyes who had been up all night, the showgirls with massive busts and sugar daddies, all of them conjectured mentally about the beat-out walker who was staring at the silver dollar Chief. He did not move, merely stared at the machine, and they wondered.

The machine was staring back at Kostner.

Three blue eyes.

The electric current had sparked through him again, as the machine had clocked down and the eyes turned up a second time, as he had won a second time. But this time he knew there was something more than luck involved, for no one else had seen those three blue eyes.

So now he stood before the machine, and waited. It

spoke to him. Inside his skull, where no one had ever lived but himself, now someone else moved and spoke to him. A girl. A beautiful girl. Her name was Maggie, and she spoke to him:

I've been waiting for you. A long time, I've been waiting for you, Kostner. Why do you think you hit the jackpot? Because I've been waiting for you, and I want you. You'll win all the jackpots. Because I want you, I need you. Love me, I'm Maggie, I'm so alone, love me.

Kostner had been staring at the slot machine for a very long time, and his weary brown eyes had seemed to be locked to the blue eyes on those jackpot bars. But he knew no one else could see the blue eyes, and no one else could hear the voice, and no one else knew about Maggie.

He thumbed in another silver dollar, and the pit boss watched, the slot machine repairman watched, the Slot Machine Floor Manager watched, three change girls watched, and a pack of unidentified players watched, from their seats.

The reels whirled, the handle snapped back, and in a second they flipped down to a halt, twenty silver dollars tokened themselves into the payoff trough, and the gong went insane again.

The Floor Manager came over and said, very softly, "Mr. Kostner, it'll take us about fifteen minutes to pull this machine and check it out. I'm sure you understand." And two slot repairmen came out of the back, hauled the Chief off its stand, and took it into the repair room at the rear of the casino.

While they waited, the Floor Manager regaled Kostner with stories of spooners who had used intricate magnets inside their clothes, of boomerang men who had attached their plastic implements under their sleeves so they could be extended on spring-loaded clips, of cheaters who had come equipped with tiny electric drills palmed in their hands and wires that slipped into the tiny drilled holes. And he kept saying he knew Kostner would understand.

But Kostner knew the Floor Manager would not understand.

When they brought the Chief back, the repairman nodded assuredly. "Nothing wrong with it. Works perfectly. Nobody's been boomin' it."

But the blue eyes were gone on the jackpot bars.

Kostner knew they would return.

They paid him off again.

He returned and played again. And again. And again. They put a "spotter" on him. He won again. And again. And again. The crowd had grown to massive proportions. Word had spread like the silent communications of the telegraph vine, up and down the strip, all the way to downtown Vegas and the sidewalk casinos where they played night and day every day of the year, and the crowd moved to him inexorably, drawn like lemmings by the odor of the luck that rose from him like musky electrical cracklings. And he won. Again and again. Thirty-eight thousand dollars. And the three blue eyes continued to stare up at him. Her lover was winning. Maggie and her Moneyeyes.

Finally, the casino decided to speak to Kostner. They pulled the Chief for fifteen minutes, for a supplemental check by experts from the slot machine company in downtown Vegas, and while they were checking it, they asked Kostner to come to the main office of the hotel.

The owner was there. His face seemed faintly familiar to Kostner. Had he seen it on television? The newspapers?

"Mr. Kostner, my name is Jules Hartshorn."

"I'm pleased to meet you."

"Quite a string of luck you're having out there."

"It's been a long time coming."

"You realize, this sort of luck is impossible."

"I'm compelled to believe it, Mr. Hartshorn."

"Um. As am I. It's happening to my casino. But we're thoroughly convinced of one of two possibilities, Mr. Kostner: one, either the machine is inoperable in a way we can't detect, or two, you are the cleverest spooner we've ever had in here."

"I'm not cheating."

"As you can see, Mr. Kostner, I'm smiling. The reason I'm smiling is at your naïveté in believing I would take your word for it. I'm perfectly happy to nod politely and say of course you aren't cheating. But no one can win thirty-eight thousand dollars on nineteen straight jackpots off one slot machine; it doesn't even have mathematical odds against its happening, Mr. Kostner. It's on a cosmic scale of improbability with three dark planets crashing into our sun within the next twenty minutes. It's on a par with Washington, Peking, and Moscow all three pushing the red button at the same micro-second. It's an impossibility, Mr. Kostner. An impossibility that's happening to me."

"I'm sorry."

"Not really."

"No, not really. I can use the money."

"For what, exactly, Mr. Kostner?"

"I hadn't thought about it, really."

"I see. Well, Mr. Kostner, let's look at it this way. I can't stop you from playing, and if you continue to win, I'll be required to pay you off. And no stubble-chinned thugs will be waiting in an alley to club you and take the money. The checks will all be honored. The best I can hope for, Mr. Kostner, is the attendant publicity. Right now, every high-roller in Vegas is in that casino, waiting for you to drop cartwheels into that machine. It won't make up for what I'm losing, if you continue the way you've been, but it will help. All I ask is that you cooperate a little."

"The least I can do, considering your generosity."

"An attempt at humor."

"I'm sorry. What is it you'd like me to do?"

"Get about ten hours' sleep."

"While you pull the slot and have it worked over thoroughly?"

"Yes."

"If I wanted to keep winning, that might be a pretty stupid move on my part. You might change the hickamajig inside so I couldn't win if I put back every dollar of that thirty-eight grand."

"We're licensed by the state of Nevada, Mr. Kostner."

"I come from a good family, too, and take a look at me. I'm a bum with thirty-eight thousand dollars in my pocket."

"Nothing will be done to that slot machine, Kostner."

"Then why pull it for ten hours?"

"To work it over thoroughly in the shop. If something as undetectable as metal fatigue or a worn escalator tooth or— we want to make sure this doesn't happen with other machines. And the extra time will get the word around town; we can use the crowd. Some of those tourists will stick to our fingers, and it'll help defray the expense of having you break the bank at this casino—on a slot machine."

"I have to take your word."

"This hotel will be in business long after you're gone, Kostner."

"That isn't much of an argument."

"It's the only one I have. If you want to get back out on that floor, I can't stop you."

"No Mafia hoods ventilate me later?"

"I haven't the faintest idea what you're talking about."

"I'm sure you haven't."

"You're got to stop reading *The National Enquirer.* This is a legally run business. I'm merely asking a favor."

"Okay, Mr. Hartshorn, I've been three days without any sleep. Ten hours will do me a world of good."

"I'll have the desk clerk find you a quiet room on the top floor. And thank you, Mr. Kostner."

"Think nothing of it."

"I'm afraid that will be impossible."

"A lot of impossible things are happening lately."

He turned to go, and Hartshorn lit a cigarette. "Oh, by the way, Mr. Kostner?"

Kostner turned. His eyes were getting difficult to focus; he was thankful for the ten hours' sleep. Those extremely weary brown eyes fastened on Hartshorn. "Yes?"

"Did you know about that slot machine? A peculiar thing happened with it about six weeks ago."

"What was that?"

"A girl died playing it. She had a heart attack, a seizure while she was pulling the handle, and died right out there on the floor."

Kostner was silent for a moment. He wanted desperately to ask Hartshorn what color the dead girl's eyes had been, but he was afraid the owner would say blue.

He paused with his hand on the office door. "Seems as though you've had nothing but a streak of bad luck on that machine."

Hartshorn smiled an enigmatic smile. "It might not change for a while, either."

Kostner felt his jaw muscles tighten. "Meaning I might die, too, and wouldn't *that* be bad luck."

Hartshorn's smile became hieroglyphic, permanent, stamped on him forever. "Sleep tight, Mr. Kostner."

In a dream, she came to him. Long, smooth thighs and soft golden down on her arms; blue eyes deep as the past, misted with a fine scintillation like lavender spiderwebs; taut body that was the only body Woman had ever had, from the very first. Maggie came to him.

Hello, I've been traveling a long time.

"Who are you?" *Kostner asked, wonderingly. He was standing on a chilly plain, or was it a plateau? The wind curled around them both, or was it only around him? She was exquisite, and he saw her clearly, or was it through a mist? Her voice was deep and resonant, or was it light and warm as night-blooming jasmine?*

I'm Maggie. I love you. I've waited for you.

"You have blue eyes."

Yes. *With love.*

"You're very beautiful."

Thank you. *With female amusement.*

"But why me? Why let it happen to me? Are you the girl who—are you the one that was sick—the one—?"

I'm Maggie. And you, I picked you, because you need me. You've needed someone for a long long time.

Then it unrolled for Kostner. The past unrolled and he saw who he was. He saw himself alone. Always alone. As a child, born to kind and warm parents who hadn't the vaguest notion of who he was, what he wanted to be, where his talents lay. So he had run off, when he was in his teens, and alone always alone on the road. For years and months and days and hours, with no one. Casual friendships, based on food, or sex, or artificial similarities. But no one to whom he could cleave, and cling, and belong. It was that way till Susie, and with her he had found light. He had discovered the scents and aromas of a spring that was eternally one day away. He had laughed, really laughed, and known with her it would at last be all right. So he had poured all of himself into her, giving her everything; all his hopes, his secret thoughts, his tender dreams; and she had taken them, taken him, all of him, and he had known for the first time what it was to have a place to live, to have a home in some-

*one's heart. It was all the silly and gentle things he laughed
at in other people, but for him it was breathing deeply of
wonder.*

*He had stayed with her for a long time, and had sup-
ported her, supported her son from the first marriage; the
marriage Susie never talked about. And then one day, he
had come back, as Susie had always known he would. He
was a dark creature of ruthless habits and vicious nature,
but she had been his woman, all along, and Kostner realized she had used him as a stopgap, as a bill-payer, till her
wandering terror came home to nest. Then she had asked
Kostner to leave. Broke, and tapped out in all the silent
inner ways a man can be drained, he had left, without even
a fight, for all the fight had been leached out of him. He had
left, and wandered West, and finally came to Las Vegas,
where he had hit bottom. And found Maggie. In a dream,
with blue eyes, he had found Maggie.*

I want you to belong to me. I love you. Her truth was
vibrant in Kostner's mind. *She was his; at last, someone
who was special was his.*

*"Can I trust you? I've never been able to trust anyone
before. Women, never. But I need someone. I really need
someone."*

It's me, always. Forever. You can trust me.

*And she came to him, fully. Her body was a declaration
of truth and trust such as no other Kostner had ever known
before. She met him on a windswept plain of thought, and
he made love to her more completely than he had known
any passion before. She joined with him, entered him,
mingled with his blood and his thought and his frustration,
and he came away clean, filled with glory.*

"Yes, I can trust you, I want you, I'm yours," he whispered to her, when they lay side by side in a dream nowhere
of mist and soundlessness. *"I'm yours."*

*She smiled, a woman's smile of belief in her man; a smile
of trust and deliverance. And Kostner woke up.*

The Chief was back on its stand, and the crowd had been
penned back by velvet ropes. Several people had played
the machine, but there had been no jackpots.

Now Kostner came into the casino, and the "spotters" got

themselves ready. While Kostner had slept, they had gone through his clothes, searching for wires, for gaffs, for spoons or boomerangs. Nothing.

Now he walked straight to the Chief, and stared at it.

Hartshorn was there. "You look tired," he said gently to Kostner, studying the man's weary brown eyes.

"I am, a little." Kostner tried a smile, which didn't work. "I had a funny dream."

"Oh?"

"Yeah . . . about a girl. . . ." He let it die off.

Hartshorn's smile was understanding. Pitying, empathic, and understanding. "There are lots of girls in this town. You shouldn't have any trouble finding one with your winnings."

Kostner nodded, and slipped his first silver dollar into the slot. He pulled the handle. The reels spun with a ferocity Kostner had not heard before and suddenly everything went whipping slantwise as he felt a wrenching of pure flame in his stomach, as his head was snapped on its spindly neck, as the lining behind his eyes was burned out. There was a terrible shriek, of tortured metal, of an express train ripping the air with its passage, of a hundred small animals being gutted and torn to shreds, of incredible pain, of night winds that tore the tops off mountains of lava. And a keening whine of a voice that wailed and wailed and wailed as it went away from there in blinding light—

Free! Free! Heaven or Hell it doesn't matter! Free!

The sound of a soul released from an eternal prison, a genie freed from a dark bottle. And in that instant of damp soundless nothingness, Kostner saw the reels snap and clock down for the final time:

One, two, three. Blue eyes.

But he would never cash his checks.

The crowd screamed through one voice as he fell heavily and lay on his face. The final loneliness . . .

The Chief was pulled. Bad luck. Too many gamblers resented its very presence in the casino. So it was pulled. And returned to the company, with explicit instructions it was to be melted down to slag. And not till it was in the hands of the ladle foreman, who was ready to dump it into the slag furnace, did anyone remark on the final tally the Chief had clocked.

"Look at that, ain't that weird," said the ladle foreman to his bucket man. He pointed to the three glass windows.

"Never saw jackpot bars like that before," the bucket man agreed. "Three eyes. Must be an old machine."

"Yeah, some of these old games go way back," the foreman said, hoisting the slot machine onto the conveyor track leading to the slag furnace.

"Three eyes, huh? How about that. Three brown eyes." And he threw the knife-switch that sent the machine down the track to the roaring inferno of the furnace.

Three brown eyes.

Three brown eyes that looked very very weary. That looked very very trapped. That looked very very betrayed. Some of these old games go way back.

Born in Ohio in 1934, Harlan Ellison's list of awards is longer than some of his stories. Among others, he has won seven Hugos, three Nebulas, and one Edgar from the Mystery Writers of America. Although he was expelled from Ohio State University for rudeness to a teacher who claimed he had no talent, Ellison's stories have been among the world's most reprinted tales. Many of his best are collected in Deathbird Stories (1983). Ellison has said, "I want people's hair to stand on end when they read my work." It does.

THREE

In the Memory Room
Michael Bishop

"This isn't my mother!" Kenny repeats, staring down at the dead woman in the Memory Room.

Kenny has a lumberjack's beard. His glasses magnify his eyes to the size of snowballs. His belly is so big that he cannot pull his maroon leather car coat tight enough to button it.

"I don't care what you guys say," Kenny tells the other eight members of Gina Callan's family arrayed behind him. "This . . . this *manikin* isn't my mother!"

"Just who the hell you think it is, then?" white-haired Uncle Sarge Lobrano asks him. "Queen Elizabeth?"

Aunt Dot, Gina's sister, rebukes her husband: "Sergio!"

"This is the wrong woman they got in here! The wrong goddamn woman! My mother was beautiful, and this person—she looks like she's hurting. Still hurting."

"Kenny, it was a painful death," Aunt Dot tries to explain. "Your mama's kidneys failed. She was retaining fluid. That's why her cheeks and jowls are so puffy."

The hostess who ushered Gina's family into the room says, "We did our best. I worked very hard to make her lifelike."

"My mother always wore glasses. We gave 'em to you. What the hell did you do with 'em?"

"Items to help make the likeness true are received at the desk, Mr. Petruzzi," the hostess tells Kenny. "Nobody passed her glasses on to me."

Kenny struggles to free his wallet from the hip pocket of his tent-sized trousers. From the wallet he extracts a photograph. "Didn't you get a picture, then? Here's the way my mother ought to look—beautiful."

39

He thrusts the photo at the hostess, a smart-looking, for-tyish woman wearing slacks and a bulky fishnet sweater. Then, gesturing hugely, he declares again, "*That's* not my mother."

Vince—Uncle Sarge and Aunt Dot's son, a high school football coach in Colorado Springs—takes his cousin's elbow. "Of course that isn't your mother, Kenny. It's only her body. Your mother's real self—her soul—is in heaven."

"I *know* where she is. But she doesn't look like *that*." Kenny flaunts the wallet photo. "This is how she looks, and this is the way I'll always remember her."

"That picture's five years old," Uncle Lyle says. "You can't expect your mother to look today the way she looked five years ago when she was in nearly perfect health."

"I can expect these bums to put the glasses we gave 'em on her, can't I?"

The hostess turns to Uncle Lyle, Gina's brother. "Mr. Sekas, I never received a photo of Mrs. Callan. Or her glasses. They never got to me."

"What you've done here," declares Kenny, "is a dis-grace."

The hostess colors. But to preserve her professional dig-nity, she purses her lips and lowers her head.

Aunt Dot squeezes forward and puts her hand on the edge of the casket. "It's not just the glasses," she tells every-one. "Gina's not wearing earrings. Sis'd never dress up in such lovely clothes without putting on her earrings."

Claudia, Vince's nineteen-year-old sister, seconds her mother: "That's right, Gina isn't Gina without her earrings."

"Gina isn't Gina because these goofballs lost the picture we gave them. And her glasses, too."

"Mr. Petruzzi," the hostess says, the Memory Room seeming to contract about her, "If you gave us a photo and some glasses, we'll find them. But no one passed them on to me, and I had to make do as well as I could without them."

"It wasn't very good, was it?"

"Get this bugger out of here," Uncle Sarge directs Vince and Frank. Frank is Uncle Lyle and Aunt Martha's son, a pharmacist in Kenny's hometown, Gunnison.

Then Sarge turns to the hostess. "Kenny's upset—we're

all upset—and you just gotta excuse him, ma'am. He depended like crazy on his mother. Even after he was this big grown man you see hulking here, he couldn't stop grabbing at her apron strings."

Like a couple of tugboats flanking the *Queen Mary*, Vince and Frank take Kenny's arms. Their huge, goggle-eyed cousin does not resist them. Instead he begins to blubber:

"She . . . she did everything for me. Loaned me money. Bought me clothes. Even if I came home at two in the morning, she'd crawl out of bed to fix me something to eat."

"She was that way to everybody," Claudia assures Kenny.

"And not just simple sandwich stuff, either. Gourmet doings. Omelets. Polenta and gravy. Steak and eggs."

Vince and Frank maneuver their cousin, the adopted son of Gina and the late Ernesto Petruzzi, toward the parlor beyond the Memory Room. Out of the pale of his dead mother's aura.

"She was my intercessor!" Kenny cries over his shoulder. "My champion when nobody else gave a damn!"

Alone with the dead woman, the hostess perches near the casket doing some careful repair work on the masklike face of Gina Sekas Petruzzi Callan. In the hermetic, off-white room, she feels again that she is inhabiting the remembered life of the deceased.

Frank Sekas's wife Melinda Jane has gone out into the February cold with Dorothy and Claudia Lobrano to buy some earrings.

All the other mourners—Uncle Sergio, Cousin Vincent, Uncle Lyle, Aunt Martha, Cousin Frank, and the distraught Kenny—have retired to the parlor, where they sit on lumpy divans or pace the worn carpet. A peculiar odor of lilies, nostalgia, and embalming fluid permeates the Memory Room.

It seems to the hostess that her subject is listening intently to her family's muted conversation.

Sergio Lobrano is saying, "It doesn't have to be open-casket, Kenny. You know that, don't you?"

"Aunt Dot wants it open."

"Now, look, let's get this straight. Your aunt's not bossing this business, and I don't want you saying afterwards that it was open-casket because that's how Aunt Dot wanted it, and your mother didn't look like herself, and blah blah blah."

"Uncle Sergio, I'm not—"

"'Cause that'd be a cheap trick, Kenny. It wouldn't be fair to your Aunt Dot and it wouldn't be fair to yourself."

"Wait a minute," Uncle Lyle objects, and Aunt Martha chimes in, "Sarge, you haven't given Kenny a chance to—"

"I don't want him blaming his aunt for making a mockery of his mother at her own funeral, that's all."

Kenny's high-pitched, indignant voice startles the hostess: "I love my Aunt Dot, Uncle Sergio! I'd never do anything to hurt her—any more'n I'd ever do anything to hurt my own mother. So what the hell're you talking here?"

"Well, I—" his uncle begins, audibly abashed.

"You didn't let me finish. I'm only saying that whatever Aunt Dot wants, *I* want. And if we both want it, how could I ever trash her for something I've okayed myself?"

"Yeah," Sarge feebly confesses. "That's different."

"You didn't let me finish."

"Kenny, I'm sorry."

"It's okay," Kenny says. "Just don't try to tell me I'd ever do somethin' to hurt Aunt Dot."

"I won't. Believe me, I won't."

Conversation lapses, and the hostess, studying Kenny's photo of his mother, makes an unobtrusive adjustment to the lines bracketing Gina Callan's mouth. A familiar claustrophobia menaces her.

Then she hears Vince say, "I wouldn't want some stranger trying to get my body presentable."

"Shhh," Aunt Martha tells him. "Not so loud."

"I want to be cremated. I want my ashes scattered on the wind over the Great Sand Dunes National Monument. It's in my will."

Sarge makes a disgusted noise.

"Can you do that?" Kenny asks. "Can you have your ashes thrown out on federal land like that?"

"Who's going to stop you?" says Vince. "You just get somebody who's willing to go out there and do it."

"It won't be me or your mother," Sarge says. "What the hell's a punk like you doing with a will?"

"Be proud of him, Sarge," Martha says. "All most young people think about today is new cars or their next skiing trip."

"Not our Vince. He thinks about becoming a pollutant in some goddamn government showcase for sand."

"What's wrong with that?" Frank asks. "I'd like to be cremated myself. Dead's dead, and it's a helluva lot cheaper than a fancy-pants show like this."

In the ever-contracting Memory Room, the hostess imagines Frank rolling his eyes at the parlor's cut-glass chandelier.

"Gina wanted a Catholic funeral," Lyle intones. "Which is why we're doing our best to give her one. Her marrying Wesley Callan, a joker with two divorces, didn't make it all that damn easy to set up, either. I had to talk to half a dozen different priests before Father McFahey agreed to it."

"And that silly fart Callan isn't even coming," Sarge grouses.

"Are you sure?" Martha asks. "I told him over the phone he'd live to regret not coming up here."

Kenny says, "Yeah, well, he told *me* he wasn't going to listen to a bunch of R.C. mumbo-jumbo. He and his holier-than-everybody cronies in Gunnison's gonna put on some sort of memorial service of their own."

"Mumbo-jumbo?" Martha says.

"Yeah, 'mumbo-jumbo.' So I said, 'You've got your own sort of mumbo-jumbo to listen to, don't you, Wes?'"

Sarge laughs. "What'd he say to that, Kenny?"

"He didn't like it. But if you treat people lousy, it stands to reason you're gonna get treated lousy back."

"Those goddamn Jehovah's Witnesses drive me bats," Frank say. "'Live Forever on Paradise Earth.' 'Blessed are the One Hundred and Forty-Four Thousand.' 'Jesus Is Actually the Archangel Michael in Disguise.' Etcetera, etcetera. Aunt Gina was a saint to put up with three years of that malarky. A bona fide saint."

"And beautiful," Kenny murmurs. "Always beautiful."

"Wes may be a Witness," Martha declares, "but when he tucks it in, they'll cremate him—hear that, Vince?—and put his ashes in a jar and stick him on a shelf right across from Gina's vault in the Tower of Memories."

"But what about me?" Kenny asks. "Where am I gonna go? They saved no place for me, Aunt Martha."

Kenny's complaint reduces everyone else to silence.

In the Memory Room, the hostess makes a tiny incision in Gina's neck, swabs the vulcanized flesh around it, and seals the cut with a special mortician's adhesive. It seems to her that, now, she and her subject are straining hard enough to hear the snow whirl out of the overcast. It clings to their turn-of-the-century building like Colorado cotton, rectangles of frozen flannel.

The door opens, and a teenage girl comes into the room with a small manila folder and a leather glasses case.

"I found these things upstairs," she says, giving them to the woman on the stool.

"Wonderful."

"What's wrong, Mrs. Dennis?"

"They'd've been a lot of help yesterday." Mrs. Dennis, the hostess, opens the envelope, removes the glossy photo, and tilts it to compare its likeness to the face undergoing renovation.

"But I wasn't here yesterday. I couldn't—"

"Never mind, Heather. Get on back upstairs."

The girl hesitates, collects herself, and leaves, going through the smoke-filled parlor past Kenny Petruzzi, the Sekases, and the Lobranos. Mrs. Dennis gets only a glimpse of the family before the door drifts shut again and she must return her attentions to the dead woman in the casket.

—Forgive my Kenny, the corpse implores her. Ernesto and I spoiled him when he was little.

He isn't little now, Mrs. Dennis rejoins.

—His thoughtless behavior isn't really his fault. He never learned any responsibility.

Why the hell didn't he?

—I couldn't have children so we adopted. We were so glad to get Kenny that we went overboard to prove it. Ernesto gave him a diamond ring when he was six. He lost it the next day.

Mrs. Dennis merely stares at the dead woman.

44

—Kenny was the only thing Wes and I ever argued about, Gina Callan continues. Except for Wes's new religion.

Aloud, Mrs. Dennis says, "Same old story. Child won't accept original parent's choice of stand-in spouse."

—It wasn't that, the corpse informs her. Kenny was almost thirty when Wes and I married. Ernesto'd been dead since Kenny was nine, and Kenny *liked* Wes. Or he did before the Witnesses got to him.

Then I had it backward, thinks Mrs. Dennis, still working on her subject's throat: It was Wes who didn't like Kenny.

—Wes liked him as a person, only he couldn't put up with him being so flighty. When we got married, Kenny was just back from Vietnam. His wife had run out on him while he was over there, and he didn't want to do nothing but play the dogs in Colorado Springs and Pueblo.

And Wes didn't approve of gambling?

—Oh, before he got converted, Wes'd play the dogs, too. It was Kenny's losing and borrowing money that drove him buggy.

But Wes loaned him money, anyway? Betting money?

—No, I loaned Kenny the money. Sometimes I just handed it to him. Sometimes he'd ask me for something to pawn. Jewelry, maybe, or silverware, and I'd give it to him so he could play his "system" and try to win back what he'd already lost.

Thinks Mrs. Dennis, No wonder Wes went buggy, Mrs. Callan. You were feeding Kenny's habit.

—It *was* a habit. A habit and an obsession. He had computer printouts and three-by-five cards about them damn dogs all over our house in Gunnison. His room downstairs . . . it looked the way an embassy looks when they have to shred their files. He was working out his "system"—A system to make him rich.

And you fell for that?

—Well, sometimes, just occasionally, he'd win. When he did, he wouldn't think to pay us back for staking him. But he'd go out and buy me a color TV set or Wes some expensive hunting equipment. That'd stick him in a hole deeper than his evening's winnings, and Wes'd start ranting about

Kenny being a numbskull and a moocher and a baby. A three-hundred-pound baby.

Painstakingly relining Gina Callan's eyes, Mrs. Dennis murmurs, "Seems like an accurate character assessment to me."

—No, wait. A month before I went into Fitzsimmons, he quit the dogs cold. Stopped going to the track. Wouldn't let his old betting buddies talk him into giving it another go. Even Wes was impressed. Even Wes.

Observes the hostess, But Wes isn't here.

—That's because my family's Catholic, and I wanted to be put to rest like a Catholic, and being a Witness has made it impossible for Wes to think about my religion without getting angry. It's got nothing to do with Kenny.

Except Kenny's Catholic, too. And hates your husband for his pious intolerance. And resents him for not being here.

—Kenny's *not* Catholic. After Wes and I married, he quit us. Now he's a Unitarian or something. Kenny hates the Catholics for refusing to let me take communion because I fell in love with and actually married a guy who'd been married twice already.

"Wheels within wheels," Mrs. Dennis tells the ceiling.

Reminisces Gina Callan:

—Our first years together, Wes had no faith but pro football. About four years ago, though, a doctor at Fitzsimmons botched the prostate surgery he needed. Wesley nearly died. These Witnesses got to him while he was suffering, talked to him, studied with him, poured their propaganda on him. He was down so far he bought it. Kenny says if only the Buddhists or the Hare Krishnas had reached him first, Wesley'd be that today instead. I wish they had.

I guess Wes was easier to take as a Denver Bronco fan than as a religious zealot?

—You bet. He wouldn't celebrate birthdays or Christmas. He wouldn't even buy me a stupid Valentine. He was afraid one of the brothers or sisters would call him "frivolous." That's when Kenny started to get fed up with *him*.

"I'm almost finished, Mrs. Callan." Mrs. Dennis leans back on her stool, studies her subject, and then removes the dead woman's glasses from their leather case and sets them on her nose, snugging the ear struts into her bouffant hairdo.

—I went into the hospital terrified, the bespectacled Gina Callan tells her hostess. I remembered how one of their lousy doctors nearly killed Wes, and *I* was afraid to die, afraid they'd push me to it the way they'd almost done him.

I suppose it's a cliché, Mrs. Dennis rejoins, but there are worse things than dying.

—Fear's one, admits the dead woman. And when I was really hurting, retaining water and so on, one of those army dorks . . . Wes called 'em *dorktors* right to their face, but they always seemed just to think he talked funny . . . came into my room and said, "Mrs. Callan, you're dying. I think you should know. You've probably only got a few more hours." He didn't ask Wes, he didn't ask Kenny, he just took it upon himself to tell me.

My God, thinks Mrs. Dennis, genuinely appalled.

—That did it. That whomped the heart right out of me. Maybe some people'd be grateful to be told, but not me. I was thinking I'd make it, but what he said was absolutely chilling. I was . . . well, the only word that says it is *horror-struck*.

Mrs. Callan, I can imagine.

—They'd been taking me on and off various monitors and kidney machines, and sticking me with needles, and running plastic tubes in and out of me, and, well, I didn't last till morning. Kenny and Wesley sat there helpless beside me as I passed on. And being dead hasn't been half so bad as going terrified into the hospital and being told by some army quack—that *dorktor*, as Wes'd call him—that I was dying.

To herself, not to the woman's corpse, Mrs. Dennis thinks, How much more of this am I going to be able to stand?

—Know what terrifies me now? What ruins the death snooze I'm entitled to after sixty-seven years working and worrying?

No, ma'am. What?

—Wes'll be okay. He's got his religion to fall back on. But what's to become of Kenny?

Thinks Mrs. Dennis consolingly, He'll be okay, too.

—No. No, he won't. He never learned any responsibility.

It was my fault, mine and Ernesto's, but poor Kenny's gonna be the one to pay for it. He's a baby. Still a baby . . .

Aunt Dot, Cousin Claudia, and Melinda Jane return from their shopping expedition. Mrs. Dennis and her subject can hear them coming down the carpeted stairs. The menfolk rise to greet them, while Aunt Martha blurts, "Those are wonderful, Dot. Those are Gina, all right. They're unquestionably Gina."

The women come crowding in, warning Kenny, Sarge, Lyle, Vince, and Frank to stay put. This is a female matter, cosmeticizing Gina, and Kenny and the guys will be allowed to look at her again only when Aunt Dot says she's presentable. Mrs. Dennis consents to their invasion—even though she cannot help feeling that they are barging into a torture chamber, not merely coming home with bangles with which to adorn their dead.

Melinda Jane shuts the door behind them.

"Ta da," says Claudia. She holds up a pair of beaten-brass earrings, with artificial pearls in the center of each clip.

"Thank God you got clip-ons," Mrs. Dennis tells her. "I know she had pierced ears, but the holes've closed up."

"Clip-ons, schlip-ons," Claudia replies. "All that matters is for 'em to look like her. These do."

"Big and jangly," says one of the aunts.

"Gina through and through," says the other.

Everyone in the Memory Room stares down at the dead woman. The hostess realizes that her subject, who stopped transmitting at the first sound of the women's return, is basking in their approval. For the first time since entering the mortuary, Gina Callan feels good about herself.

"Okay," says Aunt Dot, taking a deep breath and wiping her eyes with her sleeve. "Get Kenny in here."

Someone opens the door. The men bunch up, squeeze through, and approach the casket. Kenny shoulders his way to the front.

"Whaddaya think?" Martha asks. "Isn't that more like it?"

For a moment, Kenny merely stares. His bug eyes dart from his mother's hands to her rouged face and back again. Then he turns and, locating Mrs. Dennis, reaches out and grabs her hands.

"This is my mother," he tells her. "You goofballs finally got it right."

"Thank you. Your relatives helped."

"She's beautiful again—as beautiful as I remember."

"Thank you," repeats the hostess.

"You found her glasses. Her picture, too."

"One of our employees found them. Heather Thompson."

"Heather Thompson deserves a raise," Kenny cries. "I'm gonna buy her a box of candy. You, too. Both of you."

He releases Mrs. Dennis, turns again to the casket, and lifts his arms in a dramatic gesture of thanksgiving.

"This is my mother," he proclaims. "God bless everybody here for giving me back my mother."

Alone again with the bereaved dead woman, Mrs. Dennis sits down wearily on her stool.

—Wes never came, Gina Callan tells her. And Kenny's gonna be lost without me. Absolutely lost.

"Shut up!" the hostess shouts, trying to reclaim her room. "Do you think you're the only goddamn stiff whose troubles I've got to listen to? Is that what you think?"

Gina Sekas Petruzzi Callan ceases to transmit.

"That's better," Mrs. Dennis whispers, cupping her face in her hands. "Who the hell do you guys think you are, anyway?"

One of the newer stars of the fantasy field, Michael Bishop was born in Nebraska in 1945 to an Air Force family. After receiving a Masters in English at the University of Georgia (1968), he became a teacher at the Air Force Academy Preparatory School in Colorado, where he began his writing career. Awards received include the Science Fiction Writers of America's Nebula for "The Quickening" (1982). His shorter works have been collected in Blooded on Arachne *(1982) and* One Winter in Eden *(1984).*

Lona-Anne-Marie had passed out tracts and waited thirty years for a resurrecting God to come and raise the dead. She just didn't expect it to start with a dog.

FOUR

Resurrection

Jack Cady

Take the path behind the Kingdom Hall, the path circling back into blackberry bushes and scrub and trees—where on most mornings gray mist hangs in the tops of young fir and old madrona—and there is a clearing where most evenings a solitary man talks with dead neighbors. His name is Em, he is sixty. He always has a white dog with him. Some folks say he has two.

Lona-Anne-Marie is the only one who knows all Em's movements. Lona-Anne-Marie is stove up with eighty years, and with thirty years of door-belling, and tracts, and waiting the awful coming of a resurrecting God. She lives in a wonderland of faith. The waiting makes her beautiful. She is wrinkled and tiny and clothed in repaired things bought for a quarter at thrift shops. She can walk a little, but mostly she sits in her kitchen and watches the neighborhood. When summer sun is vague in this Pacific Northwest mist, it falls in silverish-yellow pebbles across the roof of Kingdom Hall. It isn't hard to imagine the Angel Gabriel standing astride the roof. Even we who have our doubts can think him there.

"The world is getting old and Em is aging," Lona-Anne-Marie explains. "The world is holding up pretty well, all things considered."

Behind the Kingdom Hall, and dug in beneath sheltering blackberries, lies a private cemetery. Somebody's people were buried in vague and unremembered graves: John, another John, Sarah, Esther, Timothy. The whole business sits on a bluff; and, off to the left, deer and raccoon and a black bear inhabit a deep ravine that angles down to the salt water of Puget Sound. Before young trees grew, before blackberries covered them over, those five graves looked eastward at the Sound, like planted sailors pointing boots toward the sea. A homestead once stood where now stands a broken chimney. The people died of illness. Madrona trees seeded. Some of the madrona are seventy or eighty years; hard to tell. Madrona doesn't grow like other trees. You can't count the rings.

Our neighborhood is small. A little block of apartments anchors the head of the street. People move in, then move out. Clunkity cars with mattresses strapped to roofs arrive and leave like aging gypsies. The cars are many-colored, like Joseph's coat frayed after years in one or another desert. Each time the paper mill hires or fires, people reshuffle. Faces of school children are exchanged for other schoolish faces. Beside the apartments sits Nancy's prim and puffy house with yellow shutters. The children call her "the mean lady," and children know.

"Nancy has such a pretty name," Lona-Anne-Marie ponders, sometimes to Nancy. "A body has to wonder what went wrong."

Across from Nancy's sits the ramshackle house of Jim and Lois, although Jim now lives at Odd Fellows Cemetery; he's dead these three years. Winter, summer, every week, Lois carries flowers to his grave. The ramshackle is crowded with junk on three floors. Jim collected stuff. Beside Nancy's house is the smallest house in the neighborhood, which is Lona-Anne-Marie's, and beside that, a vacant lot where a poetic lady from the apartments in years past strowed some seed. The lot is all grass and weeds and the lady's poppies, purple and red and orange and white.

Em's house sits across from Lona-Anne-Marie. Beside Em sits the nice little place with Pete and Mona. They're retired. Then comes two more vacant lots. Kingdom Hall comes at the end of the street. Beyond the Hall's parking lot there is nothing but trees, and the private cemetery; and, when the wind is wrong, the mill's smell.

"Em is learning something about graves," Lona-Anne-Marie explains, sometimes to Em. Em visits her when he's not working. "Em is learning that between the living and the dead there ain't no difference." Lona-Anne-Marie chuckles, like she was the only snapdragon in a bed of asparagus. We figure Lona-Anne-Marie can be so sure because she has eternity locked. She likes patched blue housedresses, red sweaters, the coming rebirth of the world, and garage sales. She likes children from the apartments, and she likes the overweight and worried mothers who come looking for kids. Lona-Anne-Marie's hair is whiter then Em's dog. That's white.

"Are we old and wise," Pete says, "or only old?"

"Ask me stuff like that, I'm gonna Witness." For Lona-Anne-Marie wisdom belongs somewhere in the heavens. It may descend to earth on Sunday mornings.

Through the neighborhood conversation flows. What's said to Em is later heard by Pete. Lois talks to Lona-Anne-Marie, then Nancy hears. Lona-Anne-Marie tells Nancy to stop acting mulish. About that, Mona hears. We don't talk behind the others' backs. Talk circulates like a family.

When his first dog died Em supposed himself in many ways a fool. Nancy agreed. Lona-Anne-Marie said things would mend. Pete was sympathetic. Mona worried. Lois is youngest, being fifty-eight. She baked pies.

It was not a dog that should have been in business. He was happy-go-sloppy, a dog that rode in Em's old truck. Em peddles. He sells and trades: chainsaw parts and magazines. Rope and tack and tools and books and notions. The truck sags with wants and needs and used up dreams. It carries useful stuff and other people's junk. Before Jim died, a lot of trading went on between Jim and Em.

That dog, and Em, and truck made quite a picture. The truck is more-or-less a Ford; but improved. Used to be milk truck painted green. Funny color for a milk truck. Em is skinny and hawk-nosed frowsy like the truck. He wears work clothes. The dog was shiny white, a curly tail. They held conversations, people heard. Em never even sings in church, but in that truck he sang a monotone. The dog would whine and woof. Em is modest. He never bragged except about the dog. He claimed he traded out a five buck Chevy car. "Best five dollar dog I ever owned," he'd say, and he was lying.

It was the *only* dog he'd ever owned. Like a fool, he guessed it to live forever. Inexperience can hurt.

"How can people live when they lose children?" Em asked Lona-Anne-Marie. "Because this was just my dog and I can't stand it."

"Depends on who does the losing," Lona-Anne-Marie told him. "Creation's perfect, people ain't."

"I don't know what that means."

"Let's hope you never do," Lona-Anne-Marie told him. "I never met a man so like a child."

After burying the dog beneath an apple tree, Em took up playing pool. He hung around the bars.

"He'll bring a floozy home. Expect that next." Nancy is iron-haired and skinny, but chesty. Claims nobody sees her nicest parts. This shocks Mona, tickles Lois. Lois kind of slid while Jim was dying. Got overweight. A florid smile with painful eyes. She drinks a little. Mona dyes her long hair brown. It looks nice. Tiny women don't much show their age.

"It's like he's still around," Em said to Lona-Anne-Marie. "Like he don't want to leave . . . all in my mind, of course."

"Don't count on it. You think the world's that simple?"

"It always was before," Em said. "I may retire. I'll get myself a cat and settle down. Learn to fly a rocking chair."

"Don't do it," Pete told Em when word got round. "It only *sounds* like fun." Pete is tall and sixty-eight, skinny and bald-headed. He fished for a living. Now he fixes and re-fixes on his house. The way that man can go through paint. Gallons.

Em went through a phase. Talking to his dog. With morning mist above the Kingdom Hall, Em walked the path that leads down to the graves. The dog went with him. Invisible, of course. "C'mon, mutt-dog," Em would say, and off the two walked among the trees.

"He wants a padded cell." Nancy claimed that Em was going nuts.

"He wants a woman," Lois said.

"And that's the man who says he'll get a cat? He wants another dog." The paper comes out once a week. Mona started reading classifieds.

"He's got a dog," Lona-Anne-Marie told Mona. "Tarry awhile on those puppy ads."

"He wants to give up pool and get to work." Pete figured Nancy was close to being right. He figured Em's brains were moon-scuffed. "I've seen ten-year-olds with better sense."

"I've lost people who I didn't miss as much," Em confided to Lona-Anne-Marie. "Pretending makes it better though." Em went back to work. Each morning when he climbed into his truck, he held the door until the dog jumped in. The whole thing looked natural. Lois claimed she nearly saw the dog.

"If that's the way to handle grief I'm going to try," Lois told Lona-Anne-Marie. "I'll walk through all my rooms and talk to Jim."

"There goes the neighborhood," Pete said when he was told. "This place is gonna be a looney bin."

"The preacher says that dogs don't have a soul," Em told Lona-Anne-Marie. "I think of changing churches."

"It's what you get for being Methodist."

Lois's health improved. She cut back on wine. She no longer carried flowers to Jim's grave. Autumn came with autumn rains. The path behind the Kingdom Hall became a swamp. Fat blackberries of August turned to September blue and purple pulp, while mist ran rivers through the stand of trees. We fed our woodstoves, looked toward the rain, salvation. Boot and slicker weather. Folks who love the sun don't like it here. We get a lot of wet. We get a lot of winter.

Em still walked his dog along the path. Then Jim and Lois joined them. Three people and a dancing dog, the living and the dead.

"It's getting out of hand," Pete said to Nancy.

"Maybe so," said Lona-Anne-Marie, "but Lois has quit drinkin'." Lona-Anne-Marie is rarely puzzled. When resurrection's certain, not much else is going to fool you. Still, Lona-Anne-Marie was thinking. The rebirth of the world seemed out of kilter.

Em bought a female pup with pedigree. "Because males fight," he said to Lois. "I want them to be friends."

"For what that mutt cost," Pete said, "he could of paid the taxes on his house."

The rains swept in across the western range, rains bred in Russia, the Gulf of Alaska; sou'westers coming from Japan. The roof on Kingdom Hall sat glazed and black. Em turned to motherhood and so did we.

"We're acting silly." Lona-Anne-Marie was gratified. "A man of sixty ain't too old to learn." She watched Em's patience as he trained the pup. She boiled soup bones and watched as Em, and Jim, took walks with the two dogs.

"She'll get pneumonia," Nancy said, "that's sure. They come in cold and wet." She searched her attic, found a blanket. She and Lois made the pup a bed.

Pete built a doghouse. "Big enough for *one*," he pointed out.

"I look to the redemption of the world. Not this. Right now I've got a mare's nest." Lona-Anne-Marie was always sure a resurrecting God would sweep the sky and make things new. For thirty years since her conversion she's passed out tracts.

"Jim don't explain why he's returned. Might be he can't. And I don't care." Lois started working on her weight. "I used to be nice looking."

"He really likes her." Em told everyone about his dogs. "It's going to work out fine."

"I think Em did just right, and so does Jim." Lois's eyes were nowhere near as painful. "I know you think it's crazy," she told Mona.

"I don't know what to think. There's something to it." Mona started greeting Jim, when Jim and Lois took their morning walk. It like to drove Pete wild.

"I almost, just about, can see him," Mona said. "Maybe they're not crazy."

"I don't care much for kids. I do like dogs." Nancy got maternal. She swore that Em was going to ruin the pup.

"She seems to pee a lot," Em said.

"She's got a baby bladder." Nancy went downtown, and bought a book on how to train your dog.

"How to *ruin* your dog," Pete said. "They've got that little girl downright confused."

"Maybe so," said Lona-Anne-Marie, "and maybe not. Watch where she *doesn't* jump, watch where she does."

"There's no predictin' what a pup will do." Pete watched close. The pup seemed romping with another dog. When Jim and Lois went along with Em, the pup seemed with three people. She danced in front of Jim; like he took space. She didn't run across his space.

"It's mass delusion," Pete explained. "The neighborhood is nuts, and so's my wife. I've lived beside that woman forty years. I think I've lost my mind."

"Folks get lonesome," Nancy said. "We're old. If everybody's happy why complain? The world don't care for old folks anyway. We get to act as silly as we please." Nancy didn't give a thought for Jim. She only walked along to bother Pete.

On Sunday mornings at the Kingdom Hall folks come and go like businessmen at lunch. They chomp an hour's message, then leave. Used to be, when church was over folks would stand around. They'd talk and gas and gossip, swap the news. Girls would flirt with boys, and boys would blush. There was no helter-skelter.

On Sunday mornings Lona-Anne-Marie can almost always walk to Kingdom Hall. Unless the weather's awful, or unless her rheumatism bends her. On such days, Em or Pete walks with her. They don't stay. They pick her up when services are done.

One day she walked with Jim. People took no notice. Except the people in the neighborhood. Lona-Anne-Marie leaned on Jim's arm. Her white hair puffed beneath a mended scarf. Her red coat was a thrift store hand-me-down.

"That tears it," Pete said. "I must be missin' something."

"My dog has caused the resurrection of the world." Em spoke to Lois. "Don't tell nobody yet. He died and didn't want to leave. I take no credit."

Used to be that things weren't lonesome. When church let out the old folks stood around, and counted blessings. They had families, they had friends. They know about each other back to Adam. Some were even feuding.

"It don't pay to fret about the past. I've nary chick nor child to plague me. I think about the future." Lona-Anne-Marie was optimistic. If resurrection's certain folks can plan. "It's just," said Lona-Anne-Marie, "redemption should be fancy. I thought the skies would open."

The pup grew winter fur. Along the path behind the Kingdom Hall, and on the bluff where the old chimney rose, someone cut young trees. He heard the axe-chunks carried by the wind. Winter brings us freezing rain. Our world is covered with transparent glaze.

"John's resurrected," Em explained. "His whole family. Those five graves behind the Kingdom Hall. John's putting up a cabin. John Jr.'s helping; nice young man. Esther's just a little girl, and Tim is ten. Sarah can't be more than thirty-five. Folks married younger eighty years ago." Em told all this to Pete and Jim while rummaging his truck. "I've got some stuff they're going to need. Cooking pots and such. They gotta have a stove." He turned to Jim. "I'll bet you've got a couple in your shed."

"I must be gettin' old," Pete said. "I'm tired. This dis-believing wears a fella down." The sound of axe-chunks carried from the bluff. "It won't be up to code," Pete said. "There's no permit. The sheriff's gonna come and raise some hell."

"We're past the time of sheriffs, I expect." Jim seemed certain-sure. "Woodstoves weigh a lot. We'll have to pack it down in parts. Bolt it back together on the site."

"Oh, Lord," Pete said. "I just now heard Jim's voice. Now everybody's crazy."

Used to be, miracles abounded. Every family had at least one tale of someone on the far side of death's door that death tossed back. Or maybe angels cruised the neigh-borhoods. There was a time when faith moved mountains. Pete was old enough to recollect.

"I'd ought to call the sheriff. Get this done." Nancy can be mulish. The minute Pete began to talk to Jim, Nancy balked. Her iron-gray hair looked like a puff of mist as she peered from her windows. When Em, and Jim, and Lois, and the dogs, went walking down behind the Kingdom Hall, Nancy stayed at home. "I've been playing this just like a game. Never took it serious."

"Pipe dreams come from smoke. I see no smoke."

Lona-Anne-Marie cleaned house. She washed her windows, polished up her stove. "I ain't seen Pete so lively in a while. He's finally taking interest. It's making Mona happy."

Lona-Anne-Marie washed curtains. The rebirth of the world would find her tidy. She had few words about the resurrection. "It had to happen sometime. Why not now? I've been predictin' it."

When woodsmoke rose behind the Kingdom Hall the sheriff came. Webster Smith ("Call me Web") is sheriff. He's friendly when election comes around. "There's law and folks," he says, and what he means is comfort lies in balancing the two. Web does like comfort.

"I'm not so young myself," Web said to Pete. He stood beside his car and watched the trees. Dead poppies straggled in the vacant lot, while off a-ways; two playing children looked like bouncing toys.

"Old folks imagine things. I ought to know. Try sittin' in a car night after night. Looking out for drunks." Web had walked the path, looked at the site. Nancy got so bothered she'd joined Pete. They'd waited side by side until Web got back. Web is not bad-looking, tall and built in chunky squares.

"What did you see?" Nancy frets at things, won't let them go. She's not above some flirting. Web has always been a ladies' man.

"A cabin built by axe. It's some poor duffer. Riding out the winter. Don't own a chainsaw, even."

"I'd just as leave this didn't get around. I think there's something to it." Pete winked at Jim, who only Pete could see. From up the path behind the Kingdom Hall Em walked with his two dogs.

"The folks at Kingdom Hall made no complaint. The land belongs to them. Come spring the guy will move along. Meanwhile, I won't roust him." Web had got distracted. Nancy'd pulled her shoulders back. It made her front stick out.

"None of us has got that many years." Web looked at Kingdom Hall like he was tired. "We mix up fact and memory. These days I spend a lot of time remembering my folks." Web looked where Em was coming from the trees. "I heard he bought a high-price pup. Why's he need two dogs?"

"Sweet loving God," said Nancy. Then she dropped her shoulders.

The sum of it is John and Sarah stayed, together with their kids. They feared hard times. It isn't easy, after eighty years, to make a living. They were raised with horses, not with cars; but everybody helped.

On Sundays, going to the Kingdom Hall, folks drove past and sort of looked confused. They'd wave to Pete and Em; and Em's two dogs; or maybe one. When spring rains came, a few of them began to wave at Jim.

"I got to guess," said Lona-Anne-Marie, "the skies will open soon."

In spring the rain is constant. It walks across the mountains and the Sound. It floods our gardens and the vacant lots. Hard to work the ground, the earth gets soggy. The roof of Kingdom Hall grows moss. The moss is softly green. It burns away come summer.

The pup grew to a dog and Em was thinking. "It's old folks make this happen," he told Jim. "Lona-Anne-Marie knew all along. The living and the dead are all the same. I'll get it studied out."

"Faith don't amount to squat," Pete said to Em. "Unless you're stuck with facts. Then there's something to it."

"Maybe we all died," said Em, "and none of us took notice."

In May the rains turn warm and start to thin. Our world is green. New growth tips the firs. The pines grow whitish candles. The roof of Kingdom Hall looks like a lake, reflecting trees. "It comes from being lonesome," Em told Jim. "I'd guess it's more than that, but there's a start."

"It's getting ticklish down at Kingdom Hall."

Lona-Anne-Marie still went to church. "Some folks say 'yes', and some say 'no'. Can't blame 'em much. A quiet resurrection's real surprising." Lona-Anne-Marie was feeling spry. When kids from the apartments came around, she gave them little parties.

"It's kind of cute," said Nancy. "Folks from Kingdom Hall talk resurrection. Then it comes and they don't see it. I guess it don't amount to much."

"It's having *everything,* plus lonesome." Em told Nancy, then told Pete. "Youngsters couldn't do it. Been listening to the preachers sixty years. It took my dog to teach me."

When John and Sarah took their kids to church, the congregation put its cares aside. Redemption maybe—maybe not—but here were folks who had to make a crop. The elders took a vote. They had a man come in. Tractored up the vacant lots. They brought hand tools and seed.

"I know now how it works," Em said to Pete. "Dead folks are all around."

Young folks have needs, Em claims. When they get lonesome they just chase their tails. They do those things young people have to do. Em says the resurrection always was, has always been. It just takes folks who have no wants, but feel the pain of lonesome. Em claims the skies won't open.

Lona-Anne-Marie believes they will. She waits and watches. In the vacant lots, the poppies have given way to scarlet runner beans. John and Sarah seem to have the touch. Their crop is thrifty.

John thinks Em is right, Jim isn't sure. The rest of us are waiting. When summer dawns throw silver light in patches through the trees, we watch the sky. The roof of Kingdom Hall is pebbled gold, not much has changed. On Sunday mornings folks pass to and fro. They wave and go their ways when services are done. The neighborhood falls quiet; save for children's play, while in the parking lot of Kingdom Hall two white dogs dance, or sniff at oil spots where the cars were parked.

Born in Ohio in 1932, Jack Cady was educated at the University of Louisville. A former auctioneer, truck driver, lumberjack, English professor, and newspaper publisher and editor, he writes for such diverse magazines as Overdrive *(a trucker's monthly) and* Yale Review. *In 1971 he won the Best First Story award of the* Atlantic Monthly *for "The Burning" and the National Literary Award for "Shark." His best known work is* The Jonah Watch, *about a ghostly thing that comes aboard a Coast Guard ship at night (based, he insists on a totally non-fictitious personal experience).*

No one wants to die unknown.

FIVE

The Stranger

Ambrose Bierce

A man stepped out of the darkness into the little illuminated circle about our failing campfire and seated himself upon a rock.

"You are not the first to explore this region," he said, gravely.

Nobody controverted his statement; he was himself proof of its truth, for he was not of our party and must have been somewhere near when we camped. Moreover, he must have companions not far away; it was not a place where one would be living or traveling alone. For more than a week we had seen, besides ourselves and our animals, only such living things as rattlesnakes and horned toads. In an Arizona desert one does not long coexist with only such creatures as these: one must have pack animals, supplies, arms—"an outfit." And all these imply comrades. It was perhaps a doubt as to what manner of men this unceremonious stranger's comrades might be, together with something in his words interpretable as a challenge, that caused every man of our half-dozen "gentlemen adventurers" to rise to a sitting posture and lay his hand upon a weapon—an act signifying, in that time and place, a policy of expectation. The stranger gave the matter no attention and began again to speak in the same deliberate, uninflected monotone in which he had delivered his first sentence:

"Thirty years ago Ramon Gallegos, William Shaw, George W. Kent and Berry Davis, all of Tucson, crossed the Santa Catalina mountains and traveled due west, as nearly as the configuration of the country permitted. We were prospecting and it was our intention, if we found nothing, to

push through to the Gila River at some point near Big Bend,
where we understood there was a settlement. We had a
good outfit but no guide—just Ramon Gallegos, William
Shaw, George W. Kent and Berry Davis.

The man repeated the names slowly and distinctly, as if to
fix them in the memories of his audience, every member of
which was now attentively observing him, but with a
slackened apprehension regarding his possible companions
somewhere in the darkness that seemed to enclose us like a
black wall; in the manner of this volunteer historian was no
suggestion of an unfriendly purpose. His act was rather that
of a harmless lunatic than an enemy. We were not so new to
the country as not to know that the solitary life of many a
plainsman had a tendency to develop eccentricities of con-
duct and character not always easily distinguishable from
mental aberration. A man is like a tree: in a forest of his
fellows he will grow as straight as his generic and individual
nature permits; alone in the open, he yields to the deform-
ing stresses and torsions that environ him. Some such
thoughts were in my mind as I watched the man from the
shadow of my hat, pulled low to shut out the firelight. A
witless fellow, no doubt, but what could he be doing there in
the heart of a desert?

Having undertaken to tell this story, I wish that I could
describe the man's appearance; that would be a natural
thing to do. Unfortunately, and somewhat strangely, I find
myself unable to do so with any degree of confidence, for
afterward no two of us agreed as to what he wore and how
he looked; and when I try to set down my own impressions
they elude me. Anyone can tell some kind of story; narra-
tion is one of the elemental powers of the race. But the
talent for description is a gift.

Nobody having broken silence the visitor went on to say:

"This country was not then what it is now. There was not
a ranch between the Gila and the Gulf. There was a little
game here and there in the mountains, and near the infre-
quent waterholes grass enough to keep our animals from
starvation. If we should be so fortunate as to encounter no
Indians we might get through. But within a week the purpose of the expedition had altered from discovery of wealth
to preservation of life. We had gone too far to go back, for

what was ahead could be no worse than what was behind; so we pushed on, riding by night to avoid Indians and the intolerable heat, and concealing ourselves by day as best we could. Sometimes, having exhausted our supply of wild meat and emptied our casks, we were days without food or drink; then a water-hole or a shallow pool in the bottom of an arroyo so restored our strength and sanity that we were able to shoot some of the wild animals that sought it also. Sometimes it was a bear, sometimes an antelope, a coyote, a cougar—that was as God pleased; all were food.

"One morning as we skirted a mountain range, seeking a practicable pass, we were attacked by a band of Apaches who had followed our trail up a gulch—it is not far from here. Knowing that they outnumbered us ten to one, they took none of their usual cowardly precautions, but dashed upon us at a gallop, firing and yelling. Fighting was out of the question: we urged our feeble animals up the gulch as far as there was footing for a hoof, then threw ourselves out of our saddles and took to the chaparral on one of the slopes, abandoning our entire outfit to the enemy. But we retained our rifles, every man—Ramon Gallegos, William Shaw, George W. Kent and Berry Davis."

"Same old crowd," said the humorist of our party. He was an Eastern man, unfamiliar with the decent observances of social intercourse. A gesture of disapproval from our leader silenced him and the stranger proceeded with his tale:

"The savages dismounted also, and some of them ran up the gulch beyond the point at which we had left it, cutting off further retreat in that direction and forcing us on up the side. Unfortunately the chaparral extended only a short distance up the slope, and as we came into the open ground above we took the fire of a dozen rifles; but Apaches shoot badly when in a hurry, and God so willed it that none of us fell. Twenty yards up the slope, beyond the edge of the brush, were vertical cliffs, in which, directly in front of us, was a narrow opening. Into that we ran, finding ourselves in a cavern about as large as an ordinary room in a house. Here for a time we were safe: a single man with a repeating rifle could defend the entrance against all the Apaches in the land. But against hunger and thirst we had no defense. Courage we still had, but hope was a memory.

"Not one of those Indians did we afterward see, but by the smoke and glare of their fires in the gulch we knew that by day and by night they watched with ready rifles in the edge of the bush—knew that if we made a sortie not a man of us would live to take three steps into the open. For three days, watching in turn, we held out before our suffering became insupportable. Then—it was the morning of the fourth day—Ramon Gallegos said:

" 'Señores, I know not well of the good God and what please him. I have live without religion, and I am not acquaint with that of you. Pardon, señores, if I shock you, but for me the time is come to beat the game of the Apache.'

"He knelt upon the rock floor of the cave and pressed his pistol against his temple. 'Madre de Dios,' he said, 'comes now the soul of Ramon Gallegos.'

"And so he left us—William Shaw, George W. Kent and Berry Davis.

"I was the leader: it was for me to speak.

" 'He was a brave man,' I said—'he knew when to die, and how. It is foolish to go mad from thirst and fall by Apache bullets, or be skinned alive—it is in bad taste. Let us join Ramon Gallegos.'

" 'That is right,' said William Shaw.

" 'That is right,' said George W. Kent.

"I straightened the limbs of Ramon Gallegos and put a handkerchief over his face. Then William Shaw said: 'I should like to look like that—a little while.'

"And George W. Kent said that he felt that way, too.

" 'It shall be so,' I said: 'the red devils will wait a week. William Shaw and George W. Kent, draw and kneel.'

"They did so and I stood before them.

" 'Almighty God, our Father,' said I.

" 'Almighty God, our Father,' said William Shaw.

" 'Almighty God, our Father,' said George W. Kent.

" 'Forgive us our sins,' said I.

" 'Forgive us our sins,' said they.

" 'And receive our souls.'

" 'And receive our souls.'

" 'Amen!'

" 'Amen!'

"I laid them beside Ramon Gallegos and covered their faces."

There was a quick commotion on the opposite side of the campfire: one of our party had sprung to his feet, pistol in hand.

"And you!" he shouted—"*you* dared to escape?—you dare to be alive? You cowardly hound, I'll send you to join them if I hang for it!"

But with the leap of a panther the captain was upon him, grasping his wrist. "Hold it in, Sam Yountsey, hold it in!"

We were now all upon our feet—except the stranger, who sat motionless and apparently inattentive. Someone seized Yountsey's other arm.

"Captain," I said, "there is something wrong here. This fellow is either a lunatic or merely a liar—just a plain, every-day liar whom Yountsey has no call to kill. If this man was of that party it had five members, one of whom—probably himself—he has not named."

"Yes," said the captain, releasing the insurgent, who sat down, "there is something—unusual. Years ago four dead bodies of white men, scalped and shamefully mutilated, were found about the mouth of that cave. They are buried there; I have seen the graves—we shall all see them tomorrow."

The stranger rose, standing tall in the light of the expiring fire, which in our breathless attention to his story we had neglected to keep going.

"There were four," he said—"Ramon Gallegos, William Shaw, George W. Kent and Berry Davis."

With this reiterated roll-call of the dead he walked into the darkness and we saw him no more.

At that moment one of our party, who had been on guard, strode in among us, rifle in hand and somewhat excited.

"Captain," he said, "for the last half-hour three men have been standing out there on the mesa." He pointed in the direction taken by the stranger. "I could see them distinctly, for the moon is up, but as they had no guns and I had them covered with mine I thought it was their move. They have made none, but, damn it! they have got on to my nerves."

"Go back to your post, and stay till you see them again," said the captain. "The rest of you lie down again, or I'll kick you all into the fire."

The sentinel obediently withdrew, swearing, and did not return. As we were arranging our blankets the fiery Yountsey said: "I beg your pardon, Captain, but who the devil do you take them to be?"

"Ramon Gallegos, William Shaw and George W. Kent."

"But how about Berry Davis? I ought to have shot him."

"Quite needless; you couldn't have made him any deader. Go to sleep."

Andrew Bierce was one of the first American short story writers to gain international fame. Born in Ohio in 1842, he served with distinction in the Union army during the Civil War. As a newspaperman for the San Francisco Examiner, the handsome, fearless Bierce was noted for his bitter remarks (for instance, "Friendship—a barque that will hold two in fair weather but only one in foul) collected in The Devil's Dictionary (1906), his grim tales of the Civil War Tales of Soldiers and Civilians (1891), and such horrifying stories as "The Damned Thing" and the classic "An Occurrence at Owl Creek Bridge." He vanished somewhere in Mexico in 1914; his fate is unknown to this day.

John had waited a long time and traveled a long way for revenge against the ghost that haunted him, but he still wasn't prepared for the end of the journey.

SIX

Custer's Ghost
Clark Howard

The old man learned of the anniversary ceremony entirely by accident. One of the previous night's patrons had left a newspaper on the bar, and it was still there when the old man came in early the next morning to clean up. Wiping down the bar, he had picked up the paper to throw it away, but his still quick eyes had caught a glimpse of two words that he recognized beneath a picture on the open page. The picture, of an old man like himself, meant nothing to him, but the two words beneath it had been etched in his mind for fifty years.

Stopping his work, he studied the words carefully to be certain he was not mistaken. He could not read, so he studied each letter, all fourteen of them. They spelled: WEN-DELL STEWART. When the old man was absolutely sure that the letters and words were the same as he remembered, he carefully folded the newspaper and put it in the pocket of his old, worn coat, which he had hung inside the door. Then he resumed his job of cleaning up the saloon.

Three hours later, when his work was done, the old man locked up the saloon, put on his frayed coat, and limped down the little New Mexico town's main street to a combination café-pool hall above which he had a room. He went into the kitchen of the café and showed the newspaper to Elmo, the black fry cook.

"Read this for me, please, Elmo," he said.

"I can't read, John," the black man said without embarrassment. "Ask Stella."

The old man took the newspaper to Stella, the white

69

waitress, who was filing her nails on a stool behind the cash register.

"Will you read this for me, please, Stella?" he asked.

"Sure, John. Which one? This one? Sure." Stella cleared her throat. "It says, 'Ceremony Planned for Fiftieth Anniversary of Custer Battle.' You want me to read the whole story?"

John nodded. "Yes, please."

"Sure. 'A ceremony co-mem-mor-ating the fiftieth anniversary of the Battle of the Little Bighorn and the defeat and death of General George A. Custer and his Seventh Cavalry has been scheduled for June 25, 1926, at the Custer Battlefield National Monument near Hardin, Montana. Being honored at the ceremony will be former cavalry corporal Wendell Stewart, one of the survivors of A Company, commanded by Major Marcus Reno, which was also nearly annihilated on a ridge three miles away after the Custer massacre. Stewart, one of twenty men who received the Congressional Medal of Honor for bravery that day, is believed to be the sole survivor of the Custer regiment. He is seventy-three years old.'" Stella paused and studied the old man to whom she was reading. "Say, John, you must be about the same age as him, aren't you?"

"I am almost seventy summers," John answered.

Stella cracked her chewing gum. "You sure talk funny sometimes, John. Want me to read the rest?"

"No, that is enough. Can you tell me what is the number of today?"

"You mean the date? Sure. This is yesterday's paper, so today must be Thursday, June 16, 1926."

"How many days is it until the day the newspaper speaks of?"

"Well, let's see, that would be—" Stella counted on her fingers "—nine days, not counting today." She tilted her head, raising one eyebrow curiously. "Why? You're not thinking of going up there, are you, John? It's a mighty long way."

"How long a way?"

Stella shrugged. "I don't know. A *long* long way. That's Montana and this here is New Mexico. I can tell you this: we're at the bottom of the map and that's at the top."

Two customers came in and Stella went to wait on them. John folded the newspaper and went back into the kitchen.

"How far is it to Montana?" he asked Elmo.

The fry cook smiled. "Now you asking the right man," he said proudly. "I ain't never learned to read, but, brother, I done hoboed all over this here country, top to bottom and side to side. 'Tween here and Montana you got Colorado and you got Wyoming. I expect you about twelve hundred miles. A good, long piece, my friend."

"Thank you, Elmo," the old man said.

He went out the kitchen door and limped up the back stairs, favoring his right leg. There were three rooms above the café. Elmo lived in one, an old Mexican with a government pension lived in another, and John occupied the third. Because John had dark skin, most people thought he was also Mexican, or at least part Mexican. But he was not.

In his little room, John spread the newspaper on top of a faded old bureau in which he kept his few clothes. From the bottom drawer he removed an odd-looking pouch, shaped like but slightly larger than a saddlebag, from the bottom of which hung what appeared to be, and in fact was, a brown, hairy tail. The pouch itself was also hairy, except in spots where the hair had worn off, leaving a shiny brown skin. It was a buffalo bag, and it was almost as old as John himself.

Opening the flap, John pulled out a faded blue cavalry campaign hat, its brim bent and broken, its crown crushed and lifeless. The old man straightened it out as best he could and placed it upside-down next to the picture in the newspaper. On the inside band of the hat, just barely legible after so many years, were the same fourteen letters and two words that he had found in the newspaper: WENDELL STEWART.

John shifted his eyes to the newspaper and stared at the face above the name. As he did so, he reached down and rubbed the dull, constant pain in his right leg.

So, he thought, the spirits have finally brought you to me. After fifty years.

(For many years he had used the name John Walker, but once he had been Walks-across-Prairies, a young Oglala warrior and a follower of Crazy House, his chief. His people had been members of the seven tribes which made up the great Teton Sioux Nation. He had ridden a pony bareback across the vast High Grass, the plain that stretched from the foot of the Black Hills all the way to the Rosebud in the place the blue coats called Montana.

Child, boy, and young man, he had been a Sioux.)

When the spell of the moment was over, and he no longer stared hypnotically at the photo of Wendell Stewart, the old man reached into his buffalo bag again and drew forth a crudely made but structurally solid and well crafted stone-and-pine hatchet. It was his war club of long ago, and the wood of the pine handle was so old it had petrified nearly as solid as the smooth rock that was its head. He closed his still strong right hand around the handle and held the club diagonally across his chest.

In the cracked mirror above the bureau, he looked at his old, lined face, its skin now similar in texture to the buffalo bag itself. His hair, though still thick, was white like a summer cloud. The line of his mouth had relaxed with the passage of time and no longer served to advise others of the arrogance and defiance that once burned inside him. He knew that much of the fire had gone out of him, but he was pleased to see that his eyes were still clear and alert. The spirits, he thought, always knew what they were doing. His grandfather, Many Leaves, had taught him that when he was a boy living in the tipi of one of his father's wives.

"If the great spirits did not know in which direction to go, they would not move at all," Many Leaves had told him. And added quietly, "Unlike human beings."

It was obvious to John what the spirits now wanted him to do. The picture and the words in the white man's newspaper had been his sign. He was to return to the great battlefield and meet the bluecoat called Wendell Stewart, the soldier who had wounded his right leg with a long, shiny saber and given him his limp.

For fifty years of pain, he was to kill Wendell Stewart.

The next morning when the sun began to rise, John turned his right shoulder toward the light and began walking. His buffalo bag was slung over one shoulder, and he also carried an old carpetbag he had stolen years earlier from a drummer of needles and thread. On his feet he wore his hightop white-man's shoes, but in the buffalo bag he carried the last pair of moccasins he had made for himself some ten years earlier. When he got to the High Grass, he would put on the moccasins. He walked down the street of the little New Mexico town where he had made his home for more than nine years and, without a backward glance or a regret, began his journey north.

The first day, he passed through towns called Hatch, Arrey, Caballo, and Chuchillo, and by dusk was in a place called Socorro. He did not know addition and subtraction as such, so he had no way of figuring that he had to travel 130 miles in each of the nine days he had in order to arrive at the battlefield on the day of the ceremony. He knew only that it was north and far away, and since the spirits wanted him to get there in time he *would* get there in time.

His leg hurt as he walked, as it always did, but it was advantageous in a way because his limp provided him with many rides. Farmers in wagons gave him lifts, country people driving buggies stopped for him, salesmen in Model T cars took him from town to town so they could have someone to talk to.

"Yessir, I paid three hundred and fifty dollars for this little buggy," one of them said the second day, north of Albuquerque. "Never thought I'd pay that much money for *any* car. But it's worth it. Got a self-starter—don't even have to crank it."

John merely grunted. The cost meant nothing to him. He seldom had more than a little money. Mostly he earned only enough for food, shelter, and clothing. But that had always been enough—his needs were few and simple.

His travel day began at the first hint of sunup. As soon as he was able to tell direction, he was up and moving. During the day he ate berries and other wild fruit—at night he stole corn and melons from the fields when he could and picked up a stray chicken here and there. He would have trapped small game for his meals, but he was in too much of a hurry. Nights he slept in haystacks or woods. The second night it rained and he slept under a country bridge. It had been a long time since he had slept outdoors—it was good to see the stars last thing before going to sleep.

John was pleasantly surprised that he did not dream during his journey. For fifty years, since the long-ago day of the battle, he had dreamed sporadically of Custer. Long Hair, as he had been called by Crazy Horse. Long Hair often came to him in his dreams—buckskin-clad, yellow hair flowing from under the wide-brimmed white-leather hat. In the dreams, Custer would walk directly toward him, eyes fixed, arms swinging slightly, pistols stuck in the belt of his buckskin coat. He would keep coming, growing larger and larger, seeming bent on trodding over John. Finally he would fill the boundaries of John's mind, become too big for the dream itself, and that was when John would wake up.

John was convinced that his dream image was Custer's ghost, and he hated and feared the dream. As the trip back took him closer and closer to the only place where he had ever seen Long Hair he had presumed he would be troubled by the dream every night. But he was not, and that made him even more sure of the spirits that had planned his journey.

Even without the dreams, however, he found himself thinking of Custer as he traveled.

(The time of the battle was as fresh in John's mind in 1926 as it had been immediately after it happened, in 1876. There had been 12,000 in their vast camp on the banks of the Little Bighorn back then. Tipis stretched for three miles on both sides of the river. Totanka Yotanka, the great Uncpapa medicine man, whose name translated to Sitting Buffalo, but whom the bluecoats called Sitting Bull, had summoned every tribe on the northern plains to come forward and council with him about the encroachment of the whites onto land that had been ceded to them by the Ft. Laramie Treaty of 1868.

All of South Dakota west of the Missouri River, including the sacred Black Hills and all of the Powder River country of Montana, was supposed to be theirs. It was known as the Great Sioux Reservation and Hunting Ground. There they had lived in peace with all tribes—except the unworthy Crow, of course—for eight years. Then someone had found gold in the Black Hills, and the greedy whites had swarmed in like ants to an anthill. The Sioux had lashed out to protect what the white chief had ceded to them. When the soldiers began their marches, from faraway places called Omaha and St. Paul, Sitting Bull sent word for all tribes to join him at the Little Bighorn.

For the first time ever, they came together as one people. The Uncpapa, Oglala, Miniconjou, Sans Arc, Blackfoot, Brule, even the austere, high-minded Northern Cheyenne, who considered themselves the Superior Ones. For the first time ever, their leaders, Crazy Horse, Low Dog, Gall, Black Moon, Big Road, Two Moon, and Hump, were all disenchanted with the white man at the same time. Twelve thousand people gathered to hear Sitting Bull's medicine, and of that number 4,000 were of fighting age.

Walks-across-Prairies had just turned nineteen. Since he had been a boy of eleven, there had been peace with the white-eyes. Walks-across-Prairies had never counted a coup, except among the shiftless Crow, and that certainly was no honor to boast about. When he complained to his grandfather Many Leaves about it, Many Leaves had said, "A worthy enemy is a valuable thing. But no enemy at all is even more valuable. Count coup with the buffalo, my grandson, so that an old man like me might have a new robe before the snows come."

Walks-across-Prairies had taken his grandfather's advice, and for a while he was content with his lot. But when the call came from Sitting Bull, and Crazy Horse ordered the camp struck and moved to the Little Bighorn, the young brave felt a new kind of excitement in his breast.

An excitement that meant warpaint.)

On the third day of his journey, John made it into Colorado and was picked up by an oil-truck driver going from Alamosa to Mineral Hot Springs.

"Know anything about this feller Tunney they got matched with the champ?" the man asked.

John shook his head. He did not know what the man was talking about.

"I seen a pitcher of him," the trucker said. "Looks pretty fancy to me. Ain't even got much of a beard. You know, that

Dempsey, why, he's got such a rough beard he can draw blood with it."

"This Dem-see, he is a warrior?" John asked.

"I'll say!" the truck driver laughed.

It did not bother John that even after fifty years he knew so little about the ways of the white man's world. He had not tried to learn more than he knew. He felt it was enough that he could now speak the language. Until he was twenty-five, he spoke only Sioux, because after the great battle he had followed Crazy Horse and Sitting Bull into exile in Canada. The great chiefs knew that the white government would not tolerate their great victory over the bluecoats.

"When the white-eyes defeat us, it is a victorious campaign," Many Leaves had said. "But when we defeat them, it is a massacre. The white-eyes are clever with words."

Following the battle, great trails of tribes had moved north into Saskatchewan. The chiefs knew that the bluecoats could not follow them there—some treaties they would *not* break. They planned to live on the Canadian side and return secretly to the Montana plain to hunt buffalo, which was not plentiful in Canada. But the bluecoats, ever spiteful over the "massacre," put up intense patrols all along the border—in effect, sealing it. They themselves killed buffalo for sport, but would not permit the Indian to kill it for food and hides.

Walks-across-Prairies remained in Canada for six years. For nearly all of the first year he was practically helpless from his severely wounded right leg. The woman cared for him until he could walk again. The first time he realized that he would limp the rest of his life, he cried. Then he imagined what Many Leaves, by then dead, would have said. Something like: "A man is not judged by how straight his legs are, but by how straight his heart is." That was the first of many times to come when, to bolster his spirit, he would imagine something his grandfather probably would have said.

A year after the Custer battle, he saw Crazy Horse lead one thousand of his people down to Ft. Robinson, Nebraska, and take them onto the reservation because he could not feed them. Others began to straggle after him— Gall, with his people, then Two Moon, then Low Dog. Finally, after five long years, Sitting Bull led the last forty-three tattered, starving families down to Ft. Buford, Montana, and surrendered.

Walks-across-Prairies remained in Canada another year, living alone, hunting small game to survive, fishing, occasionally making his way north to Moose Jaw to steal necessities such as rifle cartridges and salt to cure meat. When the loneliness began to gnaw at him, he left Saskatchewan and walked into Manitoba. He walked all the way across that province and entered the United States again at Pinecreek, Minnesota. For ten long but uneventful years he wandered mid-America. He crossed to Wisconsin, went over the top of Michigan, down into Indiana, over to Ohio—so far away from the High Grass that at times he thought he was in another world.

Gradually he adopted the white man's dress and began to do white man's work. He toiled in the fields for white farmers, fished off boats on Lake Huron for white fishermen, cut trees in white timber camps, herded milch cows for white dairymen. He was surprised to find that as time went by, the white-eyes regarded him with less and less animosity—and even more surprised to realize that he was beginning to feel the same about them. At all times, for years, he kept his war club handy, but he never had to hit anyone with it. It was a strange life he led, but he slowly became used to it.

Traveling now on his journey back to the Little Bighorn reminded John of his incredible lifelong pilgrimage around the United States. The little town in New Mexico where he had lived for nine years was the longest he had ever stayed in one place since his wanderings began.

At thirty-five he had been in the Midwest, at forty and forty-five in the Deep South where he learned to pick cotton. At fifty he had been shoveling coal in the engine room of a New Orleans paddleboat up and down the Mississippi. At fifty-five he had been a cook's helper on a cattle drive in Texas. At sixty he worked in the oil fields in Oklahoma, where his employer was a Cherokee millionaire.

A couple of years later he had wandered down into the desert of New Mexico because his bones had begun to ache when it rained or snowed, and he remembered Many Leaves once saying, "After a man passes his sixtieth summer he should look for a warm place to die so that he will not feel the chill of death so strongly." John found his warm place in a little desert community where he got the job cleaning up the saloon in the morning and the café-pool hall at night. For just enough money for food, clothing, and shelter. All a man needed.

When the oil-truck driver let him out in Mineral Hot Springs, John waved and said, "I hope your warrior Demsee wins his battle." The driver laughed and drove away.

That night, John found a bubbling hot spring outside town and soaked his tired old body in it for three hours. It made him feel strong again. The spirits still knew what they were doing.

On the fourth day, he passed through Poncha Springs, Colorado, walking; Buena Vista, riding a hay wagon; Leadville, on an ore truck; Dowd, walking. Day five took him out of Colorado and into Wyoming. He passed the welcome sign at the state line—he couldn't read it, but he knew he was making progress because for the first time in many years he saw purple prairie clover growing at the edge of fields. He collected some and put it into his buffalo bag to dry. He also found some wild currant flowers that day and picked fifty of their small blue-black berries.

That night, near Saratoga, he trapped a young rabbit, roasted and ate its legs, and stretched the rest of the meat out, crushed the berries all over it, poured fat from the cooked meat of the rabbit on top of that, and pounded all of it together with a rock. Then he laid it out to dry by his campfire. By morning it would be pemmican, a dry, emergency food much like beef jerky he could carry with him the rest of the trip. Afterward, he steeped the purple prairie clover in water he boiled in a tin cup and made himself some wonderful tea to warm his old bones against the night air.

On the sixth day, he made it to within twenty miles of Casper, and the next morning was given a ride on a Baptist revival bus all the way to Sheridan—more than 150 miles. With half of the day still left, he walked out of Sheridan and by late afternoon came suddenly upon the Tongue River and knew he was in the High Grass country again. Montana.

He made his bed that night on the bank of the Tongue, and for the first time in many years he dreamed not just of Custer, but of Custer's death.

("Today is a good day to fight, and a good day to die," Chief Low Dog told his warriors, who sat on the ground gathered around him the morning of the battle. Walks-across-Prairies stood nearby with Crazy Horse and other Oglalas.

"Low Dog is a fool," Crazy Horse said quietly to his group. "No day is a good day to die, but every day is a good day to fight and live. I think Low Dog has given his brain to the white man's picture box." The Sioux war chief was highly contemptuous of all the Sioux leaders who, for a few worthless trinkets, had allowed themselves to be photographed during the years of the peace. Crazy Horse himself had never permitted a picture to be taken of him. "I want no one to see my face if I cannot see theirs," he gave as his reason.

It was noon that day when Sioux scouts brought them word that Custer's regiment was crossing the plain.

"Long Hair has split his bluecoats into three forks," the leader of the scouts reported. "The captain called Ben-teen has taken one hundred twenty-five men and turned toward the foothills of the Wolf Mountains. They are moving well away from Long Hair. The other captain called Ree-no has taken one hundred forty men and crossed Rosebud Creek. He now moves in the same direction as Long Hair, who has two hundred fifteen men on the other side of the creek."

"How soon will they reach the Little Bighorn River?" Crazy Horse asked.

"When the sun is there," the scout replied, pointing to mid-sky in the west. "By three o'clock."

Gall, who was obnoxious and a braggart, spat on the ground. "Long Hair is a fool," he announced. "He will ride right into our midst."

Crazy Horse, tall and regal, with a single white feather in his hair, grunted quietly. "Long Hair is no fool. A better bluecoat does not live. But his judgment fails him when he chooses scouts. He relies on information given him by the idle-minded, no-account Crow. They are too lazy to scout more than three miles ahead of the bluecoats." He smiled. "We will lie in wait *four* miles ahead. We will lure Ree-no and his soldiers away when they reach the fork of the creek. Then we will meet Long Hair at the Little Bighorn."

And that was the way it happened. A party of forty warriors rode up on Reno's column four miles from the Little Bighorn. Custer ordered Reno to pursue them with full strength. Reno led his 140 men galloping after the forty warriors. The warriors led them three miles across the plain—where one thousand more warriors waited for them behind a knoll. Reno and his men were immediately cut off and driven up onto a bluff where they took cover and dug in.

Custer was now alone with 215 men, riding along one side of the creek that ran into the Little Bighorn. Crazy Horse, at the head of another army of one thousand warriors, waited in a low valley on the other side of the river. When the cavalry column was where Crazy Horse wanted it, the Oglala and his warriors rode up the grassy bank and across the shallow river. Custer and his men were totally, completely—and fatally—surprised.

"No white man or Indian ever fought as bravely as Custer and his men," Oglala chief Low Dog would say in an interview at the Standing Rock Agency five years later, after he had returned from Canada and surrendered. "The white soldiers stood their ground bravely and none of them made any attempt to get away. Our warriors were told not to mutilate the head white chief, for he was a brave warrior and died a brave man, and his remains should be respected."

When all but fifty of his men lay dead around him, Custer ordered his remaining soldiers to follow him to a small hill that formed the highest point on the immediate plain. There the legendary "Last Stand" took place. Crazy Horse's Sioux abandoned their ponies at this point and fought on foot, with rifles and war clubs, swarming up the low hill on all sides.

Walks-across-Prairies had counted six coup on his way up the hill. His bare chest and arms were drenched in his enemy's blood. He saw a white man in civilian clothes take a blow to the back of the head from a war club and fall dead. He didn't know until later that it was Custer's brother, Boston Custer, who had been traveling with the Seventh Cavalry as a civilian historian. A few minutes later, when there were just a few bluecoats left, perhaps a dozen, he saw a very brave captain standing shoulder-to-shoulder with Long Hair, both of them firing pistols with both hands, until finally a rifle bullet struck him in the throat and he died. That brave captain had been Tom Custer, another brother of Long Hair.

Many historians were to speculate over the decades that followed whether Custer was the last to die that afternoon. Most conclusions were that it was highly unlikely. But un- likely or not, Walks-across-Prairies knew it to be true. Custer lasted the longest that day because his men, who idolized him, fought closely around him, and took the early bullets and blows meant for him. Walks-across-Prairies had been thirty feet from Long Hair when he took the fatal bullets that killed him. It would have been good, he thought later, if Crazy Horse could have been the one to kill him—a chief deserved to die at the hand of another chief—but that was not the way that day. Walks-across-Prairies vividly remem- bered that Long Hair was killed by two warriors: Mud- between-the-Toes shot him in the right breast, and Two Dogs shot him in the left temple.

After Custer fell, Crazy Horse stood by the body and said, "Long Hair's body is sacred. It shall not be cut."

And it had not been.)

On the last day of his journey, John awoke on a low bluff near a tiny village called Lodge Grass. There was a water hole directly below the bluff, and it was for that reason that John had chosen to sleep there. He knew that in the early morning the buffalo would come to water, and he could watch them. He awoke when he heard the bulls snorting at each other, and splashing as the calves ran playfully into the water.

John sat up and for an hour watched the big, thick, some- how majestic animals as they started their day. There were about thirty of them, including the young—just enough,

John remembered, to make a good tipi for winter. It took about twenty dressed hides to make a fifteen-foot tipi, another ten for ground covering and sleeping robes.

Watching them, the old Indian nodded fondly. Then his eyes became sad. Once, he thought, there would have been a hundred or more in the herd that watered here. Now there were thirty. He sighed a deep, quiet sigh. The buffalo and the Sioux, he thought, have gone the same way. Soon both would be only memories.

When the sun was midway in the morning sky, John prepared for the day. Now that he knew where he was, he knew also how long it would take him to get where he was going. He had about three hours' easy walk across the High Grass. From his buffalo bag, he removed his moccasins and put them on, then packed the rest of his belongings.

Before he left the bluff, he searched for and found a cluster of white Dakota snowberries, and nearby some thriving bloodroot plants. Securing a quantity of each, he put them on separate flat rocks and squeezed the juices from their flowers and roots. When he was finished, he had two small portions of dye, one red and one white.

He wished he could mark his face, but he knew that a painted Indian, even an old one, would have little if any chance of getting past the modern-day bluecoats who guarded the battlefield. So he removed his shirt and streaked only his chest—one horizontal white line across the top, as he would have done his forehead, and three vertical lines drawn down from that, which would have covered his nose and each cheek. It was the Sioux symbol of life, the white line being the tribe, the three red lines being the stages of life: child, warrior, Old Person.

For the first time ever, John thought of himself as an Old Person. If life had gone on as it should have, if the whites had stayed off their land and left them alone, today he would be considered a respected elder, and would be treated with honor and dignity. Instead of having to clean out a saloon every morning.

But soon, he thought, taking the war club from his bag, he would make a place for himself in the last tales to be told around Sioux campfires. He would count one more coup— and drive the ghost of Custer from his head.

As he walked toward the half-century-old battlefield that day, John Walker/Walks-across-Prairies thought about the man he would kill.

He knew almost nothing about Wendell Stewart. They had met for only a brief, fleeting instant an hour after the Last Stand. Walks-across-Prairies and some of the other young, eager Oglalas had joined Low Dog in his assault against Major Marcus Reno and the soldiers who had been lured away from Custer. By that time, Captain Frederick Benteen and the contingent Custer had sent toward the Wolf Mountains had hurried back to reinforce Reno. The young Oglalas who had fought Custer were still fresh—it had taken them only forty-five minutes to win that battle. By then it was only four o'clock on that June afternoon. Still plenty of daylight left for fighting.

It was while Walks-across-Prairies was helping fight Reno and Benteen that a young blond-haired corporal had seized the saber of a fallen officer and slashed the right calf of Walks-across-Prairies as he had ridden through in a pony charge. Walks-across-Prairies had swung at the soldier with his war club, felt it glance off bone, and whipped his pony away with the soldier's hat caught on his war club. They had never seen each other again.

Now, after fifty years, their fight would resume.

By noon, John stood at the edge of the old battlefield where the anniversary ceremony was to take place. There were already a number of people there. They had come in Model T cars, wagons, buggies. John looked around but he didn't see anyone who resembled the newspaper picture of Wendell Stewart. He waited patiently. Under his shirt, the war paint was dry and hard on his chest. In his buffalo bag was the war club.

As he waited, the old man studied the battlefield. There were small marble stones marking where each cavalryman's body had been found. The stones formed a weaving line that snaked its way up the hill. At the top of the hill was a large monument. John walked up and stood beside a schoolboy who was looking at it.

"Is this the grave of Cus-ter?" he asked the boy.

The boy shook his head. "General Custer's not buried here. They took him back to West Point to bury."

John shook his head briefly. That was a sad thing. Long Hair would have wanted to sleep with his soldiers. John had never heard of this "West Point." He hoped it was a place of honor.

"Who lies here?" he asked the boy, touching the monument.

"The last fifty men who died with Custer," the boy said. He pointed to a cluster of markers on one side of the hill. "Those are where the last fifty died. The one at the top there is General Custer's. Just behind his is his brother's, Captain Tom Custer. Right next to that is captain Myles Keogh. His horse Comanche was the only survivor, man or animal, in this whole battle. 'Cept for Indians, of course. And see that marker 'way down at the bottom? That was General Custer's other brother, Boston Custer." The boy squinted up at the old Indian. "Anythin' else you want to know?"

John shook his head. "No. Thank you for helping me."

When the boy left, John walked over to the crest of the hill, to Custer's marker. He could still see him: white buckskin field uniform, wide-brimmed white leather hat, flowing yellow silk scarf, saber on his belt, pistol in each hand, firing down into the wall of Sioux coming up the hill, missing Mud-between-the-Toes and Two Dogs, who raised their rifles simultaneously—

"Ladies and gentlemen," a voice said through a megaphone at the bottom of the hill, "our anniversary ceremony will begin shortly. Will everyone please gather in front of the museum building."

John watched the visitors move in small groups over to the brick building at the edge of the battlefield. His eyes searched the crowd but still did not see Wendell Stewart. Frowning, he made his way back down the rise and walked around the edge of the group, studying faces but recognizing none. Finally he had gone all the way around the crowd and found himself at a side door of the small museum building. There was a young soldier there with a rifle.

"May I help you, sir?" he asked.

John's frown deepened. "Sir" was the title of respect the

84

bluecoats used when addressing their chiefs. Why would this young soldier use it when speaking to him? Perhaps his old ears had played a trick on him.

"I am looking for the old soldier called Wen-dell Stewart," John said.

"The guest of honor," said the soldier. "He's still inside. Use the front door, right around there."

John nodded. "Thank you."

"You're welcome, sir."

There, he had said it again. This time John was certain of it. The soldier had called him "sir." He had spoken to him with respect.

Still frowning, John went around to the front of the museum and entered. There were a few stragglers still inside, looking at maps and photographs and displays of uniforms and other memorabilia from the great battle. John's eyes swept the faces—and suddenly stopped, locking on the face of Wendell Stewart. The old white soldier was sitting down. A man, woman, and young girl were standing around him, their backs to John. Although it might have been his imagination, John was almost certain that the instant he recognized Stewart, he felt a sharp surge of pain where the saber had cut the tendons of his right calf.

Fifty years, and the spirits had brought them together again. For the final battle.

John's hand went into the buffalo bag and slipped the war club out. He held it at his side, handle gripped tightly. As he eased toward the small cluster of people, he made up his mind to hit Stewart at the top of the head rather than in the face. A soldier who had lived as long as Stewart had did not deserve to have his face destroyed. I will leave him his dignity and take only his life, John decided.

Slowly, he edged nearer to the man, woman, and young girl, catching only glimpses of the seated Stewart when the people around him shifted their positions. John moved past the back of the man, then the woman, then stepped easily around the young girl to face his old enemy.

And there he stopped.

Wendell Stewart was in a wheelchair. He had no right leg.

Inside John's head, he heard what he imagined Many

Leaves would have said: "It is better to have a leg that hurts for fifty years than to have no leg at all."

Wendell Stewart and the three people standing with him all stopped talking and stared at John. Stewart's eyes flicked down to the war club he held. The old white soldier tensed.

Softening, John stepped forward and held the club out to the man in the wheelchair. "I hit you in the head with this a long time ago," he said simply.

Stewart stared harder at him, frowned, then parted his lips incredulously. "And I cut your leg with Lieutenant Gibson's saber."

John nodded. "It has hurt for fifty years." He pulled the old campaign hat out of his bag. "This is yours."

Stewart took the hat and ran his fingers over it. Tears came to his eyes. The young girl knelt and gave him a hand-kerchief. "Here, Granddad."

"Where did you lose your leg?" John asked.

"On that same bluff with Reno and Benteen," the old soldier replied, wiping his eyes. "About an hour after you and I met. I was a little dizzy from the blow on the head you gave me. I didn't get out of the way fast enough and a Sioux warrior ran a lance through my thigh. By the time we got back to Ft. Lincoln two days later, I had gangrene and the post surgeon had to take it off."

"I am sorry you lost it," John said.

Stewart nodded. "I'm sorry, too, that your leg has hurt for so long."

They were next to a wide window that looked out on the markers, the hill, and the great plain beyond.

"There was room enough for everyone, red *and* white," John said.

"Yes. Yes, there was."

The young girl touched John's arm. "What's your name, sir?"

"Sir" again. John almost smiled, but checked it in time. He must maintain his dignity among these strangers, and smiling was not dignified at his age.

"I am Walks-across-Prairies," he said proudly. "Of the Oglala."

"Would you like to push my grandfather outside for the ceremony?" she asked.

"It would be a great honor."

As the old Sioux pushed the old cavalryman to the gathering outside, he asked quietly, "Do you ever dream about Custer's ghost?"

"No," Stewart replied. "I dream about Crazy Horse's ghost."

Walks-across-Prairies nodded solemnly. The spirits *did* know what they were doing.

Born in Tennessee in 1934, the son of a bootlegger, Howard Clark was raised largely in Chicago. A Marine Corps veteran, he began writing short stories for mystery magazines in the 1950s; he later wrote novels and then such true-crime books as Zebra *(1979), the story of the San Francisco serial killings. Most of his mystery stories have appeared in* Ellery Queen's Mystery Magazine, *where he won the Reader's Award for the Best Story for 1985, 1986, and 1987.* Quicksilver *(1988) is his current novel.*

The avalanche should have destroyed the mule train, but everyone in the min-
ing camp could see the mules on the mountain far above where the avalanche
had occurred. Then the men who had seen them started dying. . . .

The Mountain-Mirage
Joaquin Miller

I have set down the following facts, well known to nearly
every old gold hunter of the far northwestern states, at the
request of my old partner in the express business, T. R.
Mossman, now of Seattle, Washington. For my own part, I
do not believe in this sort of literature, and feel certain that I
could do a great deal better than write stories of this kind,
and that you could do a great deal better than read this kind
of work. So bear in mind that I do not ask you to read a line
of it, or even to believe any more than you can help believing.

It began, this ten days' storm in the Idaho Mountains,
with the "small rain" of which the Bible speaks. At first it
was only a low cloud that crept away stealthily and white
through the black tops of the tall pine trees on the mountainside only a little way above our camp. Then the clouds
grew gray and dragged heavily along on the ground and
through the long yellow grass of late autumn, as if very
weary. Then the clouds seemed to be afraid to go farther
on. They began to make familiar with our very beards. They
lay low on the grasses and stayed with us all night. They
peered in at our tent doors, and we had to keep up big fires
and to button up both tent and overcoat to keep dry. At
least this was the state of affairs as I found them on my
arrival with the express from Walla Walla on my way to Millersburgh, fifteen miles farther on up and in the heart of
Mount Idaho, where they were shovelling up gold from the
grass roots in the newly discovered Idaho mines as if it had
been wheat on a threshing floor.

I wanted to push on that night so soon as I had opened my pack, made fast to keep out the clouds, and delivered the dozen or two letters which I had chanced to have for the dozen or two men whom I found storm-bound here. But the waters were tumbling down out of the treetops. The earth was filled with water, and was flooding at every pore. It was simply absurd to attempt to force a mule up the steep and slippery mountain before me. It was as much as life was worth to attempt the pass on foot; and although I knew that the rival express, Wells Fargo, with two messengers, was close behind, I reluctantly put up for the night at the hotel tent, kept by Charles Silver, a Jew with a Nez Percé Indian woman for a wife.

At daylight next morning I found the clouds had abandoned the siege and withdrawn to the mountaintops. The air was soft and warm and still. Not a breath. Not even a bird. The air, the earth, and all things of the earth were ominously still, indeed. The clouds lay in pretty white patches, snow white, above us and all about us in the lifted distance. Through these snow white rifts and drifts the golden morning sun poured in mellow glory on the mighty mountain sides that rose above the roaring and tumbling river beyond the mouth of the creek where we lay. Our camp, or rather the dozen tents that made up this new town, was close by the mouth of White Bird Creek, made famous as the scene of the first battle in the late war with Chief Joseph, and where many a white man bit the dust.

This White Bird Creek leaps headlong with a hop and a skip and a jump away out into the roaring waters of Salmon River. This river runs into the Shoshonee or Snake River, this into the Columbia, and the Columbia into the Pacific Ocean at Astoria, as you all know.

Now, this Salmon River was, is, and will be to the end of all rivers one of the roughest, swiftest, and ruggedest in all the mountains of Idaho; and that is saying a heap.

Everything had to be carried into the new mines on the backs of either men or mules. The trail twisted and curved and corkscrewed and clung and writhed like a serpent in torment on the rocky and almost perpendicular bluff. It hung in the air along the shelving and sliding banks hundreds of feet above the foaming waters.

If a mule lost his foot-hold, good-by mule, good-by man!

As for myself, I always got off and walked along here; not infrequently taking my *cantenas,* especially if loaded with gold, on my own shoulder.

But they were making a new trail—"a tall road," it was called—high above and on better ground. In fact, it was even then completed, all but putting a bridge across the great canyon or cleft in the granite rocks dignified by the name of White Bird Creek, at the mouth of which, as said before, we were now basking in the new morning sun and congratulating ourselves that the storm was over. The new trail was only about half a mile above us, and clearly visible for a long distance.

My mule was at the door, ready. I had weighed out the dust to pay my bill at the tent hotel, and was drawing the cinch tight and strong for a hard ride, when suddenly down out of the warm sunny heavens there began to tumble hailstones as big as a hen's egg. It lasted only long enough, this cannonade of hailstones, to make my mule break away, but not till I had jerked off my *cantenas* and escaped with their precious contents to cover. Then thunder and lightning!

This lightning struck, struck and stabbed the mountain to the heart right across the river level with our faces and not five hundred feet distant. The dirt and stones and *débris* flew in the air and rained down in a deluge. The earth simply moaned with pain. The thunder was not thunder. It was the bursting open of the earth. It seemed to be the crack of doom. The cheery lightness that had been only ten minutes before was now all blackness and dismay with seams and streams of lightning. We were blinded and overcome with awe and terror.

The mountainsides, made soft as ashes from the long rain of days before, began to loosen, to roll, to rumble, then tumble headlong into the river. I now could see, or rather hear, how worlds were formed—how river courses in mountains were channelled out, filled up, or forever changed to suit the whim or fancy of the fearful gods of thunder that fashioned them.

"My goodness! My pack train—what will become of that? I told them to take the new trail; and now, my God, they are lost! they are lost!"

This was "Pike" moaning to himself in a corner of the big tent. I never knew any other name for him than Pike. He was a tall, fine-looking man, from Ohio, of middle age, good address, first class character; and possibly his real name was Pike.

Pike's pack train was the finest on the road—all mules, young and strong, and a fortune to the owner.

This storm did not last ten minutes. It was simply too terrible to last longer. If that storm had lasted ten hours, the world, or at least that portion of it where it lay, would simply have ceased to be.

Even as it was, blocks and patches of the mountain half a mile broad in places had plunged headlong out of place and left only streaming yellow streaks of clay and sand, as if the very bowels had been torn from out the earth.

Then the sun came out almost as suddenly as it had left us. Then a man, the cook, came tearing in, to where Pike was helping me tighten up the letters in my *cantenas,* a precaution against another cloud burst while on my way over the mountain, shouting at the top of his voice, "Pike's pack train! Pike's pack train safe and sound up yonder on the new trail! Come and see, Pike! Come and see!"

Silver, the man who kept the tent hotel, sprang out from behind the bar and started for the door, but his Indian wife, with blazing eyes and wild gesture, caught him and held him back.

My two hands were full just at that moment, but Pike dropped everything and rushed out, to find the whole camp craning its neck up to the new trail, where the pack train, in full view of all, was making good time up around the mountain, as if no storm had ever been.

I heard the men shout and shake hands with Pike and roar out their hearty congratulations. I heard the bell of his bell-mule between these outbursts of feeling and good fellowship. Now, mark you distinctly, I heard that bell as clearly as ever I heard any church bell. And indeed I heard that bell more clearly and more distinctly. Because, you see, in my business as carrier of letters I had to know, and know well, the sound of every mule bell on every mile of that road. For much of my riding was done by night. And then often a pack train would be half a mile off the road, for grass or water. And, even if I had nothing for either the master or the men of the train, it was my place to know where every train on the trail was, in order to answer questions of concern to merchants waiting for their goods, and all that sort of thing.

So, you see, I knew that bell of Pike's pack train. I knew the sound, the shape, the size, the quality, the very cost of it. For Pike was my friend, and he had explained when riding with me ahead of his train one day that his bell was the sweetest-and clearest-toned bell on the road because it was largely silver. He now brought the crowd in to drink at the bar. I did not drink, because I never liked liquor in those days; and then, besides that, the boys whose gold I carried had a preference for sober express men, whatever they might be themselves. But even as they drank and I completed my packing I heard that bell up above us on the mountain more distinctly than any church bell; I repeat it. For church bells, you know, are much alike, differing mainly not in quality but in volume of sound.

"Well, boy, if you don't look out, Mossman and Miller's Express will be beat by my pack train," said Pike, smiling back over his shoulder at me as he set down his tin cup at the pine bark bar and passed out of the tent.

"I'm off, Pike; good-by." and I hastily threw my *cantenas* on the saddle pommel and swung my leg across my mule, which had been brought around at the first sign of the sun.

"Say!"

"Say?"

"Tell 'em I'm O.K. and will catch the pack train before it gets to Millersburgh."

"O.K., Pike."

"Hunky dory, Miller."

My mule scrambled up the sliding and slippery hill, and I never saw genial old Pike again, nor even heard of his pack train any more, except only that it was not.

And now a paragraph of digression. I have often seen, as thousands of others have, what is called the Sahara mirage on the sandy levels of Africa. But all that is nothing compared to the weird and wondrous mirage constantly met with on the plains of America.

Not six months ago, a man at Denver, a man whom I knew to be absolutely truthful, told me that he had seen lifted up in the heavens not only entire cities, but had once seen his own house in his own town, although that town was at that moment more than fifty miles distant, with a mountain intervening!

I must admit that I have never seen anything nearly as wonderful as that in all my forty years of the plains, off and on. But I will tell you this: I have seen enough to fill a book full of most marvellous things—things of almost indescribable beauty and glory and grandeur. And the pity to me is that learned and scientific men do not take up this matter and try and explain it a little and let us really know whether these things are of this world or the next.

Now as to this mountain-mirage. Why, this mountain-mirage is as far above the mirage of the plains as the mirage of the American plains is above the mirage of Sahara. And, too, it is very rare—as rare as remarkable. And when an old mountaineer sees a mountain-mirage he is suddenly, and from that day forth to the not distant end of his days, a sober man. And yet some men live a good long time after seeing this sign hung up in the heavens of the Rocky and the Bitter Root Mountains. The only absolute conclusion connected with the tradition is that a man who once sees the mountain-mirage must, soon or late, die by violence. But to get back to the trail through the snow over the mountain to Millersburgh.

I urged my mule almost beyond his strength, as I came near the junction with the new jack trail. This was partly because I was a boy and enthusiastic, partly because I was fond of bantering and shouting back in their own tongue to the leather-clad Mexican muleteers, and partly, and no doubt mainly, because I wanted to cheer the black and handsome fellows, after the storm, with the message from Pike.

I kept continually rising up in my stirrups, and now and then leaning low to look under the long black boughs of pine that hung heavy with snow on the mountaintop. No sign. I kept listening for the clear, soft sounds of the silver bell. It was like death. And my hair stood out with terror and dismay as I came to the junction of the trails and could see not even so much as a track!

I strained my eyes so hard in the snow that day looking

ahead, looking back, looking down in the deep narrow trail in the snow before me, that I became snow blind before I reached the express office, and had to be led in by some miners whom I fortunately overtook before entirely losing my sight. This snow blindness is not painful at first. But, oh, the daggers that pierce your sockets the following night!

My older brother, who by good chance was mining at the time there, took charge of my affairs, and the next day came out of the mountains and kept on down with me as far as Lewiston, where I could have medical attendance.

And here, having saved a big bag of gold dust, I sold—or rather gave away—my half of the express line, and never again saw the mountaineers of the phantom pack train. As for the real pack train, it had perished by an avalanche bodily only a few seconds before men saw its shadow in the sun above us.

And now let me tell you what became of the men who saw that mirage. Mind you, I saw nothing—only heard the bell.

That man who came rushing in to tell Pike was the waiter cook of the crude tent hotel. He was killed by a friend of mine, whose name I will not give, from the blow of a hatchet, in that same tent. Pike was shot in the forehead and killed at that place by Matt Bloodsoe only a few days after he saw this phantom train. Bloodsoe, after killing two other men, was killed in Arizona. Si Bradley, killed in Arizona. Alex Carter, hung at Helena. Boone Helm, hung at Butte City. Whiskey Bill, hung at Bozen, I believe. I know he was hung in Montana somewhere, but am not certain of the place. Cherokee Bob, killed at Florence. Bill Willoughby, killed same time and place. Dave English, Billy Peoples, and Nelson Scott, all hung together by Vigilantes at Lewiston two months later.

I believe there was no other one present at the time the mirage was seen except myself and Silver and his Indian wife. I have been told that my partner, Mr. Mossman, was there; but he asserts, and I know, he was not. It was my business to know where he was, and I know that he was not within two hundred miles. Others, again, say that Arthur Chapman, the famous guide and friend of General Howard all through the recent Nez Percé campaign, was there at this time spoken of. He was not there, as I well know, but in

Walla Walla. He is still living, a most truthful and upright man, greatly respected, and, I believe, still with the army at the solicitation of General Miles, who succeeded General Howard in the Pacific Department.

My old partner Mossman also still lives, and visited me here within the year.

Now, this story of the mountain-mirage, as well as all stories of this phenomenon, is rare. You can read, and you can hear tell any day, of remarkable things connected with the mirage of the plains. But a mountain-mirage! Well, you will travel far before you find a man who has seen it. And no man who has not seen it believes in it the least. As for the man who has seen it—well, he is not sociable. At least he is not in the habit of going around and telling people that he is under sentence of death.

As said before, there are better tasks than either the writing or the reading of such stories as this. But back of the request that prompted the setting down of these facts lies the earnest desire for some plain commonsense reason for the mirage, in the valley or on the mountain. Let our learned men answer.

More than a quarter of a century ago, when all this was fresh in my memory, I asked a famous *savant* in Paris to explain this mountain-mirage. He put his head down and his shoulders up, and then slowly balanced his two palms in the air close up under his double chin, as if weighing some weighty proposition; but he remained silent.

Very respectfully, but very earnestly, I again entreated him to tell me what this thing they call the mountain-mirage may be. And then, very respectfully and very earnestly, he answered—

"The mountain-mirage, it is not. It is impossible."

"Then what was it the men saw?"

"I will tell you, my son." And I bowed my head as he looked me in the face for he was very serious as he said, in a voice hardly above a whisper—

"Il était un fantôme, mon fils."

A colorful novelist of Old California, Joaquin Miller was born in Indiana (in either 1839 or 1844). After running away to Califor-

nia during Gold Rush days in 1855, he lived among the Digger Indians, even joining them in raiding parties. After graduating from Columbia University in Eugene, Oregon, he was admitted to the bar but never practiced law. During his busy life he established a Pony Express service between Idaho and Oregon, published Songs of the Sierra (1871) to acclaim in England, and covered the Klondike Gold Rush for the N.Y. Journal. He died in California in 1931.

Sometimes an archaeologist finds more than pot shards and arrowheads.

EIGHT

The Resting Place

Oliver LaFarge

The possibility that Dr. Hillebrand was developing kleptomania caused a good deal of pleasure among his younger
colleagues—that is, the entire personnel of the Department
of Anthropology, including its director, Walter Klibben. It
was not that anybody really disliked the old boy. That would
have been hard to do, for he was co-operative and gentle,
and his humor was mild; he was perhaps the greatest living
authority on Southwestern archaeology, and broadly
learned in the general science of anthropology; and he was
a man who delighted in the success of others.

Dr. Hillebrand was the last surviving member of a group
of men who had made the Department of Anthropology
famous in the earlier part of the twentieth century. His ideas
were old-fashioned; to Walter Klibben, who at forty was
very much the young comer, and to the men he had
gathered about him, Dr. Hillebrand's presence, clothed with
authority, was as incongruous as that of a small, mild bron-
tosaurus would be in a modern farmyard.

On the other hand, no one living had a finer archaeological technique. Added to this was a curious intuition,
which caused him to dig in unexpected places and come up
with striking finds—the kind of thing that delights donors
and trustees, such as the largest unbroken Mesa Verde
black-on-white jar known up to that time, the famous
Biltabito Cache of turquoise and shell objects, discovered
two years before and not yet on exhibition, and, only the
previous year, the mural decorations at Painted Mask ruin.
The mural, of which as yet only a small part had been uncovered, compared favorably with the murals found at

99

Awatovi and Kawaika-a by the Peabody Museum, but was several centuries older. Moreover, in the part already exposed there was an identifiable katchina mask, unique and conclusive evidence that the katchina cult dated back to long before the white man came. This meant, Dr. Klibben foresaw gloomily, that once again all available funds for publication would be tied up by the old coot's material.

The trustees loved him. Several years ago, he had reached the age of retirement and they had waived the usual limitation in his case. He was curator of the museum, a position only slightly less important than that of director, and he occupied the Kleinman Chair in American Archaeology. This was an endowed position paying several thousand a year more than Klibben's own professorship.

Dr. Hillebrand's occupancy of these positions, on top of his near monopoly of publication money, was the rub. He blocked everything. If only the old relic would become emeritus, the younger men could move up. Klibben had it all worked out. There would be the Kleinman Chair for himself, and McDonnell could accede to his professorship. He would leave Steinberg an associate, but make him curator. Thus, Steinberg and McDonnell would have it in mind that the curatorship always might be transferred to McDonnell as the man with senior status, which would keep them both on their toes. At least one assistant professor could, in due course, be made an associate, and young George Franklin, Klibben's own prized student, could be promoted from instructor to assistant. It all fitted together and reinforced his own position. Then, given free access to funds for monographs and papers. . . .

But Dr. Hillebrand showed no signs of retiring. It was not that he needed the money from his two positions; he was a bachelor and something of an ascetic, and much of his salary he put into his own expeditions. He loved to teach, he said—and his students liked him. He loved his museum; in fact, he was daffy about it, pottering around in it until late at night. Well, let him retire, and he could still teach a course or two if he wanted; he could still potter, but Klibben could run his Department as he wished, as it ought to be run.

Since there seemed no hope that the old man would give out physically in the near future, Klibben had begun looking for symptoms of mental failure. There was, for instance, the illogical way in which Dr. Hillebrand often decided just where to run a trench or dig a posthole. As Steinberg once remarked, it was as if he were guided by a ouija board. Unfortunately, this eccentricity produced splendid results.

Then, sometimes Hillebrand would say to his students, "Now, let us imagine—" and proceed to indulge in surprising reconstructions of the daily life and religion of the ancient cliff dwellers, going far beyond the available evidence. The director had put Franklin onto that, because the young man had worked on Hopi and Zuñi ceremonials. Franklin reported that the old boy always made it clear that these reconstructions were not science, and, further, Franklin said that they were remarkably shrewd and had given him some helpful new insights into aspects of the modern Indians' religion.

The possibility of kleptomania was something else again. The evidence—insufficient so far—concerned the rich Biltabito Cache, which Dr. Hillebrand himself was enumerating, cataloguing, and describing, mostly evenings, when the museum was closed. He was the only one who knew exactly how many objects had been in the find, but it did look as if some of it might now be missing. There was also what the night watchman thought he had seen. And then there was that one turquoise bead—but no proof it had come from that source, of course—that McDonnell had found on the floor near the cast of the Quiriguá stela, just inside the entrance to the museum.

The thefts—if there had been any—had taken place in April and early May, when everyone was thinking of the end of the college year and the summer's field trips. A short time later, and quite by accident, Klibben learned from an associate professor of ornithology that old Hillebrand had obtained from him a number of feathers, which he said he wanted for repairing his collection of katchina dolls. Among them were parrot and macaw feathers, and the fluffy feathers from the breast of an eagle.

Klibben's field was not the American Southwest, but any American anthropologist would have been able to draw an obvious conclusion: turquoise, shell, and feathers of those sorts were components of ritual offerings among the modern Hopis and Zuñis, and pissibly their ancestors, whose remains Dr. Hillebrand had carried on his lifework. Dr. Klibben began to suspect—or hope—that the old man was succumbing to a mental weakness far more serious than would be evidenced by the mere stealing of a few bits of turquoise and shell.

The director made tactful inquiries at the genetics field laboratory to see if the old man had been seeking corn pollen, another component of the ritual offerings, and found that there the question of the evolution of *Zea maiz* in the Southwest was related to the larger and much vexed question of the origin and domestication of that important New World plant, so interesting to archaeologists, botanists, and geneticists. Dr. Hillebrand had been collecting specimens of ancient corn from archaeological sites for a long time— ears, cobs, and grains extending over two millenniums or more, and other parts of the plant, including some fragments of tassels. It was, Klibben thought, the kind of niggling little detail you would expect to find Hillebrand spending good time on. Dr. Hillebrand had been turning his specimens over to the plant and heredity boys, who were delighted to have them. They, in turn, had followed this up by obtaining—for comparison—seed of modern Pueblo Indian, Navajo, and Hopi corn, and planting it. It was natural enough, then, that from time to time Dr. Hillebrand should take specimens of seed and pollen home to study on his own. It might be clear as day to Klibben that the old boy had gone gaga to the point of making ritual offerings to the gods of the cliff dwellings; he still had nothing that would convince a strongly pro-Hillebrand board of trustees.

Even so, the situation was hopeful. Klibben suggested to the night watchman that, out of concern for Professor Hillebrand's health, he keep a special eye on the Professor's afterhours activities in the museum. Come June, he would arrange for Franklin—with his Southwestern interests, Franklin was the logical choice—to go along on Hillebrand's expedition and see what he could see.

Franklin took the assignment willingly, by no means unaware of the possible advantages to himself should the old man be retired. The archaeologist accepted this addition to his staff with equanimity. He remarked that Franklin's knowledge of Pueblo daily life would be helpful in interpreting what might be uncovered, while a better grounding in Southwestern prehistory would add depth to the young man's ethnographic perceptions. Right after commencement, they set out for the Navajo country of Arizona, accompanied by two undergraduate and four graduate students.

At Farmington, in New Mexico, they picked up the university's truck and station wagon and Hillebrand's own field car, a Model A Ford as archaic as its owner. In view of the man's income, Franklin thought, his hanging on to the thing was one more oddity, an item that could be added to many others to help prove Klibben's case. At Farmington, too, they took on a cook and general helper. Dr. Hillebrand's work was generously financed, quite apart from what went into it from his own earnings.

The party bounced over the horrifying road past the Four Corners and around the north end of Beautiful Mountain, into the Chinlee Valley, then southward and westward until, after having taken a day and a half to drive about two hundred miles, they reached the cliffs against which stood Painted Mask Ruin. The principal aim of the current summer's work was to excavate the decorated kiva in detail, test another kiva, and make further, standard excavations in the ruin as a whole.

By the end of a week, the work was going nicely. Dr. Hillebrand put Franklin, as the senior scientist under him, in charge of the work in the painted kiva. Franklin knew perfectly well that he was deficient in the required techniques; he would, in fact, be dependent upon his first assistant, Philip Fleming, who was just short of his Ph.D. Fleming had worked in that kiva the previous season, had spent three earlier seasons with Dr. Hillebrand, and was regarded by him as the most promising of the many who had worked under him. There was real affection between the two men.

Two of the other graduate students were well qualified to run a simple dig for themselves. One was put in charge of the untouched second kiva, the other of a trench cutting into the general mass of the ruin from the north. Franklin felt uncomfortably supernumerary, but he recognized that

that was an advantage in pursuing his main purpose of keeping a close watch on the expedition's director.

After supper on the evening of the eighth day, Dr. Hillebrand announced rather shyly that he would be gone for about four days, "to follow an old custom you all know about." The younger men smiled. Franklin kept a blank face to cover his quickened interest.

This was a famous, or notorious, eccentricity of the old man's, and one in which Drs. Klibben, McDonnell, and the rest put great hope. Every year, early in the season, Dr. Hillebrand went alone to a ruin he had excavated early in his career. There was some uncertainty as to just where the ruin was; it was believed to be one known to the Navajos as Tsekaiye Kin. No one knew what he did there. He said he found the surroundings and the solitude invaluable for thinking out the task in hand. It was usually not long after his return from it that he would announce his decision to dig in such-and-such a spot and proceed to uncover the painted kiva, or the Kettle Cave fetishes, or the Kin Hatsosi blanket, or some other notable find.

If Franklin could slip away in the station wagon and follow the old man, he might get just the information he wanted. So far, Dr. Hillebrand's activities on the expedition had evidenced nothing but his great competence. If the old man ever performed mad antique rites with stolen specimens, it would be at his secret place of meditation. Perhaps he got up and danced to the ancient gods. One might be able to sneak a photo. . . .

Dr. Hillebrand said, "I shan't be gone long. Meantime, of course, Dr. Franklin will be in charge." He turned directly to his junior. "George, there are several things on which you must keep a close watch. If you will look at these diagrams—and you, too, Phil. . . ."

Franklin and Fleming sat down beside him. Dr. Hillebrand expounded. Whether the ancient devil had done it intentionally or not, Franklin saw that he was neatly hooked. In the face of the delicacy and the probable outcome of the next few days' work, he could not possibly make an excuse for absenting himself when the head of the expedition was also absent.

Dr. Hillebrand took off early the next morning in his

throbbing Model A. He carried with him a Spartan mini-
mum of food and bedding. It was good to be alone once
more in the long-loved reaches of the Navajo country. The
car drove well. He still used it because, short of a jeep,
nothing newer had the clearance to take him where he
wanted to go.

He drove slowly, for he was at the age when knowledge
and skill must replace strength, and getting stuck would be
serious. When he was fifty, he reflected, he would have
reached T'iiz Hatsosi Canyon from this year's camp in under four hours; when he was thirty, if it had been possible
then to travel this country in a car, he would have made
even greater speed, and as like as not ended by getting lost.
He reached the open farming area outside the place where
T'iiz Hatsosi sliced into the great mesa to the south. There
were nearly twice as many hogans to be seen as when he
had first come here; several of them were square and
equipped with windows, and by some of them cars were
parked. Everything was changing, but these were good
people still, although not as genial and hospitable as their
grandparents had been when he first packed in.

He entered the narrow mouth of T'iiz Hatsosi Canyon in
the late afternoon, and by the exercise of consummate skill
drove some four miles up it. At that point, it was somewhat
wider than elsewhere, slightly under two hundred feet
across at the bottom. The heavy grazing that had so
damaged all the Navajos' land had had some effect here.
There was less grass than there used to be—but then, he
reflected, he had no horses to pasture—and the bed of the
wash was more deeply eroded, and here and there sharp
gullies led into it from the sides.

Still, the cottonwoods grew between the occasional
stream and the high, warmly golden-bluff cliffs. Except at
noon, there was shade, and the quality of privacy, almost of
secrecy, remained. In the west wall was the wide strip of
white rock from which the little ruin took its name, Tsekaiye
Kin, leading the eye to the long ledge above which the cliff
arched like a scallop shell, and upon which stood the ancient habitations. The lip of the ledge was about twenty feet
above the level of the canyon, and approachable by a talus
slope that was not too hard to negotiate. Some small ever-

greens grew at the corners of the ledge. From the ground, the settlement did not seem as if it had been empty for centuries, but rather as if its occupants at the moment happened not to be visible. The small black rectangles of doorways and three tiny squares of windows made him feel, as they had done over forty years ago, as if the little settlement were watching him.

South of the far end of the ledge, and at the level of the canyon floor, was the spring. Water seeped richly through a crack in the rock a few feet above the ground and flowed down over rock to form a pool at the base. The wet golden-brown stone glistened; small water growths clung to the crevices. In the pool itself, there was cress, and around it moss and grass rich enough to make a few feet of turf.

Here Dr. Hillebrand deposited his bedroll and his food. He estimated that he had better than two hours of daylight left. He cut himself a supply of firewood. Then he took a package out of his coffeepot. The package was wrapped in an old piece of buckskin. With this in hand, he climbed up the slope to the ruin.

The sense of peace had begun once he was out of sight of the camp at Painted Mask Ruin. It had grown when he entered T'iiz Hatsosi Canyon; it had become stronger when he stepped out of the car and glimpsed through the cottonwoods his little village, with its fourteen rooms. By the spring, it had become stronger yet, and mixed with a nostalgia of past times that was sweetly painful, like a memory of an old and good lost love. These feelings were set aside as he addressed himself to the task of climbing, which was not entirely simple; then they returned fourfold when he was in the ruin. Here he had worked alone, a green young man with a shiny new Doctor's degree, a boy-man not unlike young Fleming. Here he had discovered what it was like to step into a room that still had its roof intact, and see the marks of the smoke from the household fire, the loom ties still in place in the ceiling and floor, the broken cooking pot still in the corner.

He paid his respects to that chamber—Room 4-B; stood in the small, open, central area; then went to the roofless, irregular oval of the kiva. All by himself he had dug it out.

Could Dr. Franklin have been there, spying unseen, he

would have been most happy. From under a stone that appeared firmly embedded in the clay flooring Dr. Hillebrand took an ancient, crude stone pipe fitted with a recent willow stem. He filled it with tobacco, performed curious motions as he lit it, and puffed smoke in the six directions. Then he climbed out of the kiva on the inner side and went behind the double row of habitations, to the darker area under the convex curve of the wall at the back of the cave, the floor of which was a mixture of earth and rubbish. Two smallish, rounded stones about three feet apart inconspicuously marked a place. Sitting by it on a convenient ledge of rock, he puffed at the pipe again; then he opened the buckskin package and proceeded to make an offering of ancient turquoise beads, white and red shell, black stone, feathers and down, and corn pollen.

Sitting back comfortably, he said, "Well, here I am again."

The answer did not come from the ground, in which the bones of the speaker reposed, but from a point in space, as if he were sitting opposite Dr. Hillebrand. "Welcome, old friend. Thank you for the gifts; their smell is pleasing to us all."

"I don't know whether I can bring you any more," the archaeologist said. "I can buy new things, of course, but getting the old ones is becoming difficult. They are watching me."

"It is not necessary," the voice answered. "We are rich in the spirits of things such as these, and our grandchildren on earth still offer them to us. It has been rather for your benefit that I have had you bringing them, and I think that that training has served its purpose."

"You relieve me." Then, with a note of anxiety, "That doesn't mean that I have to stop visiting you?"

"Not at all. And, by the way, there is a very handsome jar with a quantity of beans of an early variety in it where you are digging now. It was left behind by accident when the people before the ones who built the painted kiva moved out. It belonged to a woman called Bluebird Tailfeather. Her small child ran off and was lost just as they were moving, and by the time she found him, the war chief was impatient.

However, we can come back to that later, I can see that you have something on your mind."

"I'm lonely," Dr. Hillebrand said simply. "My real friends are all gone. There are a lot of people I get on nicely with, but no one left I love—that is, above the ground—and you are the only one below the ground I seem to be able to reach. I—I'd like to take your remains back with me, and then we could talk again."

"I would not like that."

"Then of course I won't."

"I was sure of that. Your country is strange to me, and traveling back and forth would be a lot of effort. What I saw that time I visited you was alien to me; it would be to you, too, I think. It won't be long, I believe, before I am relieved of attachment to my bones entirely, but if you moved them now, it would be annoying. You take that burial you carried home ten years ago—old Rabbit Stick. He says you treat him well and have given him the smell of ceremonial jewels whenever you could, but sometimes he arrives quite worn out from his journey."

"Rabbit Stick," Dr. Hillebrand mused. "I wondered if there were not someone there. He has never spoken to me."

"He couldn't. He was just an ordinary Reed Clan man. But he is grateful to you for the offerings, because they have given him the strength he needed. As you know, I can speak with you because I was the Sun's Forehead, and there was the good luck that you were thinking and feeling in the right way when you approached me. But tell me, don't the young men who learn from you keep you company?"

"Yes. There is one now who is like a son to me. But then they have learned, and they go away. The men in between, who have become chiefs, you might say, in my Department, have no use for me. They want to make me emeritus—that is, put me on a pension, take over my authority and my rewards, and set me where I could give advice and they could ignore it. They have new ways, and they despise mine. So now they are watching me. They have sent a young man out this time just to watch me. They call him a student of the ways of your grandchildren; he spent six weeks at Zuñi once, and when even he could see that the people didn't like him, he went and put in the rest of the summer at Oraibi."

"New Oraibi or Old Oraibi?" the Sun's Forehead asked.

"New Oraibi."

The chief snorted.

"So, having also read some books, he thinks he is an ethnographer, only he calls himself a cultural anthropologist. And he is out here to try to find proof that my mind is failing." He smiled. "They'd certainly think so if they saw me sitting here talking to empty air."

The Sun's Forehead chuckled. "They certainly would. They wouldn't be able to hear me, you know." Then his voice became serious again. "That always happens, I think. It happened to me. They wanted to do things differently, when I had at last come to the point at which an Old Man talked to me. I reached it in old age—not young, as you did. They could not take my title, but they wanted to handle my duties for me, bring me enough food to live on, hear my advice and not listen to it. Struggling against them became wearying and distasteful, so finally I decided to go under. At the age I reached—about your age—it is easy to do."

"And now you say that you are about to be detached from your bones entirely? You are reaching the next stage?"

"Let us say that I begin to hope. Our life is beautiful, but for a hundred years or so now I have been longing for the next, and I begin to hope."

"How does it happen? Or is it wrong for me to know?"

"You may know. You are good, and you keep your secrets, as our wise men always did. You will see a man who has become young, handsome, and full of light. When we dance, he dances with great beauty; his singing is beautiful, and you feel as if it were creating life. Then one time when the katchinas themselves are dancing before us—not masks, you understand, the katchinas themselves—you can't find him among the watchers. Then you seem to recognize him, there among the sacred people, dancing like them. Then you think that the next time our grandchildren on the earth put on the masks and dance, that one, whom you knew as a spirit striving to purify himself, who used to tell you about his days on earth, will be there. With his own eyes he will see our grandchildren and bless them." The chief's voice trailed off, as though the longing for what he was describing deprived him of words.

"To see the katchinas themselves dancing," Dr. Hillebrand mused. "Not the masks, but what the masks stand for. . . . That would keep me happy for centuries. But then, I could not join your people. I was never initiated. I'd be plain silly trying to dance with them. It's not for me."

"For over forty years I have been initiating you," the Sun's Forehead said. "As for dancing—you will no longer be in that old body. You will not be dancing with those fragile, rheumatic bones. There is room for you in our country. Why don't you come over? Just lie down in that crevice back there and make up your mind."

"You know," Dr. Hillebrand said, "I think I will."

Both the Kleinman Professor of American Archaeology and the spirit who once had been the Sun's Forehead for the settlements in the neighborhood of T'iiz Hatsosi were thoroughly unworldly. It had not occurred to either of them that within six days after Dr. Hillebrand had left camp Dr. George Franklin would organize a search for him, and four days later his body would be found where he had died of, apparently, heart failure. Above all, it had not occurred to them that his body would be taken home and buried with proper pomp and ceremony in the appropriate cemetery. (But Philip Fleming, close to tears, resolutely overlooked the scattering of turquoise and shell in the rubbish between the crevice and the kiva.)

Dr. Hillebrand found himself among people as alien to him as they had been to the Sun's Forehead. They seemed to be gaunt from the total lack of offerings, and the means by which they should purify and advance themselves to where they could leave this life for the next, which he believed to be the final one, were confused. He realized that his spirit was burdened with much dross, and that it would be a long time before he could gather the strength to attempt a journey to the country of his friend.

His portrait, in academic gown and hood, was painted posthumously and hung in the entrance of the museum, to one side of the stela from Quiriguá and facing the reproduction of the famous Painted Kiva mural. Dr. Klibben adroitly handled the promotions and emoluments that fell under his control. Philip Fleming won his Ph.D. with honor, and was promptly offered a splendid position at Harvard. Moved by he knew not what drive, and following one or two other actions he had performed to his own surprise, Fleming went to Dr. Hillebrand's grave, for a gesture of respect and thanks.

It had seemed to him inappropriate to bring any flowers. Instead, as he sat by the grave, with small motions of his hands he sprinkled over it some bits of turquoise and shell he had held out from a necklace he had unearthed, and followed them with a pinch of pollen given him by a Navajo. Suddenly his face registered utter astonishment; then careful listening.

The following season, Fleming returned to Painted Mask Ruin by agreement with Dr. Klibben, who was delighted to get his Department entirely out of Southwestern archaeology. There he ran a trench that led right into a magnificent polychrome pot containing a store of beans of high botanical interest.

Within a few years, he stopped visiting the grave, but he was sentimentalist enough to make a pilgrimage all alone to Tsekaiye Kin at the beginning of each field season. It was jokingly said among his confreres that there he communed with the spirit of old Hillebrand. Certainly he seemed to have inherited that legendary figure's gift for making spectacular finds.

Winner of the Pulitzer prize (1929) for his Laughing Boy, *a novel of Navajo Indian life, Oliver La Farge was born in New York in 1901, educated at Groton and Harvard, and became a distinguished anthropologist and fiction writer. Serving as president of the Association on American Indian Affairs from 1933 on, he was known as an able advocate for Indian rights. Several of his best works are collected in* The Door in the Wall *(1969). He died in 1963.*

Ted was suspicious when the lot in exclusive Clay Canyon was only $1500. What was the catch?

NINE

One of the Dead
William Wood

We couldn't have been more pleased. Deep in Clay Canyon we came upon the lot abruptly at a turn in the winding road. There was a crudely lettered board nailed to a dead tree which read, LOT FOR SALE—$1500 OR BEST OFFER, and a phone number.

"Fifteen hundred dollars—in Clay Canyon? I can't believe it," Ellen said.

"Or best offer," I corrected.

"I've heard you can't take a step without bumping into some movie person here."

"We've come three miles already without bumping into one. I haven't seen a soul."

"But there are the houses." Ellen looked about breathlessly.

There indeed were the houses—to our left and our right, to our front and our rear—low, ranch-style houses, unostentatious, prosaic, giving no hint of the gay and improbable lives we imagined went on inside them. But as the houses marched up the gradually climbing road there was not a single person to be seen. The cars—the Jaguars and Mercedeses and Cadillacs and Chryslers—were parked unattended in the driveways, their chrome gleaming in the sun; I caught a glimpse of one corner of a pool and a white diving board, but no one swam in the turquoise water. We climbed out of the car, Ellen with her rather large, short-haired head stooped forward as if under a weight. Except for the fiddling of a cicada somewhere on the hill, a profound hush lay over us in the stifling air. Not even a bird moved in the motionless trees.

"There must be something wrong with it," Ellen said.

"It's probably already been sold, and they just didn't bother to take down the sign. . . . There was something here once, though." I had come across several ragged chunks of concrete that lay about randomly as if heaved out of the earth.

"A house, do you think?"

"It's hard to say. If it was a house it's been gone for years."

"Oh, Ted," Ellen cried. "It's perfect! Look at the view!" She pointed up the canyon toward the round, parched hills. Through the heat shimmering on the road they appeared to be melting down like wax.

"Another good thing," I said. "There won't be much to do to get the ground ready except for clearing the brush away. This place has been graded once. We save a thousand dollars right there."

Ellen took both my hands. Her eyes shone in her solemn face. "What do you think, Ted? What do you think?"

Ellen and I had been married four years, having both taken the step relatively late—in our early thirties—and in that time had lived in two different places, first an apartment in Santa Monica, then, when I was promoted to office manager, in a partly furnished house in the Hollywood Hills, always with the idea that when our first child came we would either buy or build a larger house of our own. But the child had not come. It was a source of anxiety and sadness to us both and lay between us like an old scandal for which each of us took on the blame.

Then I made an unexpected killing on the stock market and Ellen suddenly began agitating in her gentle way for the house. As we shopped around she dropped hints along the way—"This place is really too small for us, don't you think?" or "We'd have to fence off the yard, of course"— that let me know that the house had become a talisman for her; she had conceived the notion that perhaps, in some occult way, if we went ahead with our accommodations for a child the child might come. The notion gave her happiness. Her face filled out, the gray circles under her eyes disappeared, the quiet gaiety, which did not seem like gaiety at all but a form of peace, returned.

As Ellen held on to my hands, I hesitated. I am convinced now that there was something behind my hesitation—something I felt then only as a quality of silence, a fleeting twinge of utter desolation. "It's so safe," she said. "There's no traffic at all."

I explained that. "It's not a through street. It ends somewhere up in the hills."

She turned back to me again with her bright, questioning eyes. The happiness that had grown in her during our months of house-hunting seemed to have welled into near rapture.

"We'll call the number," I said, "but don't expect too much. It must have been sold long ago."

We walked slowly back to the car. The door handle burned to the touch. Down the canyon the rear end of a panel truck disappeared noiselessly around a bend.

"No," Ellen said, "I have a feeling about this place. I think it was meant to be ours."

And she was right, of course.

Mr. Carswell Deeves, who owned the land, was called upon to do very little except take my check for $1500 and hand over the deed to us, for by the time Ellen and I met him we had already sold ourselves. Mr. Deeves, as we had suspected from the unprofessional sign, was a private citizen. We found his house in a predominantly Mexican section of Santa Monica. He was a chubby, pink man of indeterminate age dressed in white ducks and soft white shoes, as if he had had a tennis court hidden away among the squalid, asphalt-shingled houses and dry kitchen gardens of his neighbors.

"Going to live in Clay Canyon, are you?" he said. "Ros Russell lives up there, or used to." So, we discovered, did Joel McCrea, Jimmy Stewart and Paula Raymond, as well as a cross-section of producers, directors and character actors. "Oh, yes," said Mr. Deeves, "it's an address that will look extremely good on your stationery."

Ellen beamed and squeezed my hand.

Mr. Deeves turned out to know very little about the land other than that a house had been destroyed by fire there years ago and that the land had changed hands many times since. "I myself acquired it in what may strike you as a novel way," he said as we sat in his parlor—a dark, airless box which smelled faintly of camphor and whose walls were obscured with yellowing autographed photographs of movie stars. "I won it in a game of hearts from a makeup man on the set of *Quo Vadis*. Perhaps you remember me. I had a close-up in one of the crowd scenes."

"That was a number of years ago, Mr. Deeves," I said. "Have you been trying to sell it all this time?"

"I've nearly sold it dozens of times," he said, "but something always went wrong somehow."

"What kind of things?"

"Naturally, the fire-insurance rates up there put off a lot of people. I hope you're prepared to pay a high premium—"

"I've already checked into that."

"Good. You'd be surprised how many people will let details like that go till the last minute."

"What other things have gone wrong?"

Ellen touched my arm to discourage my wasting any more time with foolish questions.

Mr. Deeves spread out the deed before me and smoothed it with his forearm. "Silly things, some of them. One couple found some dead doves. . . "

"Dead doves?" I handed him the signed article. With one pink hand Mr. Deeves waved it back and forth to dry the ink. "Five of them, if I remember correctly. In my opinion they'd sat on a wire and were electrocuted somehow. The husband thought nothing of it, of course, but his wife became so hysterical that we had to call off the transaction."

I made a sign at Mr. Deeves to drop this line of conversation. Ellen loves animals and birds of all kinds with a devotion that turns the loss of a household pet into a major tragedy, which is why, since the death of our cocker spaniel, we have had no more pets. But Ellen appeared not to have heard; she was watching the paper in Mr. Deeves' hand fixedly, as if she were afraid it might vanish.

Mr. Deeves sprang suddenly to his feet. "Well!" he cried. "It's all yours now. I know you'll be happy there."

Ellen flushed with pleasure. "I'm sure we will," she said, and took his pudgy hand in both of hers.

"A prestige address," called Mr. Deeves from his porch as we drove away. "A real prestige address."

Ellen and I are modern people. Our talk in the evenings is generally on issues of the modern world. Ellen paints a little and I do some writing from time to time—mostly on technical subjects. The house that Ellen and I built mirrored our concern with present-day aesthetics. We worked closely with Jack Salmanson, the architect and a friend, who designed a steel module house, low and compact and private, which could be fitted into the irregularities of our patch of land for a maximum of space. The interior *décor* we left largely up to Ellen, who combed the home magazines and made sketches as if she were decorating a dozen homes.

I mention these things to show that there is nothing Gothic about my wife and me: We are as thankful for our common sense as for our sensibilities, and we flattered ourselves that the house we built achieved a balance between the aesthetic and the functional. Its lines were simple and clean; there were no dark corners, and it was surrounded on three sides by houses, none of which were more than eight years old.

There were, however, signs from the very beginning, ominous signs which can be read only in retrospect, though it seems to me now that there were others who suspected but said nothing. One was the Mexican who cut down the tree.

As a money-saving favor to us, Jack Salmanson agreed to supervise the building himself and hire small, independent contractors to do the labor, many of whom were Mexicans or Negroes with dilapidated equipment that appeared to run only by some mechanical miracle. The Mexican, a small, forlorn workman with a stringy moustache, had already burned out two chain-saw blades and still had not cut halfway through the tree. It was inexplicable. The tree, the same one on which Ellen and I had seen the original FOR SALE sign, had obviously been dead for years, and the branches that already lay scattered on the ground were rotted through.

"You must have run into a batch of knots," Jack said. "Try it again. If the saw gets too hot, quit and we'll pull it down with the bulldozer." As if answering to its name, the bulldozer turned at the back of the lot and lumbered toward us in a cloud of dust, the black shoulders of the Negro operator gleaming in the sun.

The Mexican need not have feared for his saw. He had scarcely touched it to the tree when it started to topple of its own accord. Startled, he backed away a few steps. The tree had begun to fall toward the back of the lot, in the direction of his cut, but now it appeared to arrest itself, its naked branches trembling as if in agitation; then with an awful rending sound it writhed upright and fell back on itself, gaining momentum and plunging directly at the bulldozer. My voice died in my throat, but Jack and the Mexican shouted, and the operator jumped and rolled on the ground just as the tree fell high on the hood, shattering the windshield to bits. The bulldozer, out of control and knocked off course, came directly at us, gears whining and gouging a deep trough in the earth. Jack and I jumped one way, the Mexican the other; the bulldozer lurched between us and ground on toward the street, the Negro sprinting after it.

"The car!" Jack shouted. "The car!"

Parked in front of the house across the street was a car, a car which was certainly brand-new. The bulldozer headed straight for it, its blade striking clusters of sparks from the pavement. The Mexican waved his chain saw over his head like a toy and shouted in Spanish. I covered my eyes with my hands and heard Jack grunt softly, as if he had been struck in the mid-section, just before the crash.

Two women stood on the porch of the house across the street and gaped. The car had caved in at the center, its steel roof wrinkled like tissue paper; its front and rear ends were folded around the bulldozer as if embracing it. Then with a low whoosh, both vehicles were enveloped in creeping blue flame.

"Rotten luck," Jack muttered under his breath as we ran into the street. From the corner of my eye I caught the curious sight of the Mexican on the ground, praying, his chain saw lying by his knees.

In the evening Ellen and I paid a visit to the Sheffits', Sondra and Jeff, our neighbors across the canyon road, where we met the owner of the ruined car, Joyce Castle, a striking blonde in lemon-colored pants. The shock of the accident itself wore off with the passing of time and cocktails, and the three of them treated it as a tremendous joke.

Mrs. Castle was particularly hilarious. "I'm doing better," she rejoiced. "The Alfa-Romeo only lasted two days, but I held on to this one a whole six weeks. I even had the permanent plates on."

"But you mustn't be without a car, Mrs. Castle," Ellen said in her serious way. "We'd be glad to loan you our Plymouth until you can—"

"I'm having a new car delivered tomorrow afternoon. Don't worry about me. A Daimler, Jeff, you'll be interested to know. I couldn't resist after riding in yours. What about the poor bulldozer man? Is he absolutely wiped out?"

"I think he'll survive," I said. "In any case he has two other 'dozers."

"Then you won't be held up," Jeff said.

"I wouldn't think so."

Sondra chuckled softly. "I just happened to look out the window," she said. "It was just like a Rube Goldberg cartoon. A chain reaction."

"And there was my poor old Cadillac at the end of it," Mrs. Castle sighed.

Suey, Mrs. Castle's dog, who had been lying on the floor beside his mistress glaring dourly at us between dozes, suddenly ran to the front door barking ferociously, his red mane standing straight up.

"Suey!" Mrs. Castle slapped her knee. "Suey! Come here!"

The dog merely flattened its ears and looked from his mistress toward the door again as if measuring a decision. He growled deep in his throat.

"It's the ghost," Sondra said lightly. "He's behind the whole thing." Sondra sat curled up in one corner of the sofa and tilted her head to one side as she spoke, like a very clever child.

Jeff laughed sharply. "Oh, they tell some very good stories."

With a sigh Mrs. Castle rose and dragged Suey back by his collar. "If I didn't feel so self-conscious about it I'd take him to an analyst," she said. "Sit, Suey! Here's a cashew nut for you."

"I'm very fond of ghost stories," I said, smiling.

"Oh, well," Jeff murmured, mildly disparaging.

"Go ahead, Jeff," Sondra urged him over the rim of her glass. "They'd like to hear it."

Jeff was a literary agent, a tall, sallow man with dark oily hair that he was continually pushing out of his eyes with his fingers. As he spoke he smiled lopsidedly as if defending against the probability of being taken seriously. "All I know is that back in the late seventeenth century the Spanish used to have hangings here. The victims are supposed to float around at night and make noises."

"Criminals?" I asked.

"Of the worst sort," said Sondra. "What was the story Guy Relling told you, Joyce?" She smiled with a curious inward relish that suggested she knew the story perfectly well herself.

"Is that Guy Relling, the director?" I asked.

"Yes," Jeff said. "He owns those stables down the canyon."

"I've seen them," Ellen said. "Such lovely horses."

Joyce Castle hoisted her empty glass into the air. "Jeff, love, will you find me another?"

"We keep straying from the subject," said Sondra gently. "Fetch me another too, darling"—she handed her glass to Jeff as he went by—"like a good boy. . . . I didn't mean to interrupt, Joyce. Go on." She gestured toward us as the intended audience. Ellen stiffened slightly in her chair.

"It seems that there was one *hombre* of outstanding depravity," Joyce Castle said languidly. "I forgot the name. He murdered, stole, raped . . . one of those endless Spanish names with a 'Luis' in it, a nobleman I think Guy said. A charming sort. Mad, of course, and completely unpredictable. They hanged him at last for some unsavory escapade in a nunnery. You two are moving into a neighborhood rich with tradition."

We all laughed.

"What about the noises?" Ellen asked Sondra. "Have you heard anything?"

"Of course," Sondra said, tipping her head prettily. Every

inch of her skin was tanned to the color of coffee from afternoons by the pool. It was a form of leisure that her husband, with his bilious coloring and lank hair, apparently did not enjoy.

"Everywhere I've ever lived," he said, his grin growing crookeder and more apologetic, "there were noises in the night that you couldn't explain. Here there are all kinds of wildlife—foxes, coons, possums—even coyotes up on the ridge. They're all active after sundown."

Ellen's smile of pleasure at this news turned to distress as Sondra remarked in her offhand way, "We found our poor kitty-cat positively torn to pieces one morning. He was all blood. We never did find his head."

"A fox," Jeff put in quickly. Everything he said seemed hollow. Something came from him like a vapor. I thought it was grief.

Sondra gazed smugly into her lap as if hugging a secret to herself. She seemed enormously pleased. It occurred to me that Sondra was trying to frighten us. In a way it relieved me. She was enjoying herself too much, I thought, looking at her spoiled, brown face, to be frightened herself.

After the incident of the tree everything went well for some weeks. The house went up rapidly. Ellen and I visited it as often as we could, walking over the raw ground and making our home in our mind's eye. The fireplace would go here, the refrigerator here, our Picasso print there. "Ted," Ellen said timidly, "I've been thinking. Why don't we fix up the extra bedroom as a children's room?"

I waited.

"Now that we'll be living out here our friends will have to stay overnight more often. Most of them have young children. It would be nice for them."

I slipped my arm around her shoulders. She knew I understood. It was a delicate matter. She raised her face and I kissed her between her brows. Signal and counter-signal, the keystones of our life together—a life of sensibility and tact.

"Hey, you two!" Sondra Sheffits called from across the street. She stood on her front porch in a pink bathing suit, her skin brown, her hair nearly white. "How about a swim?"

"No suits!"

"Come on, we've got plenty."

Ellen and I debated the question with a glance, settled it with a nod.

As I came out onto the patio in one of Jeff's suits, Sondra said, "Ted, you're pale as a ghost. Don't you get any sun where you are?" She lay in a chaise lounge behind huge elliptical sunglasses encrusted with glass gems.

"I stay inside too much, writing articles," I said.

"You're welcome to come here any time you like"—she smiled suddenly, showing me a row of small, perfect teeth— "and swim."

Ellen appeared in her borrowed suit, a red one with a short, limp ruffle. She shaded her eyes as the sun, glittering metallically on the water, struck her full in the face.

Sondra ushered her forward as if to introduce my wife to me. "You look much better in that suit than I ever did." Her red nails flashed on Ellen's arm. Ellen smiled guardedly. The two women were about the same height, but Ellen was narrower in the shoulders, thicker through the waist and hips. As they came toward me it seemed to me that Ellen was the one I did not know. Her familiar body became strange. It looked out of proportion. Hairs that on Sondra were all but invisible except when the sun turned them to silver, lay flat and dark on Ellen's pallid arm.

As if sensing the sudden distance between us, Ellen took my hand. "Let's jump in together," she said gaily. "No hanging back."

Sondra retreated to the chaise lounge to watch us, her eyes invisible behind her outrageous glasses, her head on one side.

Incidents began again and continued at intervals. Guy Relling, whom I never met but whose pronouncements on the supernatural reached me through others from time to time like messages from an oracle, claims that the existence of the living dead is a particularly excruciating one as they hover between two states of being. Their memories keep the passions of life forever fresh and sharp, but they are able to relieve them only at a monstrous expense of will and energy which leaves them literally helpless for months or sometimes even years afterward. This was why materializations and other forms of tangible action are relatively rare. There are of course exceptions, Sondra, our most frequent translator of Relling's theories, pointed out one evening with the odd joy that accompanied all of her remarks on the subject; some ghosts are terrifically active—particularly the insane ones who, ignorant of the limitations of death as they were of the impossibilities of life, transcend them with the dynamism that is exclusively the property of madness. Generally, however, it was Relling's opinion that a ghost was more to be pitied than feared. Sondra quoted him as having said, "The notion of a haunted house is a misconception semantically. It is not the house but the soul itself that is haunted."

On Saturday, August 6, a workman laying pipe was blinded in one eye by an acetylene torch.

On Thursday, September 1, a rockslide on the hill behind us dumped four tons of dirt and rock on the half-finished house and halted work for two weeks.

On Sunday, October 9—my birthday, oddly enough— while visiting the house alone, I slipped on a stray screw and struck my head on a can of latex paint which opened up a gash requiring ten stitches. I rushed across to the Sheffits'. Sondra answered the door in her bathing suit and a magazine in her hand. "Ted?" She peered at me. "I scarcely recognized you through the blood. Come in, I'll call the doctor. Try not to drip on the furniture, will you?"

I told the doctor of the screw on the floor, the big can of paint. I did not tell him that my foot had slipped because I had turned too quickly and that I had turned too quickly because the sensation had grown on me that there was someone behind me, close enough to touch me, perhaps, because something hovered there, fetid and damp and cold and almost palpable in its nearness; I remember shivering violently as I turned, as if the sun of this burning summer's day had been replaced by a mysterious star without warmth. I did not tell the doctor this nor anyone else.

In November Los Angeles burns. After the long drought of summer the sap goes underground and the baked hills seem to gasp in pain for the merciful release of either life or death—rain or fire. Invariably fire comes first, spreading through the outlying parts of the country like an epidemic, till the sky is livid and starless at night and overhung with dun-colored smoke during the day.

There was a huge fire in Tujunga, north of us, the day Ellen and I moved into our new house—handsome, severe, aggressively new on its dry hillside—under a choked sky the color of earth and a muffled, flyspeck sun. Sondra and Jeff came over to help, and in the evening Joyce Castle stopped by with Suey and a magnum of champagne.

Ellen clasped her hands under her chin. "What a lovely surprise!"

"I hope it's cold enough. I've had it in my refrigerator since four o'clock. Welcome to the canyon. You're nice people. You remind me of my parents. God, it's hot. I've been weeping all day on account of the smoke. You'll have air conditioning I suppose?"

Jeff was sprawled in a chair with his long legs straight in front of him in the way a cripple might put aside a pair of crutches. "Joyce, you're an angel. Excuse me if I don't get up. I'm recuperating."

"You're excused, doll, you're excused."

"Ted," Ellen said softly. "Why don't you get some glasses?"

Jeff hauled in his legs. "Can I give you a hand?"

"Sit still, Jeff."

He sighed. "I hadn't realized I was so out of shape." He looked more cadaverous than ever after our afternoon of lifting and shoving. Sweat had collected in the hollows under his eyes.

"Shall I show you the house, Joyce? While Ted is in the kitchen?"

"I love you, Ellen," Joyce said. "Take me on the whole tour."

Sondra followed me into the kitchen. She leaned against the wall and smoked, supporting her left elbow in the palm of her right hand. She didn't say a word. Through the open door I could see Jeff's outstretched legs from the calves down.

"Thanks for all the help today," I said to Sondra in a voice unaccountably close to a whisper. I could hear Joyce and Ellen as they moved from room to room, their voices swelling and dying: "It's all steel? You mean everything? Walls and all? Aren't you afraid of lightning?"

"Oh, we're all safely grounded, I think."

Jeff yawned noisily in the living room. Wordlessly Sondra put a tray on the kitchen table as I rummaged in an unpacked carton for the glasses. She watched me steadily and coolly, as if she expected me to entertain her. I wanted to say something further to break a silence which was becoming unnatural and oppressive. The sounds around us seemed only to isolate us in a ring of intimacy. With her head on one side Sondra smiled at me. I could hear her rapid breathing.

"What's this, a nursery? Ellen, love!"

"No, no! It's only for our friends' children."

Sondra's eyes were blue, the color of shallow water. She seemed faintly amused, as if we were sharing in a conspiracy—a conspiracy I was anxious to repudiate by making some prosaic remark in a loud voice for all to hear, but a kind of pain developed in my chest as the words seemed dammed there, and I only smiled at her foolishly. With every passing minute of silence, the more impossible it became to break through and the more I felt drawn into the intrigue of which, though I was ignorant, I was surely guilty. Without so much as a touch she had made us lovers.

Ellen stood in the doorway, half turned away as if her first impulse had been to run. She appeared to be deep in thought, her eyes fixed on the steel, cream-colored doorjamb.

Sondra began to talk to Ellen in her dry, satirical voice. It was chatter of the idlest sort, but she was destroying, as I had wished to destroy, the absurd notion that there was something between us. I could see Ellen's confusion. She hung on Sondra's words, watching her lips attentively, as if this elegant, tanned woman, calmly smoking and talking of trifles, were her savior.

As for myself, I felt as if I had lost the power of speech entirely. If I joined in with Sondra's carefully innocent chatter I would only be joining in the deception against my wife; if I proclaimed the truth and ended everything by bringing it into the open . . . . but what truth? What was there in fact to bring into the open? What was there to end? A feeling in the air? An intimation? The answer was nothing, of course. I did not even like Sondra very much. There was something cold and unpleasant about her. There was nothing to proclaim because nothing had happened. "Where's Joyce?" I asked finally, out of a dry mouth. "Doesn't she want to see the kitchen?"

Ellen turned slowly toward me, as if it cost her a great effort. "She'll be here in a minute," she said tonelessly, and I became aware of Joyce's and Jeff's voices from the living room. Ellen studied my face, her pupils oddly dilated unter the pinkish fluorescent light, as if she were trying to penetrate to the bottom of a great darkness that lay beneath my chance remark. Was it a code of some kind, a new signal for her that I would shortly make clear? What did it mean? I smiled at her and she responded with a smile of her own, a tentative and formal upturning of her mouth, as if I were a familiar face whose name escaped her for the moment.

Joyce came in behind Ellen. "I hate kitchens. I never go into mine." She looked from one to the other of us. "Am I interrupting something?"

At two o'clock in the morning I sat up in bed, wide awake. The bedroom was bathed in the dark red glow of the fire which had come closer in the night. A thin, autumnal veil of smoke hung in the room. Ellen lay on her side, asleep, one hand cupped on the pillow next to her face as if waiting for something to be put in it. I had no idea why I was so fully awake, but I threw off the covers and went to the window to check on the fire. I could see no flame, but the hills stood out blackly against a turgid sky that belled and sagged as the wind blew and relented.

Then I heard the sound.

I am a person who sets store by precision in the use of words—in the field of technical writing this is a necessity. But I can think of no word to describe that sound. The closest I can come with a word of my own invention is "vlump." It came erratically, neither loud nor soft. It was, rather, pervasive and without location. It was not a *solid* sound. There was something vague and whispering about it, and from time to time it began with the suggestion of a sigh—a shuffling dissipation in the air that seemed to take form and die in the same instant. In a way I cannot define, it was mindless, without will or reason, yet implacable. Because I could not explain it immediately I went to seek an explanation.

I stepped into the hall and switched on the light, pressing the noiseless button. The light came down out of a fixture set flush into the ceilings and diffused through a milky plastic-like Japanese rice paper. The clean, indestructible walls rose perpendicularly around me. Through the slight haze of smoke came the smell of the newness, sweet and metallic— more like a car than a house. And still the sound went on. It seemed to be coming from the room at the end of the hall, the room we had designed for our friends' children. The door was open and I could see a gray patch that was a west window. Vlump . . . vlump . . . vlumpvlump. . . .

Fixing on the gray patch, I moved down the hall while my legs made themselves heavy as logs, and all the while I repeated to myself, "The house is settling. All new houses settle and make strange noises." And so lucid was I that I believed I was not afraid. I was walking down the bright new hall of my new steel house to investigate a noise, for the house might be settling unevenly, or an animal might be up to some mischief—raccoons regularly raided the garbage cans, I had been told. There might be something wrong with the plumbing or with the radiant-heating system that warmed our steel and vinyl floors. And now, like the responsible master of the house, I had located the apparent center of the sound and was going responsibly toward it. In a second or two, very likely, I would know. Vlump vlump. The gray of the window turned rosy as I came near enough to see the hillside beyond it. That black was underbrush and that pink the dusty swath cut by the bulldozer before it had run amok. I had watched the accident from just about the spot where I stood now, and the obliterated hole where the tree had been, laid firmly over with the prefabricated floor of the room whose darkness I would eradicate by touching with my right hand the light switch inside the door.

"Ted?"

Blood boomed in my ears. I had the impression that my heart had burst. I clutched at the wall for support. Yet of course I knew it was Ellen's voice, and I answered her calmly. "Yes, it's me."

"What's the matter?" I heard the bedclothes rustle.

"Don't get up, I'm coming right in." The noise had stopped. There was nothing. Only the almost inaudible hum of the refrigerator, the stirring of the wind.

Ellen was sitting up in bed. "I was just checking on the fire," I said. She patted my side of the bed and in the instant before I turned out the hall light I saw her smile.

"I was just dreaming about you," she said softly, as I climbed under the sheets. She rolled against me. "Why, you're trembling."

"I should have worn my robe."

"You'll be warm in a minute." Her fragrant body lay against mine, but I remained rigid as stone and just as cold, staring at the ceiling, my mind a furious blank. After a moment she said, "Ted?" It was her signal, always hesitant, always tremulous, that meant I was to roll over and take her in my arms.

Instead I answered, "What?" just as if I had not understood.

For a few seconds I sensed her struggling against her reserve to give me a further sign that would pierce my peculiar distraction and tell me she wanted love. But it was too much for her—too alien. My coldness had created a vacuum she was too unpracticed to fill—a coldness sudden and inexplicable, unless . . .

She withdrew slowly and pulled the covers up under her chin. Finally she asked, "Ted, is there something happening that I should know about?" She had remembered Sondra and the curious scene in the kitchen. It took, I knew, great courage for Ellen to ask that question, though she must have known my answer.

"No, I'm just tired. We've had a busy day. Good-night, dear." I kissed her on the cheek and sensed her eyes, in the shadow of the fire, searching mine, asking the question she could not give voice to. I turned away, somehow ashamed because I could not supply the answer that would fulfill her need. Because there was no answer at all.

The fire was brought under control after burning some eight hundred acres and several homes, and three weeks later the rains came. Jack Salmanson came out one Sunday to see how the house was holding up, checked the foundation, the roof and all the seams and pronounced it tight as a drum. We sat looking moodily out the glass doors onto the patio—a flatland of grayish mud which threatened to swamp with a thin ooze of silt and gravel the few flagstones I had set in the ground. Ellen was in the bedroom lying down; she had got into the habit of taking a nap after lunch, though it was I, not she, who lay stark awake night after night explaining away sounds that became more and more impossible to explain away. The gagging sound that sometimes accompanied the vlump and the strangled expulsion of air that followed it were surely the result of some disturbance in the water pipes; the footsteps that came slowly down the hall and stopped outside our closed door and then went away again with something like a low chuckle were merely the night contracting of our metal house after the heat of the day. Through all this Ellen slept as if in a stupor; she seemed to have become addicted to sleep. She went to bed at nine and got up at ten the next morning; she napped in the afternoon and moved about lethargically the rest of the time with a Mexican shawl around her shoulders, complaining of the cold. The doctor examined her for mononucleosis but found nothing. He said perhaps it was her sinuses and that she should rest as much as she wanted.

After a protracted silence Jack put aside his drink and stood up. "I guess I'll go along."

"I'll tell Ellen."

"What the hell for? Let her sleep. Tell her I hope she feels better." He turned to frown at the room of the house he had designed and built. "Are you happy here?" he asked suddenly.

"Happy?" I repeated the word awkwardly. "Of course we're happy. We love the house. It's . . . just a little noisy at night, that's all." I stammered it out, like the first word of a monstrous confession, but Jack seemed hardly to hear it. He waved a hand. "House settling." He squinted from one side of the room to the other. "I don't know. There's something about it. . . . It's not right. Maybe it's just the weather . . . the light. . . . It could be friendlier, you know what I mean? It seems cheerless."

I watched him with a kind of wild hope, as if he might magically fathom my terror—do for me what I could not do for myself, and permit it to be discussed calmly between two men of temperate mind. But Jack was not looking for the cause of the gloom but the cure for it.

"Why don't you try putting down a couple of orange rugs in this room?" he said.

I stared at the floor as if two orange rugs were an infallible charm. "Yes," I said, "I think we'll try that."

Ellen scuffed in, pushing back her hair, her face puffy with sleep. "Jack," she said, "when the weather clears and I'm feeling livelier, you and Anne and the children must come and spend the night."

"We'd like that. After the noises die down," he added satirically to me.

"Noises? What noises?" A certain blankness came over Ellen's face when she looked at me now. The expression was the same, but what had been open in it before was now merely empty. She had put up her guard against me; she suspected me of keeping things from her.

"At night," I said. "The house is settling. You don't hear them."

When Jack had gone, Ellen sat with a cup of tea in the chair where Jack had sat, looking out at the mud. Her long purple shawl hung all the way to her knees and made her look armless. There seemed no explanation for the two white hands that curled around the teacup in her lap. "It's a sad thing," she said tonelessly. "I can't help but feel sorry for Sondra."

"Why is that?" I asked guardedly.

"Joyce was here yesterday. She told me that she and Jeff have been having an affair off and on for six years." She turned to see how I would receive this news.

"Well, that explains the way Joyce and Sondra behave toward each other," I said, with a pleasant glance straight into Ellen's eyes; there I encountered only the reflection of the glass doors, even to the rain trickling down them, and I had the eerie sensation of having been shown a picture of the truth, as if she were weeping secretly in the depths of a soul I could no longer touch. For Ellen did not believe my innocence; I'm not sure I still believed in it myself; very likely

Jeff and Joyce didn't either. It is impossible to say what Sondra believed. She behaved as if our infidelity were an accomplished fact. In its way it was a performance of genius, for Sondra never touched me except in the most accidental or impersonal way; even her glances, the foundation on which she built the myth of our liaison, had nothing soft in them; they were probing and sly and were always accompanied by a furtive smile, as if we merely shared some private joke. Yet there was something in the way she did it—in the tilt of her head perhaps—that plainly implied that the joke was at everyone else's expense. And she had taken to calling me "darling."

"Sondra and Jeff have a feebleminded child off in an institution somewhere," Ellen said. "That set them against each other, apparently."

"Joyce told you all this?"

"She just mentioned it casually as if it were the most natural thing in the world—she assumed we must have known. . . . But I don't want to know things like that about my friends."

"That's show biz, I guess. You and I are just provincials at heart."

"Sondra must be a very unhappy girl."

"It's hard to tell with Sondra."

"I wonder what she tries to do with her life. . . . If she looks for anything—outside."

I waited.

"Probably not," Ellen answered her own question. "She seems very self-contained. Almost cold . . ."

I was treated to the spectacle of my wife fighting with herself to delay a wound that she was convinced would come home to her sooner or later. She did not want to believe in my infidelity. I might have comforted her with lies. I might have told her that Sondra and I rendezvoused downtown in a cafeteria and made love in a second-rate hotel on the evenings when I called to say that I was working late. Then the wound would be open and could be cleaned and cured. It would be painful of course, but I would have confided in her again and our old system would be restored. Watching Ellen torture herself with doubt, I was tempted to tell her those lies. The truth never tempted me: To have admitted that I knew what she was thinking would have been tantamount to an admission of guilt. How could I suspect such a thing unless it were true? And was I to explain my coldness by terrifying her with vague stories of indescribable sounds which she never heard?

And so the two of us sat on, dumb and chilled, in our watertight house as the daylight began to go. And then a sort of exultation seized me. What if my terror were no more real than Ellen's? What if both our ghosts were only ghosts of the mind which needed only a little common sense to drive them away? And I saw that if I could drive away my ghost, Ellen's would soon follow, for the secret that shut me away from her would be gone. It was a revelation, a triumph of reason.

"What's that up there?" Ellen pointed to something that looked like a leaf blowing at the top of the glass doors. "It's a tail, Ted. There must be some animal on the roof."

Only the bushy tip was visible. As I drew close to it I could see raindrops clinging as if by a geometrical system to each black hair. "It looks like a raccoon tail. What would a coon be doing out so early?" I put on a coat and went outside. The tail hung limply over the edge, ringed with white and swaying phlegmatically in the breeze. The animal itself was hidden behind the low parapet. Using the ship's ladder at the back of the house I climbed up to look at it.

The human mind, just like other parts of the anatomy, is an organ of habit. Its capabilities are bounded by the limits of precedent; it thinks what it is used to thinking. Faced with a phenomenon beyond its range it rebels, it rejects, sometimes it collapses. My mind, which for weeks had steadfastly refused to honor the evidence of my senses that there was Something Else living in the house with Ellen and me, something unearthly and evil, largely on the basis of insufficient evidence, was now forced to the subsequent denial by saying, as Jeff had said, "fox." It was, of course, ridiculous. The chances of a fox's winning a battle with a raccoon were very slight at best, let alone what had been done to this raccoon. The body lay on the far side of the roof. I didn't see the head at all until I had stumbled against it and it had rolled over and over to come to rest against the parapet where it pointed its masked, ferret face at me.

Only because my beleaguered mind kept repeating, like a voice, "Ellen mustn't know, Ellen mustn't know," was I able to take up the dismembered parts and hurl them with all my strength onto the hillside and answer when Ellen called out, "What is it, Ted?" "Must have been a coon. It's gone now," in a perfectly level voice before I went to the back of the roof and vomited.

I recalled Sondra's mention of their mutilated cat and phoned Jeff at his agency. "We will discuss it over lunch," I told myself. I had a great need to talk, an action impossible within my own home, where every day the silence became denser and more intractable. Once or twice Ellen ventured to ask, "What's the matter, Ted?" but I always answered, "Nothing." And there our talk ended. I could see it in her wary eyes; I was not the man she had married; I was cold, secretive. The children's room, furnished with double bunks and wallpaper figured with toys, stood like a rebuke. Ellen kept the door closed most of the time though once or twice, in the late afternoon, I had found her in there moving about aimlessly, touching objects as if half in wonder that they should still linger on after so many long, sterile months; a foolish hope had failed. Neither did our friends bring their children to stay. They did not because we did not ask them. The silence had brought with it a profound and debilitating inertia. Ellen's face seemed perpetually swollen, the features cloudy and amorphous, the eyes dull; her whole body had become bloated, as if an enormous cache of pain had backed up inside her. We moved through the house in our orbits like two sleepwalkers, going about our business out of habit. Our friends called at first, puzzled, a little hurt, but soon stopped and left us to ourselves. Occasionally we saw the Sheffitses. Jeff was looking seedier and seedier, told bad jokes, drank too much and seemed always ill at ease. Sondra did most of the talking, chattering blandly on indifferent subjects and always hinting by gesture, word or glance at our underground affair.

Jeff and I had lunch at the Brown Derby on Vine Street under charcoal caricatures of show folk. At a table next to ours an agent was eulogizing an actor in a voice hoarse with trumped-up enthusiasm to a large, purple-faced man who was devoting his entire attention to a bowl of vichyssoise.

"It's a crazy business," Jeff said to me. "Be glad you're not in it."

"I see what you mean," I replied. Jeff had not the faintest idea of why I had brought him there, nor had I given him any clue. We were "breaking the ice." Jeff grinned at me with that crooked trick of his mouth, and I grinned back. "We are friends"—presumably that is the message we were grinning at each other. Was he my friend? Was I his friend? He lived across the street; our paths crossed perhaps once a week; we joked together; he sat always in the same chair in our living room twisting from one sprawl to another; there was a straight white chair in his living room that I preferred. Friendships have been founded on less, I suppose. Yet he had an idiot child locked off in an asylum somewhere and a wife who amused herself with infidelity by suggestion; I had a demon loose in my house and a wife gnawed with suspicion and growing remote and old because of it. And I had said, "I see what you mean." It seemed insufferable. I caught Jeff's eye. "You remember we talked once about a ghost?" My tone was bantering; perhaps I meant to make a joke.

"I remember."

"Sondra said something about a cat of yours that was killed."

"The one the fox got."

"That's what you said. That's not what Sondra said."

Jeff shrugged. "What about it?"

"I found a dead raccoon on our roof."

"Your roof!"

"Yes. It was pretty awful."

Jeff toyed with his fork. All pretense of levity was at an end. "No head?"

"Worse."

For a few moments he was silent. I felt him struggle with himself before he spoke. "Maybe you'd better move out, Ted," he said.

He was trying to help—I knew it. With a single swipe he had tried to push through the restraint that hung between us. He was my friend; he was putting out his hand to me.

And I suppose I must have known what he'd suggest. But I could not accept it. It was not what I wanted to hear. "Jeff, I can't do that," I said tolerantly, as if he had missed my point. "We've only been living there five months. It cost me twenty-two thousand to build that place. We have to live in it at least a year under the GI loan."

"Well, you know best, Ted." The smile dipped at me again.

"I just wanted to talk," I said, irritated at the ease with which he had given in. "I wanted to find out what you knew about this ghost business."

"Not very much. Sondra knows more than I do."

"I doubt that you would advise me to leave a house I had just built for no reason at all."

"There seems to be some sort of jinx on the property, that's all. Whether there's a ghost or not I couldn't tell you," he replied, annoyed in his turn at the line the conversation was taking. "How does Ellen feel about this?"

"She doesn't know."

"About the raccoon?"

"About anything."

"You mean there's more?"

"There are noises—at night. . . ."

"I'd speak to Sondra if I were you. She's gone into this business much more deeply than I. When we first moved in, she used to hang around your land a good deal . . . just snooping . . . particularly after that cat was killed . . ." He was having some difficulty with his words. It struck me that the conversation was causing him pain. He was showing his teeth now in a smiling grimace. Dangling an arm over the back of his chair he seemed loose to the point of collapse. We circled warily about his wife's name.

"Look, Jeff," I said, and took a breath, "about Sondra . . ."

Jeff cut me off with a wave of his hand. "Don't worry, I know Sondra."

"Then you know there's nothing between us?"

"It's just her way of amusing herself. Sondra's a strange girl. She does the same thing with me. She flirts with me but we don't sleep together." He picked up his spoon and stared at it unseeingly. "It started when she became preg-

135

nant. After she had the boy, everything between us
stopped. You know we had a son? He's in a sanitarium in
the Valley."

"Can't you do anything?"

"Sure. Joyce Castle. I don't know what I'd have done
without her."

"I mean divorce."

"Sondra won't divorce me. And I can't divorce her. No
grounds." He shrugged as if the whole thing were of no
concern at all to him. "What could I say? I want to divorce
my wife because of the way she looks at other men? She's
scrupulously faithful."

"To whom, Jeff? To you? To whom?"

"I don't know—to herself, maybe," he mumbled.

Whether with encouragement he might have gone on I
don't know, for I cut him off. I sensed that with the enigmatic
remark he was giving me my cue and that if I had chosen to
respond to it he would have told me what I had asked him
to lunch to find out—and all at once I was terrified; I did not
want to hear it; I did not want to hear it at all. And so I
laughed in a quiet way and said, "Undoubtedly, undoubtedly," and pushed it behind the closed door of my mind
where I had stored all the impossibilities of the last
months—the footsteps, the sounds in the night, the mutilated raccoon—or else, by recognizing them, go mad.

Jeff suddenly looked me full in the face; his cheeks were
flushed, his teeth clamped together. "Look, Ted," he said,
"can you take the afternoon off? I've got to go to the sanitarium and sign some papers. They're going to transfer the
boy. He has fits of violence and does . . . awful things. He's
finally gotten out of hand."

"What about Sondra?"

"Sondra's signed already. She likes to go alone to visit
him. She seems to like to have him to herself. I'd appreciate
it, Ted—the moral support. . . . You don't have to come in.
You can wait in the car. It's only about thirty miles from
here, you'd be back by dinnertime. . . ." His voice shook,
tears clouded the yellow-stained whites of his eyes. He
looked like a man with fever. I noticed how shrunken his
neck had become as it revolved in his collar, how his head
caved in sharply at the temples. He fastened one hand on

my arm, like a claw. "Of course I'll go, Jeff," I said. "I'll call the office. They can get along without me for one afternoon."

He collected himself in an instant. "I'd appreciate it, Ted. I promise you it won't be so bad."

The sanitarium was in the San Fernando Valley, a complex of new stucco buildings on a newly seeded lawn. Everywhere there were signs that read, PLEASE KEEP OFF, FOLKS. Midget saplings stood in discs of powdery earth along the cement walks angling white and hot through the grass. On these walks, faithfully observing the signs, the inmates strolled. Their traffic, as it flowed somnolently from one avenue to another, was controlled by attendants stationed at intersections, conspicuous in white uniforms and pith helmets.

After a time it became unbearably hot in the car, and I climbed out. Unless I wished to pace in the parking lot among the cars, I had no choice but to join the inmates and their visitors on the walks. I chose a nearly deserted walk and went slowly toward a building that had a yard attached to it surrounded by a wire fence. From the slide and the jungle gym in it I judged it to be for the children. Then I saw Jeff come into it. With him was a nurse pushing a kind of cart railed around like an oversized toddler. Strapped into it was "the boy."

He was human, I suppose, for he had all the equipment assigned to humans, yet I had the feeling that if it were not for the cart the creature would have crawled on his belly like an alligator. He had the eyes of an alligator too—sleepy, cold and soulless—set in a swarthy face and a head that seemed to run in a horizontal direction rather than the vertical, like an egg lying on its side. The features were devoid of any vestige of intelligence; the mouth hung open and the chin shone with saliva. While Jeff and the nurse talked, he sat under the sun, inert and repulsive.

I turned on my heel and bolted, feeling that I had intruded on a disgrace. I imagined that I had been given a glimpse of a diseased universe, the mere existence of which constituted a threat to my life; the sight of that monstrous boy with his cold, bestial eyes made me feel as if, by stumbling on this shame I somehow shared in it with Jeff. Yet I told myself that the greatest service I could do him was to pretend that I had seen nothing, knew nothing, and not place on him the hardship of talking about something which obviously caused him pain.

He returned to the car pale and shaky and wanting a drink. We stopped first at a place called Joey's on Hollywood Way. After that it was Cherry Lane on Vine Street, where a couple of girls propositioned us, and then a stop at the Brown Derby again, where I had left my car. Jeff downed the liquor in a joyless, businesslike way and talked to me in a rapid, confidential voice about a book he had just sold to Warner Brothers Studio for an exorbitant sum of money—trash in his opinion, but that was always the way—the parasites made it. Pretty soon there wouldn't be any good writers left: "There'll only be competent parasites and incompetent parasites." This was perhaps the third time we had had this conversation. Now Jeff repeated it mechanically, all the time looking down at the table where he was painstakingly breaking a red swizzle stick into ever tinier pieces.

When we left the restaurant, the sun had gone down, and the evening chill of the desert on which the city had been built had settled in. A faint pink glow from the vanished sun still lingered on the top of the Broadway Building. Jeff took a deep breath, then fell into a fit of coughing. "Goddamn smog," he said. "Goddamn city. I can't think of a single reason why I live here." He started toward his Daimler, tottering slightly.

"How about driving home with me?" I said. "You can pick your car up tomorrow."

He fumbled in the glove compartment and drew out a packet of small cigars. He stuck one between his teeth where it jutted unlit toward the end of his nose. "I'm not going home tonight, Ted friend," he said. "If you'll just drop me up the street at the Cherry Lane I'll remember you for life."

"Are you sure? I'll go with you if you want."

Jeff shook a forefinger at me archly. "Ted, you're a gentleman and a scholar. But my advice to you is to go home and take care of your wife. No, seriously. Take care of her, Ted. As for myself I shall go quietly to seed in the Cherry

Lane Café." I had started toward my car when Jeff called out to me again. "I just want to tell you, Ted friend. . . . My wife was once just as nice as your wife. . . ."

I had gone no more than a mile when the last glimmer of light left the sky and night fell like a shutter. The sky above the neon of Sunset Boulevard turned jet black, and a sickly half-moon rose and was immediately obscured by thick fog that lowered itself steadily as I traveled west, till at the foot of Clay Canyon it began to pat my windshield with little smears of moisture.

The house was dark, and at first I thought Ellen must have gone out, but then seeing her old Plymouth in the driveway I felt the grip of a cold and unreasoning fear. The events of the day seemed to crowd around and hover at my head in the fog; and the commonplace sight of that car, together with the blackness and silence of the house, sent me into a panic as I ran for the door. I pushed at it with my shoulder as if expecting it to be locked, but it swung open easily and I found myself in the darkened living room with no light anywhere and the only sound the rhythm of my own short breathing. "Ellen!" I called in a high, querulous voice I hardly recognized. "Ellen!" I seemed to lose my balance; my head swam; it was as if this darkness and silence were the one last iota that the chamber of horrors in my mind could not hold, and the door snapped open a crack, emitting a cloudy light that stank of corruption, and I saw the landscape of my denial, like a tomb. It was the children's room. Rats nested in the double bunks, mold caked the red wallpaper, and in it an insane Spanish don hung by his neck from a dead tree, his heels vlumping against the wall, his foppish clothes rubbing as he revolved slowly in invisible currents of bad air. And as he swung toward me, I saw his familiar reptile eyes open and stare at me with loathing and contempt.

I conceded: It is here and It is evil, and I have left my wife alone in the house with It, and now she has been sucked into that cold eternity where the dumb shades store their plasms against an anguished centenary of speech—a single word issuing from the petrified throat, a scream or a sigh or a groan, syllables dredged up from a lifetime of eloquence to slake the bottomless thirst of living death.

And then a light went on over my head, and I found myself in the hall outside the children's room. Ellen was in her nightgown, smilng at me. "Ted? Why on earth are you standing here in the dark? I was just taking a nap. Do you want some dinner? Why don't you say something? Are you all right?" She came toward me; she seemed extraordinarily lovely; her eyes, a deeper blue than Sondra's, looked almost purple; she seemed young and slender again; her old serenity shone through like a restored beacon.

"I'm all right," I said hoarsely. "Are you sure you are?"

"Of course I am," she laughed. "Why shouldn't I be? I'm feeling much, much better." She took my hand and kissed it gaily. "I'll put on some clothes and then we'll have our dinner." She turned and went down the hall to our bedroom, leaving me with a clear view into the children's room. Though the room itself was dark, I could see by the hall light that the covers on the lower bunk had been turned back and that the bed had been slept in. "Ellen," I said. "Ellen, were you sleeping in the children's room?"

"Yes," she said, and I heard the rustle of a dress as she carried it from the closet. "I was in there mooning around, waiting for you to come home. I got sleepy and lay down on the bunk. What were you doing, by the way? Working late?"

"And nothing happened?"

"Why? What should have happened?"

I could not answer; my head throbbed with joy. It was over—whatever it was, it was over. All unknowing Ellen had faced the very heart of the evil and had slept through it like a child, and now she was herself again without having been tainted by the knowledge of what she had defeated; I had protected her by my silence, by my refusal to share my terror with this woman whom I loved. I reached inside and touched the light button; there was the brave red wallpaper scattered over with toys, the red-and-white curtains, the blue-and-red bedspreads. It was a fine room. A fine, gay room fit for children.

Ellen came down the hall in her slip. "Is anything wrong, Ted? You seem so distraught. Is everything all right at the office?"

"Yes, yes," I said. "I was with Jeff Sheffits. We went to see his boy in the asylum. Poor Jeff; he leads a rotten life." I told Ellen the whole story of our afternoon, speaking freely in my house for the first time since we had moved there. Ellen listened carefully as she always did, and wanted to know, when I had finished, what the boy was like.

"Like an alligator," I said with disgust. "Just like an alligator."

Ellen's face took on an unaccountable expression of private glee. She seemed to be looking past me into the children's room, as if the source of her amusement lay there. At the same moment I shivered in a breath of profound cold, the same clammy draft that might have warned me on my last birthday had I been other than what I am. I had a sense of sudden dehydration, as if all the blood had vanished from my veins. I felt as if I were shrinking. When I spoke, my voice seemed to come from a throat rusty and dry with disuse. "Is that funny?" I whispered.

And my wife replied, "Funny? Oh, no, it's just that I'm feeling so much better. I think I'm pregnant, Ted." She tipped her head to one side and smiled at me.

All the editors know about William Wood is that he is the author of a fine story of dark, ghostly horrors invading a house in the rainswept California hills.

Hobo Harold Skidmore was very sick, and when farmer Plone offered Harold use of his old log cabin, Harold eagerly accepted, even if the cabin had this odd habit of disappearing.

TEN

The Ghosts of Steamboat Coulee

Arthur J. Burks

I

𝔸 heartless brakeman discovered me and kicked me off the train at Palisades. I didn't care greatly. As well be dropped here in Moses Coulee like a bag of spoiled meal as farther up the line. When a man knows he has but a short time to live, what matters it? Had I not been endowed with a large modicum of my beloved father's stubbornness I believe I should, long ere this, have crawled away into some hole, like a mongrel cur, to die. There was no chance to cheat the Grim Reaper. That had been settled long ago, when, without a gas mask, I had gone through a certain little town in Flanders.

My lungs were just about done. Don't think I am making a bid for sympathy. I know a sick man seldom arouses in the breast of strangers any other emotion than disgust.

But I am telling this to explain my actions in those things which came later.

After leaving the train at Palisades I looked up and down the coulee. Where to go? I hadn't the slightest idea. Wenatchee lay far behind me, at the edge of the mighty Columbia River. I had found this thriving little city unsympathetic and not particularly hospitable. I couldn't, therefore, retrace my steps. Besides, I never have liked to go back over lost ground. I saw the train which had dropped me

143

crawl like a snake up the steep incline which led out of the coulee. I hadn't the strength to follow. I knew that I could never make the climb.

So, wearily, I trudged out to the road and headed farther into the coulee, to come, some hours later, to another cul-de-sac. It was another (to me impossible) incline, this time a wagon road. I have since learned that this road leads, via a series of three huge terraces bridged by steep incline, out of Moses Coulee. It is called The Three Devils—don't ask me why, for it was named by the Siwash Indians.

At the foot of this road, and some half-mile from where it began to climb, I saw a small farmhouse, from the chimney of which a spiral of blue smoke arose lazily into the air. Here were folks, country folks, upon whose hospitality I had long ago learned to rely. Grimy with the dust of the trail, damp with perspiration, red spots dancing in the air before my eyes because of the unaccustomed exertion to which I had compelled myself, I turned aside and presently knocked at the door of the farmhouse.

A housewife answered my knock and nervously motioned me enter. I was shortly pointed to a seat at the table to partake of the tasty viands brought forth. When I had finished eating I arose from my place and was about to ask her what I might do in payment for the meal, when I was seized with a fit of coughing which left me faint and trembling; and I had barely composed myself when the woman's husband and a half-grown boy entered the house silently and looked at me.

"How come a man as sick as you is out on the road afoot like this?" demanded the man.

I told them my story, and that I had neither friends nor family, nor abode. While I talked they exchanged glances with one another, and when I had finished the husband looked at me steadily for a long moment.

"Is there a chance for you to get well?" he asked finally.

"I am afraid not." I tried to make my voice sound cheerful.

"Would you like to find a place where nobody'd bother you? A place where you could loaf along about as you wished until your time came?"

I nodded in answer to the question. The man strode to the door and pointed.

"See there?" he asked. "That's the road you came here on, against that two hundred foot cliff. Opposite that cliff, back of my house, is another cliff, thirteen hundred feet high. Matter of fact, my place is almost surrounded by cliffs, don't need to build fences, except where the coulee opens away toward Columbia River, which is some lot of miles away from here. Cliffs both sides of it, all the way down. No other exit, except there!"

As he spoke he swung his extended forearm straight toward the cliff to the north.

"See what looks like a great black shadow against the face of the cliff, right where she turns to form the curve of the coulee?"

"Yes, I see it."

"Well, that ain't a shadow. That's the entrance to another and smaller coulee which opens into this one. It is called Steamboat Coulee, and if you look sharp you can see why."

I studied that black shadow as he pointed, carefully, running my eyes over the face of the cliff. Then I exclaimed suddenly, so unexpectedly did I discover the reason for the name. Right at the base of that black shadow was a great pile of stone, its color all but blending with the mother cliff unless one looked closely; and this mass of solid rock, from where we stood in the doorway of the farmhouse, looked like a great steamboat slowly emerging from the cleft in the giant walls!

"Good Lord!" I exclaimed. "If I didn't know better I would swear that was a boat under steam!"

"It's fooled a lot of folks," returned the farmer. "Well, that coulee entrance is on my land, so I guess I have a right to make this proposition to you. Back inside that coulee about two miles is my old log cabin that could easy be made livable. Just the place for you, and I could send in what little food you would need. It's kind of cool at night, but in the daytime the sun makes the coulee as hot as an oven, and you could loaf all day in the heat. There are plenty of big rocks there to flop on and—who knows—maybe you'd even get well!"

"I thank you, sir," I said, as politely as I could; "you are very kind. I accept your offer with great pleasure. May I know to whom I am indebted for this unusually benevolent service?"

The man hesitated before answering.

"What difference does a name make? We don't go much on last names here. That there is Reuben, my boy, and this is my wife, Hildreth. My own name is Plone. You can tell us what to call you, if you wish, but it don't make much difference if you don't care to."

"My name is Harold Skidmore, late of the U. S. Army. Once more allow me to thank you, then I shall go into my new home before it gets so dark I can't find it."

"That's all right. Reuben will go along and show you the place. Hillie will put up a sack of grub for you—enough to last a couple of days—and tote it in tomorrow. You'll probably be too sore from your walk to come out for a while—and we may be too busy to take any in to him."

The woman dropped her arms to her side and moved into the kitchen to do the bidding of Plone. Plone! What an odd name for a man! I studied him as, apparently having forgotten me, he stared moodily down the haze-filled coulee. I tried to see what his eyes were seeking, but all I could tell was that he watched the road by which I had come to this place—watched it carefully and in silence, as though he expected other visitors to come around the bend which leads to the Three Devils. He did not turn back to me again; and when, ten minutes or so later, Reuben touched my arm and started off in the direction of Steamboat, Plone was still staring down the road.

I studied the territory over which we traveled. Though I knew absolutely nothing about farming, I would have sworn that this ground hadn't been cultivated for many years. It had been plowed once upon a time, but the plowing had been almost obliterated by scattered growths of green sagebrush which had pushed through and begun to thrive, while in the open Reuben and I struggled through regular matted growths of wild hollyhocks, heavy with their fiery blooms. Plone's farm was nothing but a desert on the coulee floor.

We were approaching Steamboat Coulee entrance, and the nearer we strode the less I liked the bargain I had made, for the huge maw looked oddly like a great open mouth that might take one in and leave no trace. But those red spots were dancing before my eyes again and may have helped me to imagine things.

When we reached the gap its mouthlike appearance was not so pronounced, and the rock which had looked like a steamboat did not resemble a steamboat at all. The floor of this coulee was a dry stream-bed which, when the spring freshets came, must have been a roaring torrent.

Before entering I looked back at the house of Plone, and shouted in amazement.

"Reuben! Where is the house? I can see all of that end of the coulee, and your house is not in sight!"

"We come over a rise, a high one, that's all," he replied carelessly; "if we go back a piece we can see the house. Only we ain't got time. I want to show you the cabin and get back before dark. This coulee ain't nice to get caught in after dark."

"It isn't?" I questioned. "Why not?"

But Reuben had begun the entrance to Steamboat Coulee and did not answer. I was very hesitant about following him now, for I knew that he had lied to me. We hadn't come over any rise, and I should have been able to see the farmhouse!

I liked this coulee less and less as we went deeper into it. Walls rose straight on either hand, and they were so close that they seemed to be pressing over upon me. The stream-bed narrowed and deepened. On its banks grew thickets of wild willow, interspersed with clumps of squaw-berry bushes laden with pink fruit. Behind these thickets arose the talus slope of shell-rock.

I studied the slopes for signs of pathways which might lead out in case a heavy rain should fill the stream bed and cut off my retreat by the usual way, but saw none. I saw instead something that filled me with a sudden feeling of dread, causing a sharp constriction of my throat. It was just a mottled mass on a large rock; but as I looked at it the mass moved, untwisted itself, and a huge snake glided out of sight in the rocks.

147

"Reuben," I called, "are there many snakes in this coulee?"

"Thousands!" he replied without looking back. "Rattlers, blue racers and bull whips—but mostly rattlers. Keep to your shanty at night and stay in the stream-bed in the daytime and they won't be any danger to you!"

Well, I was terribly tired, else I would have turned around and quitted this place—yes, though I fell dead from exhaustion ten minutes later. As it was I followed Reuben, who turned aside finally and climbed out of the stream-bed. I followed him and stood upon a trail which led down a gloomy aisle into a thicket of willows. Heavy shadows hung in this moody aisle, but through these I could make out the outline of a squatty log cabin.

Ten minutes later I had a fire going in the cracked stove which the house boasted, and its light was driving away the shadows in the wall. The board floor was well laid—no cracks through which venturesome rattlers might smell me out. I made sure of this before I would let Reuben get away, and that the door could be closed and bolted.

"Well," said Reuben, who had stood by while I put the place rapidly to rights, "you'll be all right now. Snug as a bug in a rug—if you ain't afraid of ghosts!"

His hand had dropped to the doorknob as he began to talk, and when he had uttered this last sinister sentence he opened the door and slipped out before I could stop him. Those last six words had sent a chill through my whole body. In a frenzy of fear which I could not explain, I rushed to the door and looked out, intending to call Reuben back.

I swear he hadn't had time to reach that stream-bed and drop into it out of sight; but when I looked out he was nowhere to be seen, and when I shouted his name until the echoes rang to right and left through the coulee, there was no answer! He must have fairly flown out of that thicket!

I closed the door and barred it, placed the chair back under the doorknob, and sat down upon the edge of the bed, gazing into the fire.

What sort of place had I wandered into?

For a time the rustling of the wind through the willows outside the log cabin was my only answer. Then a gritty grating sound beneath the floor, slow and intermittent, told me that a huge snake, sluggish with the coolness of the evening, was crawling there and was at that moment scraping alongside one of the timbers which supported the floor.

I was safe from these, thank God!

The feeling of security which now descended upon me, together with the cheery roaring of the fire in the stove, almost lulled me to sleep as I sat. My eyes were closing wearily and my head was sinking upon my breast. . . .

II

A cry that the wildest imagination would never have expected to hear in this place, came suddenly from somewhere in the darkness outside.

It was a cry as of a little baby that awakes in the night and begs plaintively to be fed. And it came from somewhere out there in the shell-rock of the talus slopes.

Merciful heaven! How did it happen that a wee small child such as I guessed this to be had wandered out into the darkness of the coulee? Whence had it come? Were there other inhabitants in Steamboat? But Plone had not mentioned any. Then how explain that eery cry outside? A possible explanation, inspired by frayed nerves, came to me, and froze the marrow in my bones before I could reason myself out of it.

"If you ain't afraid of ghosts!"

What had Reuben of the unknown surname meant by this remark? And by what means had he so swiftly disappeared after he had quitted my new home?

Just as I asked myself the question, that wailing cry came again, from about the same place, as near as I could judge, on the talus slope in rear of my cabin. Unmistakably the cry of a lost baby, demanding by every means of expression in its power, the attention of its mother. Out there alone and frightened in the darkness, in the heart of Steamboat Coulee, which Reuben had told me was infested by great numbers of snakes, at least one kind of which was venomous enough to slay.

Dread tugged at my throat. My tongue became dry in my mouth, cleaving to the palate. I knew before I opened the door that the coulee was now as dark as Erebus, and that moving about would be like groping in some gigantic pocket. But there was a feeble child out there on the talus slope, lost in the darkness, wailing for its mother. And I prided myself upon being at least the semblance of a man.

Mentally girding myself, I strode to the door and flung it open. A miasmatic mist came in immediately, cold as the breath from a sunless marsh, chilling me anew. Instinctively I closed the door as though to shut out some loathsome presence—I know not what. The heat of the fire absorbed the wisps of vapor that had entered. I leaned against the door, panting with a nameless terror, when, from the talus slope outside, plain through the darkness came again that eery wailing.

Gulping swiftly, swallowing my terrible fear, I closed my eyes and flung the door wide open. Nor did I close it until I stood outside and opened *my* eyes against an opaque blanket of darkness. When Plone had told me the coulee was cold after nightfall, he had not exaggerated. It was as cold as the inside of a tomb.

The crying of the babe came again, from directly behind my cabin. The cliff bulked large there, while above its rim, high up, I made out the soft twinkling of a pale star or two.

Before my courage should fail me and send me back into the cheery cabin, thrice cheery now that I was outside it, I ran swiftly around the cabin, nor stopped until I had begun to clamber up the talus slope, guided by my memory of whence that wailing cry had come. The shell-rock shifted beneath me, and I could hear the shale go clattering down among the brush about the bases of the willows below. I kept on climbing.

Once I almost fell when I stepped upon something round, which writhed beneath my foot, causing me to jump straight into the air with a half-suppressed cry of fear. I was glad now that the coulee was cold after nightfall, else the snake, were it by chance a rattler, could have struck me a death-blow. The cold, however, made the vile creature sluggish.

When I thought I had climbed far enough I bent over and tried to pierce the heavy gloom, searching the talus intently for a glimpse of white—white which should discover to me the clothing of the baby which I sought. Failing in this, I remained quiet, waiting for the cry to come again. I waited amid a silence that could almost be felt, a silence lasting so long that I began to dread a repetition of that cry. What if there were no baby—flesh and blood, that is? Reuben had spoken of ghosts. Utter nonsense! No grown man believes in ghosts! And if I didn't find the child before long the little tot might die of the cold. Where had the child gone? Why this eery silence? Why didn't the child cry again? It was almost as though it had found that which it sought, there in the darkness. That cry had spoken eloquently of a desire for sustenance.

If the child did not cry, what was I to believe? Who, or what, was suckling the baby out on the cold talus slope?

I became as a man turned to stone when the eery cry came again. It was not a baby's whimper, starting low and increasing in volume; it was a full-grown wail as it issued from the unseen mouth. And it came from at least a hundred feet higher up on the talus! I, a grown man, had stumbled heavily in the scramble to reach this height; yet a baby so small that it wailed for its milk had crept a hundred feet farther up the slope! It was beyond all reason; weird beyond the wildest imagination. But undoubtedly the wailing of a babe.

I did not believe in ghosts. I studied the spot whence the wail issued, but could see no blotch of white. Only two lambent dots, set close together, glowing like resting fireflies among the shale. I saw them for but a second only. Undoubtedly mating fireflies, and they had flown.

I began to climb once more, moving steadily toward the spot where I had heard the cry.

I stopped again when the shell rock above me began to flow downward as though something, or somebody, had started it moving. What, in God's name, was up there at the base of the cliff? Slowly, my heart in my mouth, I climbed on.

There was a rush, as of an unseen body, along the face of the talus. I could hear the contact of light feet on the shale; but the points of contact were unbelievably far apart. No baby in the world could have stepped so far—or jumped. Of course the cry might have come from a half-witted grown person; but I did not believe it.

The cry again, sharp and clear; but at least two hundred

yards up the coulee from where I stood, and on about a level with me. Should I follow or not? Did some nocturnal animal carry the babe in its teeth? It might be; I had heard of such things, and had read the myth of Romulus and Remus. Distorted fantasies? Perhaps; but show me a man who can think coolly while standing on the talus slopes of Steamboat after dark, and I will show you a man without nerves—and without a soul.

Once more I took up the chase. I had almost reached the spot whence the cry had come last, when I saw again those twin balls of lambent flame. They seemed to blink at me— off and on, off and on.

I bent over to pick up a bit of shale to hurl at the dots, when, almost in my ears, that cry came once more; but this time the cry ended in a spitting snarl as of a tomcat when possession of food is disputed!

With all my might I hurled the bit of shale I had lifted, straight at those dots of flame. At the same time I gave utterance to a yell that set the echoes rolling the length and breadth of the coulee. The echoes had not died away when the coulee was filled until it rang with that eery wailing—as though a hundred babies cried for mothers who did not come!

Then—great God!—I knew!

Bobcats! The coulee was alive with them! I was alone on the talus, two hundred yards from the safe haven of my cabin, and though I knew that one alone would not attack a man in the open, I had never heard whether they hunted in groups. For all I knew they might. At imminent risk of breaking my neck, I hurled myself down the slope and into the thicket of willows at the base. Through these and into the dry steam-bed I blundered, still running. I kept this mad pace until I had reached the approximate point where the trail led to my cabin, climbed the bank of the dry stream and sought for the aisle through the willows.

Though I searched carefully for a hundred yards on each hand I could not find the path. And I feared to enter the willow thicket and beat about. The ominous wailing had stopped suddenly, as though at a signal, and I believed that the bobcats had taken to the trees at the foot of the talus. I studied the dark shadows for dots of flame in pairs, but could see none. I knew from reading about them that bob-cats have been known to drop on solitary travelers from the limbs of trees. Their sudden silence was weighted with ponderous menace.

I was afraid—*afraid!* Scared as I had never been in my life before—and I had gone through a certain town in Flanders without a gas mask.

Why the sudden, eery silence? I would have welcomed that vast chorus of wailing, had it begun again. But it did not.

When I crept back to the bank of the stream-bed a pale moon had come up, partly dispelling the shadows in Steamboat Coulee. The sand in the stream-bed glistened frostily in the moonlight, making me think of the blinking eyes of a multitude of toads.

Where, in Steamboat, was the cabin with its cheery fire? I had closed the door to keep my courage from failing me, and now there was no light to guide me.

It is hell to be alone in such a place, miles from the nearest other human being.

I sat down on the high bank, half sidewise so that I could watch the shadows among the willows, and tried mentally to retrace my steps, hoping that I could reason out the exact location of the cabin in the thicket.

Sitting as I was, I could see for a hundred yards or so down the stream-bed. I studied its almost straight course for a moment or two, for no reason that I can assign. I saw a black shadow dart across the open space, swift as a breath of wind, and disappear in the thicket on the opposite side. It was larger than a cat, smaller than the average dog. A bob-cat had changed his base hurriedly, and in silence.

Silence! That was the thing that was now weighing upon me, more even than thought of my failure to locate the little cabin. Why had the cats stopped their wailing so suddenly, as though they waited for something? This thought deepened the feeling of dread that was upon me. If the cats were waiting, for what were they waiting?

Then I breathed a sigh of relief. For, coming around a bend in the stream-bed, there strode swiftly toward me the figure of a man. He was a big man who looked straight before him. He walked as a country man walks when he hurries home to a late supper. Then there were other people in this coulee, after all!

But what puzzled me about this newcomer was his style of dress. He was garbed after the manner of the first pioneers who had come into this country from the East. From his high-topped boots, into which his trousers were tucked loosely, to his broad-brimmed hat, he was dressed after the manner of those people who had vanished from this country more than a decade before my time. An old prospector evidently, who had clung to the habiliments of his younger days. But he did not walk like an old man; rather he strode, straight-limbed and erect, like a man in his early thirties. There was a homely touch about him, though, picturesque as he was; for he smoked a corncob pipe, from the bowl of which a spiral of blue smoke eddied forth into the chill night air. I knew from this that, did I call to him, his greeting in return would be bluffly friendly.

I waited for him to come closer, hoping that he would notice me first. As he approached I noticed with a start that two huge revolvers, the holsters tied back, swung low upon his hips. People nowadays did not carry firearms openly. In an instant I had decided to let this stranger pass, even though I spent the remainder of the night on the bank of the dry stream. Sight of those savage weapons had filled me with a new and different kind of dread.

Then I started as another figure, also of a man, came around the selfsame bend of the watercourse, for there was something oddly familiar about that other figure. He moved swiftly, his body almost bent double as he hurried forward. As he came around the bend and saw the first man who had come into my range of vision, he bent lower still.

As he did so the moonlight glowed dully on something that he carried in the crook of his arm. I knew instantly that what he carried was a rifle. Once more that chill along my spine, for there was no mistaking his attitude.

He was stalking the first man, furtively, and there was murder in his heart!

It did not take his next action to prove this to me. I knew it, even as the second man knelt swiftly in the sand of the watercourse and flung the rifle to his shoulder, its muzzle pointing at the man approaching me.

I cried out with all the power of my shattered lungs. But the man ahead, all unconscious of the impending death at his heels, paid me absolutely no attention. He was no more than twenty yards from me when I shouted, yet he did not turn his head. For all the attention he paid me I might as well have remained silent. It was as though he were stone-deaf.

I shouted again, waving my arms wildly. Perhaps he could not see me because of the shadows at my back. Still he did not see me. I whirled to the kneeling man, just as a sheet of yellow flame leaped from the muzzle of his rifle. The first man was right in front of me when the bullet struck him. He stopped, dead in his tracks. I guessed that the bullet had struck him at the base of the skull. Even so, he whirled swiftly, and both his guns were out. But he could not raise them to fire. He slumped forward limply, and sprawled in the sand.

I had not heard the report of the rifle, for simultaneously with that spurt of flame the bobcats had begun their wailing once more, drowning out the sound.

With a great cry, whose echoes could be heard in the coulee even through the wailing of the bobcats, I sprang to my feet and ran, staggering, down the watercourse, in the direction of what I thought was Steamboat's entrance.

Long before I had reached it my poor body failed me and I fell to the sandy floor, coughing my lungs away, while scarlet stains wetted the sand near my mouth.

III

When I awoke in the sand the sun was shining. Some sixth sense told me to remain motionless, warning me that all was not well. Without moving my head I rolled my eyes until I could see ahead in the direction I had fallen. In falling my right hand had been flung out full length, fingers extended.

Imagine my fear and horror when I saw, coiled up within six inches of my hand, a huge rattlesnake! His head was poised above the coil, while just behind it, against the other arc of the vicious circle, the tip of the creature's tail, adorned with an inch or more of rattles, hummed its fearful warning.

With all my power I sprang back and upward. At the

same time the bullet head, unbelievably swift, flashed toward my hand and—thank God!—safely beneath it! Stretched helplessly now to its full length, the creature's mouth, with its forked tongue, had stopped within a scant two inches of where my face had been.

Before the rattler could return and coil again I had stepped upon the bullet head, grinding it deep into the sand, and when the tail whipped frantically against my leg I seized it and hurled the reptile with all my might, out of the stream bed into the shell-rock. Even as I did it I wondered where I had found the courage; and what had kept me from moving while unconscious. Had I moved I might never again have awakened.

I climbed the bank of the dry stream to look for the entrance to my log cabin which I believed to lay ahead of me, but kept well away from the thickets for fear of snakes. With the sun high in the heavens, turning the coulee into a furnace, the snakes came out by hundreds to bask upon the shale, and as I passed, they coiled and warned me away with myriad warnings. I did not trespass upon their holdings.

After I had plodded along for fully an hour I knew that I must be quite close to the rock which gave Steamboat its name; but still I had not found the pathway leading to the log cabin. Evidently I had already passed it.

Even as I had this thought I came upon a path leading into the shadows of the willow thicket—a path that seemed familiar, even though, from the stream bed, I could not see the cabin. With a sigh, and much surprised that I had, last night, traveled so far in my hysterical terror, I turned into this path and increased my pace.

I came shortly to pause, chilled even though the sun was shining. For at the end of the mossy trail there was no cabin; but a cleared plot of ground adorned with aged mounds and rough-hewn crosses! Rocks were scattered profusely over the mounds and, I guessed, had been placed to foil the creatures which otherwise would have despoiled the bodies resting there. There was a great overhang of the cliff wall, bulging out over the little graveyard, and from the overhang came a steady drip of moisture. Slimy water lay motionless in a pool in the center of the plot. Mossy green were the stones. Mudpuppies scurried into the deeps as I stopped and stared, turning the water to a pool of slime.

How uneasy I felt in this place! Why had such a remote location been chosen as a cemetery, hidden away here from the brightness of God's sunshine? Nothing but shadow-filled silence, except for the dripping of the water from the overhang.

I hurried back to the stream bed and continued on my way.

Another hour passed, during which, my body racked with continual coughing, I suffered the torments of the damned. Those red dots were dancing before my eyes again, and nothing looked natural to me. The sunning snakes in the shale seemed to waver grotesquely—twisting, writhing, coiling. Here, on the cliff, was a row of ponderous palisades; but they seemed to be ever buckling and bending, as though shaken by an earthquake.

Then, far ahead, I saw the rock at the entrance. With a sob of joy I began to run—only to stop when I reached the pile, with a cry of hopelessness and despair. For the rock, unscalable even to one who possessed the strength to climb, now filled the coulee from lip to lip, while on my side of the pile there nestled a little lake, clear and pellucid, into which I could look, straight down, for what I guessed must have been all of twenty feet!

Some great shifting of the walls, during the night, had blocked the entrance, entombing me in Steamboat Coulee with all its nameless horrors!

There was no one to see me, so I flung myself down at the edge of the pool and wept weakly, bemoaning my terrible fate.

After a time I regained control of my frayed nerves, arose to my knees and bathed my throbbing temples. Sometime, somehow, I reasoned, Plone would find a way to reach me. There was nothing to do now but return and search again for my cabin. Plone had said that Hildreth would bring supplies to me—and I felt that they would know how to get in by some other way. They had lived in the coulee and should know their way about.

Wearily I began the return march. It never occurred to me to note that the sun went ahead of me on its journey into the west. I can only blame my physical condition for not noting this. Had I done so I would have realized at once that I had gone in the wrong direction, and that straight ahead of me lay freedom. I had gone to the head of the coulee, straight in from Steamboat Rock, and when I found the coulee blocked at the end had thought the entrance closed against me.

But I did not note the sun.

I strode wearily on, and found the cabin with ridiculous ease.

Inside, awaiting my coming, sat Hildreth, the wife of Plone! She said nothing when I opened the door, just sat on the only chair in the house and looked at me. I spoke to her, thanking her for the sack of provisions which I saw on the rickety shelf on the wall beyond the door. Still she said nothing. Just stared at me, unblinking.

I asked her about leaving this place and she shook her head, as though she did not catch my meaning.

"For God's sake, Hildreth!" I cried. "Can't you speak?"

For it had come to me that I had never heard her speak. When I had first entered the farmhouse she had placed a meal for me, and had bidden me eat of it. But I remembered now that she had done so by gestures with her hands.

In answer now to my question she opened her mouth and pointed into it with her forefinger. Hildreth, the wife of Plone, had no tongue!

Did you ever hear a tongueless person try to speak? It is terrible. For after this all-meaning gesture there came a raucous croak from the mouth of Hildreth—wordless, gurgling, altogether meaningless.

I understood no word; but the eyes of the woman, strangely glowing now, were eloquent. She pointed toward the door, trying to warn me of something, and stamped her foot impatiently when I did not understand. I saw her foot move as she stamped it—but failed to notice at the time that the contact of her foot with the board floor made no noise! Later I remembered it.

When I shook my head she arose from her chair and strode to the door, flinging it wide. Then she pointed up the coulee in the direction I had entered originally. Again that raucous croak, still meaningless. Once more I shook my head.

Was there something by the entrance that menaced me?

I was filled with dread of the unknown, wished with all my soul that I could understand what this woman was trying to say to me.

I stepped back, to search about the place for paper, so that, with the aid of a pencil which I possessed, she might write what she had to tell me. I found it and turned back to the woman, who had watched me gravely while I searched. Noting the paper she shook her head, telling me mutely that she could not write.

Then Plone, his face as dark as a thundercloud, stood in the doorway! To me he paid no attention. His eyes, glowering below heavy brows, burned as he stared at the woman. In her eyes I could read fright unutterable. She gave one frightened croak and turned to flee. But she could not go far, for she fled toward the bare wall opposite the open door. Plone leaped after her, and when I jumped between them, he flung me to the floor, where I bumped my head and lay stunned for a moment.

In that horrifying instant I realized why the murderer looked familiar last night. It was Plone! I half arose and whirled around to see what aid I could offer Hildreth. But they had vanished just like Reuben had the night before.

Trembling in every fiber of my being I strode to the back wall and ran my hand over the rough logs. They were as solid, almost, as the day the cabin had been built. To me this was a great relief. I was beginning to fear that I had stumbled into a land of wraiths and shadows or was hallucinating and I should not have been surprised if the logs had also proved to be things of shadow-substance, letting me through to stand amazed upon the shell-rock behind the cabin.

But here was one place in the coulee of shadows that was real.

I went to the door, locked and barred it. Then I returned and lighted the stove to disperse the unnatural chill that hovered in the room. After this I searched out my food and wolfed some of it ravenously. Another thought came to me:

if Reuben, Plone and Hildreth were nothing but fantasies, where had I procured this food, which was real enough and well cooked? Somewhere in my adventures since being kicked off the train at Palisades there must be a great gap I had tried to fill in. What had happened, really, in that blank space?

Having eaten, I stepped to the door and looked out. If I again went forth into the stream bed in any attempt to get out of the coulee, I should never reach it before dark. What would it mean to my tired reason to be caught in the open, in the midst of this coulee, for another terrible night? I could not do it.

Again I secured the door. Nothing *real* could get in to bother me—and even now I reasoned myself out of positive belief in ghosts. The hallucinations which had so terrified me had undoubtedly been born of my sickness.

Convinced of this at last I lay down on the rough cot and went to sleep.

IV

When I awoke suddenly in the night, the fire had burned very low and a heavy chill possessed the cabin. I had a feeling that I was not the only occupant of my abode; but, striving to pierce the gloom in the cabin's corners, I could see nothing.

In the farthest corner I saw the pale, ghostly lineaments of a woman! Just the face, shimmering there in the gloom, oddly, but neither body nor substance. The face of Hildreth, wife of Plone! Then her hands, no arms visible, came up before her face and began to gesture. Her mouth opened and I imagined I again heard that raucous croak of the tongueless. Again her eyes were eloquent, mutely giving a warning which I could not understand.

Fear seizing me in its terrible grip, I leaped from my bed and threw wood on the fire, hoping to dispel this silent shadow. When the light flared up the head shimmered swiftly and began to fade away; but not before I saw a pair of hands come forth from nowhere and fasten themselves below that head, about where the neck should have been.

Hands that were gnarled and calloused from toil on an unproductive farm—the work-torn hands of the killer, Plone!

Then the weird picture vanished and I was alone with my fantasies.

I had scarcely returned to my seat on the bed, sitting well back against the wall so that my back was against something solid, when the wailing of lost babies broke out again on the talus slopes outside. I had expected this to happen after nightfall; but the reality left me weak and shivering, even though I knew that the animals that uttered the mournful wails were flesh and blood. The wailing of bobcats, no matter how often it is heard, always brings a chill that is hard to reason away. Nature certainly prepared weird natural protections for some of her creatures!

Then the wailing stopped suddenly—short off. And the silence was more nerve-devastating than the eery wailing.

Nothing for many minutes. Then the rattle of sliding talus, as the shale glided into the underbrush.

This stopped, and a terrible silence pressed down upon me.

Then my cabin shook with the force of the wind that suddenly swooped through the coulee. It rattled through the eaves, shook the door on its hinges, while the patter-patter on the roof told me of showers of sand which the wind had scooped up from the bed of the dry stream. The wind was terrific, I thought; but ever it increased in power and violence.

The patter on the roof and the rattle in the eaves began to take on a new significance; for the patter sounded like the scamper of baby feet above my head, while the wailing about the eaves sounded like the screaming of people who are tongueless. The door bellied inward against the chair back as though many hands were pressed against it from outside, seeking entrance. Yet I knew that there was no one outside.

Then, faint and feeble through the roaring of the wind, I caught that eery cry in the night. It was the despairing voice of a woman, and she was calling aloud, hopelessly, for help! I shivered and tried not to hear. But the cry came again, farther now, as though the woman were being dragged away from me.

In God's name! What woman could be abroad in such a night?

The cry again. No man, fear the shadows as he might, could ignore that pitiful plea and call himself a man again.

I gritted my teeth and ran to the door, flinging it open. A veritable sea of flying sand swept past me; but through the increased roar came plainly that cry for help. I left the door open this time, so that the light would stream out and guide my return.

On the bank of the dry stream I stopped.

And before and below me I saw Hildreth, wife of Plone, fighting for her very life with her brutal husband! She was groveling on her knees at his feet—his hands were about her throat. As she begged for mercy I could understand her words. She had a tongue, after all! Then Plone, holding Hildreth with his left hand, raised his right and, crooking it like a fearful talon, poised it above the face of Hildreth.

He did a ghastly, unbelievable thing. I can not tell it. But when his hand came away her words were meaningless, gurgling—the raucous croaking of a person who had no tongue.

Frenzied with horror at what Plone had done, I leaped into the dry stream and ran forward—to bring up short in the middle of the sandy open space, staring aghast.

For I was all alone—no Hildreth, the tongueless—no Plone with the calloused hands! Once more a hallucination had betrayed me.

Screaming in fear I sprang out of the stream-bed and rushed toward the cabin, only to dart off the trail as I saw another man walk out of the cabin's light. He was dressed very much as had been the man whom I had seen fall before the murderous rifle of Plone last night. But he was older, stooped slightly under the weight of years. I heard him sigh softly, as a man sighs whose stomach is comfortably filled with food.

He walked toward the stream-bed, following the path through the thicket.

He had passed me when a malevolently leering figure followed him from the cabin—and that figure was Reuben, the feral son of Plone! Reuben, as his father had stalked that other unfortunate, stalked the aged man who preceded him. The latter passed a clump of service berry bushes and paused on the lip of the dry stream. He had scarcely halted when out of the clump of service berries stepped Plone himself, moving stealthily, like a cat that stalks a helpless, unsuspecting bird!

The older man half turned as though he heard some slight sound, when Plone, with the silent fury of the bobcat making a kill, leaped bodily upon his back and bore him to the ground, where the two of them, fighting and clawing, rolled into the sand below.

Reuben began to run when his father closed with the stranger, and I was right at his heels when he leaped over the edge to stop beside the silent combatants. Then he bent to assist his father.

The end was speedy. For what chance has an aged man, taken by surprise, against two determined killers? They slew him there in the sand, while I, my limbs inert because of my fright, looked on, horror holding me mute when I would have screamed aloud.

Their bloody purpose accomplished, Reuben and Plone methodically began to turn the pockets of the dead man inside out. The contents of these they divided between themselves. This finished, in silence, the murderers, taking each an arm of the dead man, began to drag the body up the sandy stretch toward the end of the coulee—the closed end.

Still I stood, as one transfixed.

Then I became conscious of a low, heart-breaking sobbing at my side. Turning, I saw the figure of Hildreth standing there, tragedy easily readable in her eyes, wringing her hands as her eyes followed the figures of her husband and her son. Then she extended her hands in a pleading gesture, calling the two who dragged the body.

She began to follow them along the stream-bed, dodging from thicket to thicket on the bank as though she screened her movements from Plone and Reuben. I watched her until her wraithlike form blended with the shadows in the thickets and disappeared from view.

As I watched her go, and saw the figures of Plone and

Reuben passing around a sharp bend in the dry stream, there came back to my memory a mental picture of a grave-yard located in perpetual shadow, adorned with rotting crosses upon which no names were written. Slimy stones at the edge of a muddy pool populated by serpentine mud-puppies.

Turning then, I hurried back to the cabin, whose door remained open—to pause aghast at the threshold, staring into the interior.

At a table in the center of the room—a table loaded with things to eat, fresh and steaming from the stove—sat an-other stranger, this time a man dressed after the manner of city folk. His clothing bespoke wealth and refinement, while his manner of eating told that he was accustomed to choicer food than that of which necessity now compelled him to partake. Daintily he picked over the viands, sorting judi-ciously, while near the stove stood Hildreth, her eyes wide with fright and wordless entreaty.

Reuben stood in a darkened corner and his eyes never left the figure of the stranger at the table. As he stared at this one I saw his tongue come forth from his mouth and de-scribe a circle, moistening his lips, anticipatorily, like a cat that watches a saucer of cream.

Plone, too, was silently watching, standing just inside the door, with his back toward me. As I watched him he moved slightly, edging toward the table.

Then Plone was upon the stranger, a carving knife, snatched from the table, in his hand.

But why continue? I had seen this same scene, slightly varied, but a few minutes before, in the sand of the dry stream.

Crouching there in the darkness I guessed what the wraith of Hildreth had tried to tell me. Going back in my memory I watched her lips move again. And as they moved I read the words she would have uttered. As plain as though she had spoken I now understood the warning.

"As you value the life God has given you—*do not stay in this cabin tonight!*"

The cabin was a trap! The ghosts of Reuben and Plone—for surely they must be ghosts—knew where it was, and could shimmer through its walls, to slay me at their will. By chance, I had escaped being murdered by going outside both nights. But until I escaped the coulee, I could be found and killed.

For hours I trembled in the shadows, afraid to move, while Reuben and Plone carried forward their ghastly work. Many times during those hours did I see them make their kill. Ever it was Plone who commanded, ever it was Reuben who stood at his father's side to assist. Ever it was Hildreth who raised her hand or her voice in protest.

Then, suddenly, she was back in the cabin with Reuben and Plone. She told the latter something, gesturing vehemently as she spoke. These gestures were simple, easy to understand. For she pointed back down the coulee, in the direction of Steamboat Rock. Somehow I knew that what she tried to tell him was that she had gone forth and told the authorities what he and Reuben had done. Plone's face became black with wrath. Reuben's turned to the pasty gray of fear which is unbounded. Both sprang to the door and stared down the coulee. Then Plone leaped back to Hildreth, striking her in the face with his fist. She fell to the floor, groveling on her knees at his feet. He dragged her forth into the trail, along it to the stream bed and, as I crept toward the edge, repeated that terrible scene I had witnessed once before.

Reuben advanced to the lip of the dry stream as Plone fought with Reuben's mother. He paid them no heed, however, but shaded his eyes with his hand as he gazed into the west in the direction of Steamboat Rock. Then he gestured excitedly to Plone, pointing down the coulee.

Plone was all activity at once. With Reuben at his heels and Hildreth stumbling farther in the rear, they rushed to the cabin and began to throw rough packs together, one each for Reuben and Plone.

But in the midst of their activities they paused and stared at the doorway where I stood transfixed. Then, slowly, though no one stood there except myself, they raised their hands above their heads, while Hildreth crouched in a corner, wild-eyed, whimpering.

Plone and Reuben suddenly lurched toward me, haltingly, as though propelled by invisible hands. Their hands were at their sides now as though bound there securely by ropes. Outside they came, walking oddly with their hands still at their sides.

They stopped beneath a tree which had one bare limb, high up from the ground—a strong limb, white as a ghost in the moonlight. Reuben and Plone looked upward at this limb, and both their faces were gray. Hildreth came out and stood near by, also looking up, wringing her hands, grief marring her face that might once have been beautiful.

Reuben and Plone looked at each other and nodded. Then they looked mutely at Hildreth, as though asking her forgiveness. After this they turned and nodded toward no one that I could see, as though they gestured to unseen hangmen.

I cried aloud, even though I had foreseen what was to come, as both Plone and Reuben sprang straight into the air to an unbelievable height, to pause midway to that bare limb; their necks twisted at odd angles, their bodies writhing grotesquely.

I watched until the writhing stopped. Until the bodies merely swayed, as though played upon by vagrant breezes sweeping in from the sandy dry stream.

Then, for the last time, I heard the piercing, wordless shriek of a tongueless woman. I swerved to look for Hildreth, and saw a misty, wraithlike shadow disappear among the willows, flashing swiftly out of sight up the coulee.

Hildreth had gone, and I was alone, swaying weakly, nauseated, staring crazily up to two bodies which oscillated to and fro as though played upon by vagrant breezes.

Then the bodies faded slowly away as my knees began to buckle under me. I sank to the ground before the cabin, and darkness descended once more.

When I regained consciousness I opened my eyes, expecting to see those swaying bodies in the air above me. There were no bodies. Then I noted that my wrists were close together, held in place by manacles of shining steel.

From the cabin behind me came the sound of voices— voices of men who talked as they ate—noisily. Behind the cabin I could hear the impatient stamping of horses.

I lay there dully, trying to understand it all.

Then two men came out of the cabin toward me. One of them chewed busily upon a bit of wood in lieu of a toothpick. Upon the mottled vest of this one glistened a star, emblem of the sheriff. The second man I knew to be his deputy.

"He's awake, I see, Al," said the first man as he looked at me.

"So I see," said the man addressed as Al.

Then the sheriff bent over me.

"Ready to talk, young man?" he demanded.

It must have mystified this one greatly when I leaped suddenly to my feet and ran my hands over him swiftly. How could they guess what it meant to me to learn that these two were flesh and blood?

"Thank God!" I cried. Then I began to tremble so violently that the man called Al, perforce, supported me with a burly arm about my shoulders. As he did so his eyes met those of the sheriff and a meaningful glance passed between them.

The sheriff passed around the cabin, returning almost at once with three horses, saddled and bridled for the trail. The third horse was for me. Weakly, aided by Al, I mounted.

Then we clambered down into the dry stream and started toward Steamboat Rock.

I found my voice.

"For what am I wanted, sheriff?" I asked.

"For burglarious entry, son," he replied, not unkindly. "You went into a house in Palisades, while the owner and his wife were working in the fields, and stole every bit of food you could lay your hands on. There's no use denying it, for we found the sack you brought it away in, right in that there cabin!"

"But Hildreth, the wife of Plone, gave me that food!" I cried. "I didn't steal it!"

"Hildreth? Plone?" The sheriff fairly shouted the two names.

Then he turned and stared at his deputy—again that meaningful exchange of glances. The sheriff regained control of himself.

"This Hildreth and Plone," he began, hesitating strangely, "did they have a son, a half-grown boy?"

167

"Yes! Yes!" I cried eagerly. "The boy's name was Reuben! He led me into Steamboat Coulee!"

Then I told them my story, from beginning to end, sparing none of the unbelievable details. When I had finished, the two of them turned in their saddles and looked back into the coulee, toward the now invisible log cabin we had left behind. The deputy shook his head, muttering, while the sheriff removed his hat and scratched his poll. He spat judiciously into the sand of the dry stream before he spoke.

"Son," he said finally, "if I didn't know you was a stranger here I would swear that you was crazy as a loon. There ain't a darn thing real that you saw or heard, except the rattlesnakes and the bobcats!"

I interrupted him eagerly.

"But what about Plone, Hildreth and Reuben?"

"Plone and Reuben," he replied, "were hanged fifteen years ago! Right beside that cabin where we found you! Hildreth went crazy and ran away into the coulee. She was never seen again."

I waited, breathless, for the sheriff to continue.

"Plone and Reuben," he went on, "were the real bogy men of this coulee in the early days. They lived in that log cabin. Reuben used to lure strangers in there, where the two of them murdered the wanderers and robbed their dead bodies, burying them afterward in a gruesome graveyard farther inside Steamboat Coulee. Hildreth, so the story goes, tried to prevent these murders; but was unable to do so. Finally she reported to the pioneer authorities—and Plone cut her tongue out as punishment for the betrayal. God knows how many unsuspecting travelers the two made away with before they were found out and strung up without trial!"

"But how about Plone's farm in Moses Coulee, outside Steamboat, and the farmhouse where I met the family?"

"It's mine," replied the sheriff. "There's never been a house on it to my knowledge. I foreclosed on it for the taxes, and the blasted land is so poor that even the rattlesnakes starve while they are crawling across it!"

"But I saw it as plainly as I see you!"

"But you're a sick man, ain't you? You never went near the place where you say the house was. We followed your footprints, and they left the main road at the foot of the Three Devils, from which they went straight as a die, to the mouth of Steamboat Coulee! They was easy to follow, and if I hadn't had another case on I'd have picked you up before you ever could have reached the cabin!"

Would to God that he had! It would have saved me many a weird and terrifying nightmare in the nights which have followed.

There the matter ended—seemingly. The sheriff, not a bad fellow at all, put me in the way of work which, keeping me much in the open beneath God's purifying sunshine, is slowly but surely mending my ravished lungs. After a while, there will come a day when I shall no longer be a sick man.

But ever so often, I raise my eyes from my work, allowing them to wander, against my will, in the direction of that shadow against the walls of Moses Coulee—that shadow out of which seems slowly to float the stony likeness of a steamboat under reduced power. And I wonder.

Born on a farm in Washington state in 1898, Arthur J. Burks served in the Marines in World War I. During the 1930s, he began writing for the pulp magazines, becoming so prolific that he became one of the fabulous "million-words-a-year writers." His novelette, Salute for Sunny, *was the most popular story Sky Fighters ever ran. His stories collected in* Black Medicine (1966) *are based on his experiences in the Carribean as an aide-decamp to Gen. Smedley Butler. He died in 1974.*

Judith loved both Mike and Jason, but only one of them truly loved her. She would find out which only after their plane went down.

ELEVEN

That Which Hath Wings

Paul Gallico

. . . for a bird of the air shall carry the voice, and that which hath wings shall tell the matter.

Ecclesiastes 10:20.

Judith drove over to Glendale Airport that morning to see her men off on a ferry job to Salt Lake City, with no sense whatever of premonition. None of them at any time felt any. Indeed, to Judith there was never anything of the supernatural about the affair. She was, after all, the level-headed daughter of a Glendale doctor. Everything that happened seemed to her natural and even logical, with the possible exception of the thing that occurred in the depth of her own soul and what was revealed to her there.

Her father, Dr. Amos Shorrell, even, was inclined to suggest a form of self-hypnosis, a semicataleptic state induced by altitude and lack of oxygen, but to Judith, with her warmth and great, deep-seated womanliness—above all, her capacity for and belief in love between human beings—it was much simpler and much more elemental. She was of the modern breed born into a world that has added to its life the uncharted dimensions of the sky. She grew up with a consciousness of its mysteries.

Jason and Mike were flying a DC-3 over to Salt Lake City to replace one that had developed a cough in a port motor.

Judith always drove to the airport when Jason took off on a run. She would kiss him good-by and then stand outside the gates waiting for that moment when the big ship went by her on the take-off run, roaring like all the dragons of antiquity.

When the wind was right, so that it ran past the administration building, she would, for a second, catch a glimpse of Jason's wonderful profile, seen through the window of the control cabin, and see him raise his right hand to the peak of his cap. It was his farewell to her, his love, because he would not take his eyes off the runway.

Of Mike Trant, Jason Hawks's copilot, she would see nothing, but it was a comfort to know that he was there—funny, ugly Michael with the harsh, dark face and the great, kindly heart. She had a feeling that when the two were together nothing could happen to either of them. She loved them both, deeply and tenderly, but she was in love with Jason.

She sometimes wondered to herself whether she had chosen Jason because he was, among other things, so strikingly handsome while she herself was plain. For Judith was not a beauty as beauties are accounted in the market. She was plain, but she had the deep, inner beauty of soul and character that so illuminates a plain exterior. She was going on twenty-seven. Her mother had died when she was fifteen, and she had lived with her father since that time. When Judith fell in love with and became engaged to Jason Hawks, Doctor Shorrell slipped quietly into the background and became the friend of her lover, and of Mike Trant as well.

For both men had been Judith's suitors. It had been a gay, bright courtship conducted by the two pilots. Jason Hawks was dramatically handsome. Mike Trant was as gentle and kind as he was ugly. Jason was gay and vital, and seething with life and spirit, and flying the big tin geese was meat and drink to him. If he was not so sensitive or imaginative as Trant, he made up for it with vitality and sheer male attractiveness. Judith's magnificence had cut through to him, though perhaps not to the extent that it had reached Mike Trant. No man can love beyond his own ability to estimate another human being, and above all he cannot love beyond the power of his imagination. To Mike, who had a lot of Irish in him, Judith's grave, deep wells of feminine power, her store of tenderness and the welling inner beauty that she had were like music, like ancient songs.

The relations of the three were by no means a triangle, chiefly because of Mike Trant's extraordinary nature. He was that rare type of man occasionally encountered who is happiest when he is doing something for others, no matter how trivial. Mike had made his run, so to speak, for Judith, and had failed. Jason Hawks was his friend. Judith was the woman he loved and would always love. And therefore he was content in the joy they took in each other. Because he loved them both, he was happy in their company, and they in his. Judith adored Mike, and a good deal of their splendid relations was due to her fine sense of tact and fitness. She never hurt him by carelessness. She had long had a curious feeling that somehow their three lives were bound up together.

Once, in a serious moment when the three had been drawn even closer together by the washing out of a ship and several passengers on a mountainside, where they had been found dead after an eight-day search, Mike Trant had said, curiously and apparently incongruously, "If we ever crack up a ship, Jude, don't waste time looking for us on the ground."

Judith's brow wrinkled and her dark head cocked a little to one side as she thought. "No?" she said finally. "Where?"

Mike pointed overhead. "Get yourself plenty of altitude, Jude, if you ever come to look for us, because that's where we'll be."

Jason grinned and said, "Mike has a quaint notion that he and I are going to heaven, if that's what he means."

But the frown and the puzzled look had remained on Judith's face for some time, because she wasn't at all sure that was what Mike had meant.

She parked her little roadster in the pilot's enclosure and went into the waiting room, where she ran into Swampy Smith, the instructor for the Red Arrow School, who said, "Hello, monkey! When are you going to learn to fly?"

Swampy was an old-timer and was allowed to take liberties. He was one of the last great barnstormers. He could probably outfly any pilot on the field and might have been a senior pilot in the airline service, but his old barnstormer's pride wouldn't let him give in to ground direction. He called the airline pilots glorified chauffeurs and made a living out of the Red Arrow Hangar down at one end of the field, teaching beginners how to hoist a couple of training jalopies around the field without killing themselves.

Judith grinned so that her eyes disappeared and said, "Now, you know I'd never make a flyer, Swampy. I'm a female." Swampy was notoriously against women ever being allowed at the stick of any kind of flying machine. "Have you seen Jason or Mike around?"

He led her out to the apron of the No. 5 gate, where the empty DC-3 stood ready for flight. Jason and Mike were checking papers with the dispatcher.

"My brave birdmen," said Judith. "Were they going to fly all alone to Salt Lake City without any pretty stewardess?"

"There's a fog over Los Colopitos," said Swampy.

It was January, but the sky over Glendale was brilliantly blue and cloudless, the sun warm.

"Darling," said Jason, "can you bear to see your hero in one of his less dramatic moments?" Then in answer to Swamp's remark, "We're not going that way. Mike and I are going sightseeing."

The freight man came out of the office and said, "Hey, dopes! There's some air express to go. Oranges and grapefruit and a couple of crates of avocados. Joe's bringing it out."

"Pack camels," said Judith unfeelingly, and watched them stow the crates.

Mike Trant made her a low bow. "Hawks and Trant, Expressing and Trucking, Furniture Moved. Call upon us any time."

When they were ready to go aboard, Judith went through the little ceremony they always had. She kissed Jason on his mouth with all longing and frankness and passion; then she went to Mike and kissed him on the cheek gently, because it brought her close to his ear, where she could whisper, "Take care of him, Mike."

Judith grinned into Mike's wizened, ugly face as he gave

her the usual wink. For a moment they stood there, the plain girl and the ugly man, holding each other by both arms and looking into each other's face.

Then the two pilots got into the big ship and flew right into the low yellow afternoon sun, and Judith saw Jason's hand to his cap as he coursed by, and even caught a glimpse of Mike's uneven profile outlined behind his, like two heads on a medallion. Because they were flying into the sun, the ship was a black outline, a huge beetle, and then a dark flying cross that grew smaller and smaller until it vanished after the last faint whisper from its motors had died away.

And that was the end of it, except for the faint message out of the fog, snow and storm, received at Las Vegas, asking for help and directions. Then those stopped. The ship never arrived at Salt Lake City or anywhere else. It vanished somewhere into the Sierra Nevadas.

The most terrible time for Judith was the uncertain routine days of the search. Because she was Judith, there was no attempt made to conceal matters from her. As a matter of fact, one of the dispatchers called her up at eleven o'clock that night and said, "Hello, Jude? This is Crandall. You'd better get over here. There's some trouble."

And that first night she spent in the radio room, staring with her dark eyes at the black metal boxes with their dials and indicators and knobs, those boxes that were so silent except for cracklings and hummings, but from which might suddenly come forth the voice of the man she loved. It never came, nor was there any news of any kind. Only one thing was certain: By four o'clock in the morning the vanished ship was no longer in the air.

There was no search that morning, or that day, because the fog had swept down from the north and blanketed the area. Doctor Shorrell took his daughter home and made her get some sleep.

The next day the fog lifted, and the machines from Los Angeles and Las Vegas and Salt Lake City and Reno climbed into the air and swept the snowbound passes and the black walls and precipices of the mountains. Swampy Smith took off in his own pride and joy, his powerful open-

175

cockpit Hornung-Eagle that could achieve a ceiling of twenty-one thousand feet. Because they had said they planned to avoid Los Colopitos, and he remembered what Jason had said about going sightseeing, he ranged across to Kingman and then headed north across the Grand Canyon and combed the sides of the Wasatch Mountains. He returned after two days with nothing to report.

Curiously, it was at the end of the seventh day, when the search officially ended and hope was abandoned until spring and the melting of the snows might reveal the wreckage to some passing ship or chance prospector or sheep herder, that the conviction came to Judith that the men were still alive.

It was that same night, following the announcement that the search had been abandoned, that Doctor Shorrell entered his house after a late call. It was past three in the morning. He tiptoed upstairs wearily and passed Judith's room, the door of which was open. And he thought, in the first shock of hearing her voice from the darkness, that she was speaking to him. There was breathless agony and pleading in her voice.

She said, "Oh, louder . . . louder! I can't hear you." He stopped in surprise. She spoke again, sharply first, then trailing away to a despairing whisper: "Jason! Jason. . . . Michael. . . . Oh, I can't hear you any more. . . . I can't hear you."

Her father stepped into her room quickly and snapped the wall switch. She was sitting up in bed with her hands to her head, her hair lifted away from her ears and her eyes wide and dark and staring raptly into distances beyond all walls, the fixed stare of intense concentration of one who is listening.

She did not hear her father or notice that the light was on until he said, "Judith, darling," and came over to her bed. Then she made a quick motion as though to silence his steps, and suddenly turned a wild face to him and cried, "Father! Jason. . . . Mike. . . . I—I can't hear him any more." Then she clung to him and began to shake.

He stroked her hair gently and said, "Poor Judith. The dead?"

Judith cried, "No! No, the living. Not dead. They're alive

somewhere. He—he spoke to me. I heard—I felt him; and then I couldn't hear or feel any more."

"Who was it?" asked the doctor quietly. "Jason?"

Judith was frowning deeply and there was a puzzled expression on her face. She answered hesitatingly, "I—I don't know. It was one of them. It must have been Jason. But I don't know."

The doctor studied his daughter. There were no signs of hysteria. "What did he say? Was there a message?"

Judith still had her hands pressed to her temples and she shook her head slowly and repeated after him, "Message? I don't know," and continued to shake her head. Then suddenly she stopped and sat up and looked at her father and said flatly, "They're damned sick of eating avocados."

The doctor nodded his head gravely. "If they were alive they would be living on the fruit they were carrying."

Suddenly Judith wilted, the tension of her body relaxed. She began to sob. She shook her father by the lapels and pleaded with him:

"Father, give me something—something to take that will let them get through to me again. Please, father. There's so much around—so many things—I can't hear them any more. Help me. Help me, please."

The doctor went downstairs and secured a mild sedative to quiet her nerves. He gave it to her and then remained with her until she dropped quietly off to sleep. He remained awake for a long time, but there were no further sounds from her room, nor did she say anything more when she came downstairs the next morning.

Judith tried to rationalize her experience. She knew that it had not been a vivid dream, that she had not been asleep. Because she was her father's daughter and had been brought up in an atmosphere of medicine, she was quite ready to mistrust her own senses, and question the possible tricks that might be played by a hurt and distraught mind.

Now, in the hard light of morning, she was not sure whether she had actually heard something or whether a thought had permeated her. But the life line to which she clung was the ridiculous, logical incongruity of the message that had remained with her. She had nothing but contempt for the departed who rattled tambours, blew trumpets and chose long-defunct Indians to deliver their messages. But she had a great feeling of strength and power in the love that was between her and Jason, and, she added to herself, Mike too. She had felt it as an actual force that bound them together, far beyond words and phrases, or even physical contact. Somehow she would have mistrusted any other message. They had been living on avocados and were fed up with them. It was like both of them.

She was puzzled because she was not certain who had spoken to her. She had been almost sure that it was Jason, but she thought it strange that there had been nothing that made the identification positive.

She set out to reason her way coldly to a solution, because it was necessary to combat the almost panicky excitement there was within her. If she gave way to it, it might forever destroy the hope she now had of finding them. She must not again show the panic to which she had given way with her father, the night of the occurrence.

She sat in her study and summoned logic. She began with the premise that Jason and Michael were alive. They must be injured or they would have come out. They must have been trying to communicate with her for many days. Then their communication had not been an accident. But her reception, even of the fragment, had been an accident. Somehow, for that brief electric moment, the lines had been cleared. What had clogged them for the rest of the time? Had it been she? Or her situation? She tested herself, recalling the sleepless nights she had spent. Surely she had been in tune, had lain there raw and suffering. Was the house shutting her in? Might she be closer if she went into an open field? She felt no nearer a solution, and the need for speed was driving her close to panic. They could not live forever on the food they had.

She began to tremble, and her head felt compressed as though by shrinking loops of steel. Her feeling of loss was gone, but in its place was the awful sense of futility and inadequacy that was blocking her from answering a cry for help.

And then suddenly, with all the deep, sonorous clarity of a great ringing bell, a bell that pealed joy and freedom, there came to her the curious half-forgotten thing that Michael Trant had said to her: "If we ever crack up a ship, Jude, don't waste time looking for us on the ground."

It brought her up standing, flushed and breathing hard, her eyes burning like lamps set in windows for loved ones, and in her ears the tocsin rang: "Earthbound! Earthbound! Earthbound! Search for them where they dwell!" She would find Swampy. Swampy would take her there where she could find them again.

When Judith drove up to the Red Arrow Hangar, Swampy recognized her car and strolled over.

"Swampy," she cried, "I want to go up! Will you take me? High!"

Swampy said, "O.K., monkey. Want to air out a little, eh? You're smart. We'll take the Eagle and go after a little altitude. Nothing like airing out when you're feeling low."

He got her helmet and goggles and a warm leather jacket and strapped her in. They were at five thousand feet and moving on to six when Judith's eyes found the altimeter in the front cockpit. She began calling on Jason. She called to him with her voice and with her being. She called to Mike too. And she leaned her head against the front of the cockpit and cried bitterly, the tears gathering inside her goggles. There was no reply. There was no repetition of the vital vivid experience of the night before.

At ten thousand feet she had a better grip on herself. The earth was half hidden by broken cloud banks. She forced herself to calm. Perhaps she had been overeager. There was but one sensation of which she was definitely conscious, and that was a sense of freedom, of having shed so much of the terrible load the earth places upon us. It was not only a physical liberation that she experienced, but a psychic and spiritual one as well. She was going through the lift and exaltation that come to all depressed people when they air out, as Swampy expressed it. There is no haven as sweet and gentle as the sky for the sick and the sore in spirit. But free as she felt from the million and one cross currents of the life below, she could get no answer from the men she called.

At thirteen thousand feet she noted that the nose of the ship was no longer high and that the pitch of the motor had changed. She turned around and looked at Swampy, and

pointed upward with one hand. He shook his head in nega-
tion, and when she pointed again, insistently, he suddenly
cut the gun and shouted at her above the sound of the idling
motor and the high tune of the wind in the wires:

"That's enough! Haven't got any oxygen aboard! It's
freezing up there!"

She turned around, and Swampy let the ship drop earth-
ward, motorless, in a flat glide. And suddenly, with a rush as
though it had swooped upon her, and only for a brief second, the man she loved was with her, and then he was
gone, blocked off, shut out as though a door had slammed.
There had been no message, but she knew that her name
had been called and that for one brief moment she had
been conscious of a love such as she had never known before.

The opening and shutting of the door had been so rapid
and decisive that she whipped around instinctively to look at
Swampy. She saw that he was shaking his head like a fighter
who has been stunned.

He grinned at her and said, "I was dozing off. Hang on,
monkey, we're going down."

And then Judith understood and knew what she must do.

When they rolled up to the line, Swampy helped her out to
the ground. "Feel better?" he said.

Judith was as taut as piano wire, and she saw herself
moving as though she were detached and in a dream. She
said, "Swampy, I want to learn how to fly."

The pilot grinned at her fondly and said, "Okay, baby. I
thought you'd get around to it someday. When do you want
to start—tomorrow? We can get you your student license,
and Doc Steadman can give you your physical in the morning."

Judith put her arm on Swampy's shoulder, and he was
surprised at the power of the grip of her fingers. She spoke
to him slowly in a low, clear voice, as if in that way he might
understand. "Swampy, I want to learn at once. Now. I've
got to be able to fly. Don't ask me any questions. Just help
me. Every minute counts. How long will it take?"

Swampy looked at her curiously, no longer smiling. There
was something so powerful and pathetic in her earnestness.

"You've got to have fifty hours to get a license," he said gravely. He was weighing her and the stuff she was made of. "You'll find you won't want to do more than a couple of hours a day, maybe three. It's damn hard work, and tiring."

"I'll do ten hours, Swampy. More. Fourteen. I must. I must." She was in such a panic inside her that he might not understand, might block her through not understanding. And yet if she tried to tell him—

He was suddenly sharply suspicious, and said, "What is this, baby? You haven't any nonsense in mind about Jason and Mike? The best pilots in the country looked for them."

"No," said Judith. "No nonsense about Jason and Mike. Word of honor, Swampy. I want to fly the Eagle alone. In time, Swampy—while there's still time. Will you trust me? Will you help me?"

Swampy looked at his wrist. It was two o'clock. "Come on, baby," he said, and nodded with his head toward her car. He got into the driver's seat and drove across the field to the office of the doctor who looked after the health of the pilots. When Doctor Steadman came out he said, "Student pilot, doc. Give her the works. She starts when you're finished with her."

The next days were to Judith nightmarish because of the reiterance of detail. She lived with a roaring engine in her ears, and the jumpy motions of the little training ship, and the sight of Swampy's helmeted head in front of her eyes, and his signals, and the sudden jars of countless landings. She was, of course, useless the first two hours, simply because of the tension created by her terrific concentration on the job, until Swampy broke it by making her fly in rhythm to his arm motions, which he waved to a timed beat like a conductor leading an orchestra. They rested fifteen minutes after each hour, for, though Judith begrudged the time, Swampy insisted upon it.

He took her home at dusk and she went to bed without eating, and was asleep almost at once. She was back at the hangar at eight in the morning, grim, determined, tight-lipped.

At three o'clock Swampy turned her loose and stood gray-faced on the field below while she did her first three solo turns. The solo flight brought Judith the confidence she

had lacked, but gave her none of the joy and great exultation that attend the student's first solitary attempt. To her it
was merely one step on the way to the accomplishment of
her task.

The hours and days that followed were dream hours and
dream days. When Swampy was busy with other pupils she
rattled around the air alone, cutting endless circles and figure eights above the airport, learning to keep a wary eye on
the incoming transports, getting the feel of her ship. She
flew thirteen hours one day, and twelve the next. She
learned night flying by the giant airport floodlights.
She learned how to handle more power. She soloed everything in the Red Arrow Hangar, including Swampy's beloved Hornung-Eagle, and when she felt the powerful beast
under her single control, and made it hoist her to four thousand feet, she smiled for the first time and cried, "Coming
Jason! . . . Mike! . . . Coming—coming!"

The strain was refining her. She was drawn and white,
and had lost weight, but for her own purposes she was glad
of that, and ate very little. She was tired all the time, even
after a night's sleep. She took her license in four and a half
days. By that time she was flying so well that she went
through the test as routine.

When she rolled up to the line after the last landing,
Swampy was shocked to see how she looked. Her eyes
seemed larger because they glowed out of the white hollows
of her face and were deeply shadowed underneath.

Swampy, too, was close to the end of his nervous control.
It had not been easy for him, either. He said, "All right,
baby. You're a pilot. You've done it. Now go home and get
some rest."

Judith climbed stiffly out of the cockpit. "What day is
this?" she asked.

"Friday."

Judith counted days off to herself on her fingers, and fear
came into her eyes. "So long; so long. Swampy! I want the
Eagle tonight. After dark. Please. For an hour."

"Nothing doing, baby. You get some rest. You can fly it
tomorrow."

"Swampy!" Her cry was almost animal in its pain. "Must I
go down on my knees?"

Swampy caught her. "All right, monkey," he said. "Whatever you say. Try to get some sleep. Come back at nine o'clock. I'll have her ready for you."

When she came back at nine, the squat, strong red ship was standing on the line with the motor idling. Swampy was standing beside her with a 'chute in his hands and offered it to her.

She shook her head. "No. Straight flying."

She was bulky with sweaters and warm clothing which Swampy should have noticed. She climbed into the cockpit and strapped herself in, tried the controls and roared the engines once. Swampy came over, looking worried. "What's up, baby? What are you up to?"

For a moment Judith had a pang. The Eagle was his darling. Suddenly she leaned her head down over the side and said, "Swampy! Get Turner, the traffic manager, to come over. I'll be back in an hour. Maybe two. I want to see him."

She began to ease the throttle forward gently.

"Judith!" cried Swampy suddenly in fright. "What are you up to? Where are you going?"

Her goggled and helmeted head came up bravely and her cry rang clearly above the accelerating engine. "To find Jason! To find Jason and Mike! Stand clear!"

Before Swampy could shout more than, "Judith! Come back, monkey!" she roared the red ship up into the night sky and the waiting stars.

She felt joyous immediately she had freed herself of the earth, and for the sheer power and movement of the upward rush she hauled herself aloft on her prop until she remembered to flatten out and continue her ascent in the long circles Swampy had taught her. By that time the airport was already a tiny patch of floodlight. She turned her face from the earth and looked to the stars.

She was ready. She felt purified by her work of the past days, and if they were there she would find them. She would climb so high that not a single stray cross current from the teeming millions of humans below should interfere. If her love was still alive that night and called to her, she would hear him.

She thought first of Jason and the firm feel of his arms

and shoulders beneath his coat and his beloved man smell, his light, far-away-looking eyes and his wonderfully clean mouth. Because she was for the first time alone at night, suspended between heaven and earth, she knew for the first time, too, why her men belonged to and in the sky.

Judith let her thoughts dwell on gentle Mike and his great heart, and he, too, belonged to those clean, sweet, free upper reaches because he was warm and kindly, and kindness was to him a habit. She could not think of Mike as dead, nonexistent. Jason was—well, Jason; but Mike was so simple and magnificent a person, an anchor and a rock. Her altimeter clocked eight thousand feet. She studied her instrument board, throttled back on the engine a bit and continued to climb.

Jason and Mike. It was the search for Jason that was drawing her into the sky, but it had been Mike who had told her where she would find them, Michael, whose depth and strength and fineness were such that he had found things aloft that Jason, perhaps, never even dreamed of. She exulted suddenly in them, and cried as she climbed, though she could hardly hear herself above the sweet, deep tone of the motor, "Coming! Oh, coming, coming!"

At thirteen thousand feet she flattened out for a moment. It was a landmark. To that height she had been with Swampy. What lay above was uncharted. She found herself floating between firmament and firmament. Starlight above, earthlight below, the earth lights topaz and twinkling, the stars diamond blue and white. She noted the great wall of the mountain ranges that ran to the edge of the long valley of lights beneath the San Bernardinos. Thirteen thousand feet. Not yet, not yet. Above, it was more certain. Above, they would be. There she would hear them.

Again she tilted the nose of the ship upward. The climb was slower now. It took longer to notch the altimeter needle. She resisted the temptation to sharpen the angle. At fifteen thousand feet she found that she was breathing more rapidly and that suddenly she was drowsy. She remembered that Swampy had dozed for a moment with her in the ship, and she shook her head to clear it. There was a pressure at the base of her neck. She rapped her knuckles sharply on the side of the ship so that the pain would help to keep her awake. She had hauled herself to sixteen thousand feet, and not until she tried to smile at the triumph did she realize that her face was stiff with the bitter cold.

Higher. Higher. "Get yourself plenty of altitude, Jude, if you ever come to look for us!" Had that been Mike speaking to her? She shook her head. No. She had said it to herself. She passed seventeen thousand without even noticing it, because she was fighting her body that was gasping for oxygen.

The cold was like the stabbing of knives now, and her fingers were numb on the stick and her feet on the rudder bars. But she could still work them. She kept on.

Past nineteen thousand her distress became almost unbearable, and she had to fight desperately every second against the hot rasping pain in her chest and the giddiness in her head and the deadening, numbing cold. Because the needle refused to move, she increased the climbing angle. Her goal was twenty thousand, and the figure on the dial had a magic that drew her on beyond any suffering. Light and darkness flashed before her eyes, and bright flashing spears darted through her head. Only through suffering shall you attain— To love greatly is to suffer. Go higher, higher. . . . For countless centuries men had been turning their eyes upward to the sky, always upward.

She was there. She had reached it. The needle had touched twenty thousand, dropped back, went forward again and stayed. She reached for the throttle, but felt nothing. She saw that her hand was on it, the fingers crooked, and pulled back. The roar died away to a gentle hissing. Somehow she eased the ship into gliding position, lifted her face upward and cried aloud through her bleeding lips, "Jason! Jason! . . . Mike! I'm here!"

She strained and wrestled at the strap of her safety belt with the force of the effort she was making. With what was left of her senses, she was striving to make of her body a great receiving set. He came to her immediately, with a rush and a warmth of enveloping love so strong and vivid that she felt it almost physically, and in her reeling brain grew the pictures of where they were, the half-shattered plane on its belly on the flat, steep, rocky, half-snow-covered slope, the twin peaks that towered above them and the mountain that was shaped like a Spanish woman, mantilla-draped.

She heard no sound actually but the high whine of the frosty wind on the taut wires, and the voice that spoke to her played upon her the way the wind played upon the wires, an antiphony in deep tones of pain and anguish and love. For the man who had come through to her was badly hurt, and with the last of his strength she knew that he was sending out his love to find her and bring her to them.

The plane rocked and tossed in its descent from the high cold silences, as shaken and racked as the soul of Judith. She knew that her lover was dying and, dying, was flinging out to her and enveloping her with the great, flowing waves of his love.

The pictures suddenly became fainter and interrupted, and she cried aloud for him to come back to her, to leave with her this love that was filling her with such unutterable sweetness and beauty.

And then the universe through which she was tumbling rocked with her name. It rang from every star and shattered every silence, twice called, once in agony, the last time in farewell:

"Judith! Judith!"

And then it was gone, and with it every sensation of connection. It was not that she could no longer hear it or feel it. It was no longer there. She sickened and nearly died with the sense of loss, and the world turned upon her, whirling, topaz upon diamond, diamond upon topaz, and great shapeless darknesses; and with a shock she realized that the ship was spinning, wrapping up tighter and tighter.

She would have let it spin in and crash her into the peace of never-lifting night, but there was something she still had to know. Sobbing, she fought the stick forward and pressed a rudder pedal and pulled out, but immediately fell into another, and fought again, and conquered, and this time gunned the ship into flying level. She saw that she was very close to the ground, with the airport lights a little to the north. She flew to them and circled until the floodlights came on, and, with what remained of her strength and senses, slipped and bounced it in to a landing. She was unconscious before the ship stopped rolling.

But she came to, when they were lifting her out of the cockpit. She saw faces that she knew—Swampy Smith, Turner, the traffic manager, two other pilots.

She cried, "Swampy! Swampy! I know where they are! I've found them! Jason and Mike! You must go to them!"

She was lying on the ground and Swampy was wiping the blood from her face with his silk neck scarf. He said, "Hush, child. What in God's name have you done to yourself?"

"No!" Judith cried again. "You must listen to me! I've found them! One is dead! The other is still alive! You must go to him!"

Turner knelt at her side and asked, "Which one is still living, Miss Shorrell?"

Judith knew then that she had to face it. "I don't know. I don't know. I don't dare know. It must be—Oh, I don't know. I must know."

She began to sob hysterically. Her father broke through the circle, took her in his arms and held her, gave her a whiff of ammonia salts.

Swampy said, "She says she's found them."

The doctor stroked her head and said quietly, "Judith— where are they?"

She closed her eyes for a moment to bring back the pictures. "To the north—north of Las Vegas, in Utah. Past the Twin Peaks. On a slope. The ship is lying flat. One wing is torn off. You can see her if you pass to the west of the mountain shaped like a Spanish woman wearing a mantilla."

Turner was shaking his head slowly and regretfully, but Swampy Smith suddenly yelled, "Jupiter! Mount Dolores!"

Turner said sadly, "It's impossible." He shrugged. "Poor child. Grief. Brooding."

"A fire," Judith said. "Smoke drifting upwards. Many crates and boxes broken open. The cabin is intact."

Swampy jumped to his feet. "Damn it!" he shouted at Turner and the two pilots. "You office flyers! What do you know about the air? . . . I'll go, Judith. If I leave now, I can make it by dawn. If they're there, I'll find them."

He was rewarded many times over by her smile.

"They're there," she said, and closed her eyes. She was

187

being carried into the pilots' room when she heard the zooming roar of Swampy's takeoff in the Red Eagle.

She remained there overnight. She was still there the next day shortly after eleven when Swampy came rocketing down out of the sky in a diving landing and fishtailed right for the administration building, dodging a taxiing transport. He was out on a wing while it was still rolling, waving an arm. Someone raced in and got Judith. She came out in time to see him running toward them, shouting, "Found 'em! Found 'em! They're there! One of them is still alive!"

"Which?" Judith spoke the word.

Swampy stood before her. "I—honey, I'm sorry. I couldn't tell. I couldn't get low enough. I just saw him wave. I spotted the country. It was where you said they'd be. They can be reached through Chowatchie Pass. We'll have him out in twenty-four hours. I'm—I'm sorry I couldn't tell, honey."

But by this time Judith was sure she knew.

She would not let herself hope. All through the terrible suspense of the weary trek on horseback from Almores through Chowatchie Pass, she told herself dully that Jason was dead. He had cried her farewell, but before he died he had shared with her such love as few women can know from man. A hundred times she thought back to the great, soaring, singing strength that had come winging to her through the air, the tenderness and passion that had filled her and stirred her in response to such love as she had never before known, and she thought that she had loved Jason as utterly as any woman can love.

Jason, then, was dead, and because so much of her was dead, too, she was able to go on and see for herself. Yes, see for herself. She caught herself on that phrase. Why, if she was certain? Why had she not waited until the news was confirmed by wire from the searching party? Why had she come? What were those terrible fears and doubts that welled up darkly from deep inside her like the great sighing bubbles in ancient tar pits?

There was a sudden shout from up front and a shot. They had been traveling a narrow trail on the side of a steep, bare, rocky slope. The caravan of men and horses and the lone girl stopped and looked. Over the hill, around the bend, they could see ascending a thin streamer of smoke. With a rush, they spurred their horses forward and came around the corner. The silver ship was there, on the slope side, on her belly, the undercarriage washed out. One wing was torn off. There were broken crates of oranges and grapefruit and avocados strewn about. A little way from the ship a fire barely smoldered. Two figures lay there, one on either side, motionless. The party rushed forward wildly, shouting, Doctor Steadman in the lead. Now that it was to be, Judith found herself calm. She watched the doctor bend over both figures.

Then he straightened up with a little cry and said, "Jason's still alive. He's still breathing. We've got a chance to pull him through. But Mike—Mike's gone."

So that now at last she knew. Beyond any doubt or recall. The others crowded around the doctor working over Jason. Judith went slowly over to the other still figure, knelt in the snow and gazed at him and marveled at the great beauty that had come upon the face that had been so ugly, the beauty that must have come when he said good-by to her.

Yes, it had been Michael who had got through to her, because of the kind of man he was and because of the way he loved her. Michael who had been with her on that unforgettable night. Michael who always had been, who always would be. She wondered how long she had known it was Michael she loved. Oh, for a long, long time. Had it not always been Michael? When they disappeared—she must have known then. And the first night in her home when Michael reached her. She had been blinded by her feelings for Jason or she would have known who it was.

Michael, Michael, always Michael. Every question was answered now. Yes, each and every one was answered fully by the mute clay there that she had loved. All, with possibly one exception. There was a cry from the other group and it opened up a little. It was Swampy who called to her, "Judith! Jason's coming around! Come here!"

That was the question to which she knew no answer. Still kneeling by Michael's side, she stared over at them through the mist of tears that came at last, and did not know whatever she would do.

189

"Judith!" Swampy called again. "Jason's coming to! He's all right!"

She rose very slowly to her feet. "Yes," she said. "Poor Jason. Poor, poor Jason."

Born in New York City in 1898, novelist and film writer Paul Gallico was educated at the University of Columbia and first gained fame as a sportswriter for the New York Daily News. *His best columns were collected in* Farewell to Sports *(1938). Turning to fiction full time, his* The Snow Goose *(1941) was the first of forty books and several hundred stories in such slick magazines as the* Saturday Evening Post *and* Cosmopolitan. *His bestseller,* The Poseidon Adventure *(1969), was made into a blockbuster film and provided him a luxurious life until his death in Monaco in 1976.*

Gram kept wandering away from the retirement home, but it took a very special private investigator to find out where she was going.

TWELVE

In the Shade
Edward Bryant

Keeping a tail on the taxi ahead of me was the easy part. Staying discreet about it wasn't. The white cab and my Audi were the only two vehicles on the graveled road, and the twin rooster tails of dust rose at least ten yards into the cloudless sky. I did my best, lagging back about half a mile. Only a blind driver could have failed to spot me. However, I'm not exactly Nancy Drew, and the taxi driver didn't ferry a desperate criminal. The woman he carried away from the town and into the summer morning was a seventy-one-year-old grandmother whose daughter was terrified that Gram O'Brien might be hurting herself.

Alice Mary O'Brien had not been young when I first met her while I was a little girl. Even then, everyone called her Gram, including Marge, her last-born. Marge had been my best friend in eighth grade, and we had intermittently kept in touch, though the miles and decades had inexorably drawn us apart.

I thought of Gram as a marvelously tough and plain-spoken pioneer woman whose parents had moved from Wisconsin to Wyoming in a team-drawn wagon shortly before the First World War. By that time there were no Indian raids or anything else quite as melodramatic, but life was still frontier-precarious with drought, blizzards, timber wolves and the influenza epidemic of 1919. Most of Gram's brothers and sisters had not survived infancy.

Over decades, the O'Briens hewed out an increasingly fruitful life on their ranch along the fertile bottomlands of the Trapper River. Part of the measure was that more children,

191

and then grandchildren, survived. Some of the offspring moved away to less sage-choked pastures. Others stayed with the original land. Gram married the neighbor boy at the height of the Great Depression. When Gram's father died just after Pearl Harbor, her husband and she moved into the big old house on the river. And when her husband died shortly after the election of John F. Kennedy, Gram took back the O'Brien name. She was proud of it.

Gram O'Brien lived happily as the family matriarch for another twenty years. Then came the troubled time when the power company fixed on Stubblefield as the site of a 1,500-megawatt coal-fired generating plant. The boilers and the cooling system needed considerable water, and that was where the Trapper River came in. Graystone Dam entered construction; the waters of the reservoir began to back up.

She fought it down to the wire in the courts, but the companies with their giant machinery and high-powered law firms won. The crews came in with bulldozers and chain saws and felled the thick old cottonwoods along the river. At the end, Gram would not move, no matter what the entreaties of Marge or her other children, or the grandchildren. On the final morning, the sheriff's deputies used fire axes to batter down Gram's door. Then, because they both feared and respected her, and because everyone knew her, they let Gram watch from the sheriff's car, at her own request, as the dozers moved in and the walls of the O'Brien house collapsed inward.

The new world of the changing West had defeated Gram. The question in a lot of minds was whether the defeat was permanent.

Gram signed herself into Riverview Manor, the new, clean, well-managed senior citizens' development in town. She had her own room in bright, decorator colors. O'Brien money would ensure that she was cared for. She could grow older gracefully, and finally die.

In the meantime, Gram lived on as the O'Brien land drowned beneath the spreading surface of Graystone Reservoir. As the first unit of the power plant went on-line and the six-hundred-foot stack belched steam, the slow flood overcame the original banks of the Trapper River.

I had seen the dry boneyards of stacked branches when I drove up the Interstate from Denver, but at first hadn't realized where the trees had come from. All I knew was that someone would have a lot of winter firewood. I'd made no direct connection as I looked north across town and watched the steady blinking of the aircraft-warning strobes on the three stacks.

Once in Stubblefield, I settled myself in a stark room at the Trapper Peak Motel and phoned Marge. She sounded glad to hear from me, for all the strain evident in her voice.

"Angie, can you come over right away? Not if you're too tired, but—"

"I'm walking out the door," I said. "Just give me directions."

Marge's trailer was parked in one of the mobile-home warrens that now claimed to be a suburb of the town. The development sprawled across what had been wheatfields and horse pastures when I'd lived in Stubblefield years before. In the twilight, the trailers gleamed like an underwater colony of mollusks. I found Marge's number and parked behind an old red Ford four-by-four. Out of my car, I edged past a beautiful husky on a frayed rope. The dog didn't give me a second look.

Marge answered the door as though she had been waiting on the knock. I thought she was approaching her forties well. Never the slimmest girl in junior high, she was getting a little hefty around the hips. But Marge's face was arresting. She'd told me once there was American Indian blood back a few generations. Time had tautened the skin over her cheeks, delineating a bone structure I envied.

We hesitated, time making us awkward. Then she hugged me. "Angie, it's so good to see you." She smelled fresh, smelled of pine and sun-dried laundry. "Thanks for coming."

Marge introduced me to her two Manx cats. The husky outside was Roger. Marge's sixteen-year-old daughter was on an overnight hike at the church camp on Trapper Peak.

She started talking a nervous streak, settling me on the living room couch and filling two schooner glasses with beer. At first I waited patiently for the nervous flood to abate.

"How's Gram?" I finally said.

"Gram?" Marge looked away from my eyes and toyed with the stem of her glass.

"Your mother. Remember?" I smiled.

"I'm worried sick."

"I figured that," I said. "You didn't sound terrific on the phone. You also didn't tell me anything."

Marge's cheeks went red. "I thought you'd think I was silly to worry at all."

"About *what?*" I said in exasperation. "Level with me."

"I think you can help me. I've heard you can help."

I looked at her quizzically.

"People always talked, Angie."

"Don't be coy," I said. "Come on. You were always a straight-arrow."

She met my gaze again. "You're a witch," she said.

"Of course I am. And now that you're divorced, you manage a hardware store, right?"

Marge nodded. She began to smile too. "Grommets and spells don't seem like the same ballpark."

" 'I can't fix a dripping faucet with magic," I said. "Now, what about Gram?"

Marge leaned back into the cushions, obviously starting to relax. Still, I thought I saw a spark of the modern rationalist burning back somewhere behind her eyes. On some level, Marge didn't believe my powers went any further than my MasterCard. On another level, she believed in and feared the powers. But she had sought me out.

"My mother's in the old people's home, you know that, right?" I nodded. "She keeps . . . disappearing," Marge said. "It's honest-to-God vanishing, and it happens almost every day."

"Maybe she just walks out the door."

"Nobody sees her go," said Marge.

"But she comes back?"

"So far."

"And safe?"

"Yes. So far."

"What's the problem?" I said.

"Gram's an old woman," Marge said. "She could get hurt

on her own. God knows where she goes. Nobody else does."

"So you want me to trace your mother's playing hooky?"

"Wherever she goes," said Marge. "Yes."

"Sure you don't need a professional detective?"

"Hired one up from Cheyenne. Not too bright, but he should have been good enough. Didn't tell me anything."

"So why me?"

Marge said desperately, "I feel like I need you."

And that was why I was driving down the graveled road to Graystone Dam and Reservoir, keeping a moderate distance behind the taxi which carried Gram O'Brien.

As for Gram's disappearing from Riverview Manor, well, I played a hunch. I had left Marge's early so I could make business hours in town. I stopped at the rock shop and bought a small chunk of iron ore from the Sunrise Mine. My toolbox furnished a file so I could supplement the ore with filings from a rusted cast-iron stove from the junkpile behind the motel. The nearest liquor store didn't have wine imported from much farther away than Boise, but that was all right. Back in my room, I used an immersion heater to boil the ore and filings in milk. Then I decanted the liquid into a plastic glass of wine. I debated for a moment, then put the mixture away until the morning. Luckily there was a second empty cup. I drank the rest of the wine and watched a Clint Eastwood movie on TV before dropping into an untroubled slumber.

In the morning, I had no appetite, but forced myself to go out to a cafe for a short stack and a glass of milk. Potions don't sit well on an empty stomach. Then I returned to the room and downed the concoction I'd fixed the night before. Up to a certain degree of fascination—of enchantment—I should have clear sight. I brushed my teeth twice.

At eight o'clock, I parked my Audi in a corner of the asphalt parking lot that commanded a view of the Manor from two sides. Shortly before ten, I saw a familiar figure stroll out of the rear firedoor. Hair gray as slate and rolled up beneath a scarf, Gram looked little different from my memories of her from the 'sixties. Stouter, maybe, but her posture was still as ramrod-rigid.

Gram walked right past an aide taking out some trash. The aide looked through her, oblivious to the woman's presence.

She stepped quickly down the walk to the street and turned west. I waited thirty seconds, then started the Audi and followed her. Gram walked until she came to the telephone booth beside the Texaco station. She made a call; ten minutes later, one of the town's two taxis pulled up. I recognized Petey Winston looking gray and emaciated, the same as he had when he drove school buses while I was growing up. The taxi pulled away and I followed.

The road to the dam led past the three blocky generating units of the power station. Closer to the reservoir, it was lined with candy-striped metal poles, each with an attached plate that read TRAPPER RIVER STATION WATER SUPPLY HORIZONTAL CURVE, or WATER SUPPLY AIR VACUUM VALVE, or WATER SUPPLY BLOWOFF, or any of a dozen other esoteric designations. I took time to notice those things, hanging back, pretending to have no interest in the vehicle ahead. Besides, I'm always curious about other people's arcana.

I crossed a rise and saw the reservoir lying to my left. The water held the startling deep blue of the sky before a storm. Stratified layers of sandstone lay in streaks of tan and beige upslope from the waterline. The earthen dam sprawled new, the blade-cuts in the soil raw, the cubical concrete pumping station stark and unfinished. Someday the drowned valley would be a community recreation area. A rough reef of brown fill segregated a long, narrow slash of water that would become a small marina.

We passed a flagwoman in her red safety vest, sitting reading *The Dead Zone* beside a chocolate-colored van. She glanced up and pointed to her CAUTION sign. I slowed down. No one in the taxi ahead seemed to have noticed the admonition.

Another quarter mile, and the road coiled closer to the water, passing a compound enclosed in hurricane fence. An unlikely row of potted palm trees lined the south side of one of the construction trailers. Doubtful in this climate—I knew that. But almost anything might happen in this hushed valley. I couldn't identify any of them directly, but my intuitions were beginning to push buttons.

Eventually the road would be paved, completed, and would lead across the top of the dam. Not yet. The road ended at the foot of the newly dozed hill rising against the east.

I saw brake lights flicker through the dust. I slalomed between the red and yellow rag flags tacked to lath, pulled off the road, and parked. Then I got out of the Audi and stood beside the hood. A few hundred yards closer to the dam, the taxi slewed around in its dirty cloud and roared back toward me. As he passed my car, Petey Winston smiled and waved. Momentarily at a loss, I waved back.

The dust began to settle and I saw Gram O'Brien. She walked briskly down the gentle slope toward the water. The sun dazzle gleamed like burnished armor.

Gram O'Brien waded into the water.

Was it safe? asked an inner voice. Of course not. Were the deadfalls all snagged out and safely hauled away? I had seen the wooden mausoleum along the Interstate.

The reservoir was up to her shoulders. To her neck.

Swimming? I thought. Fully clothed? What was she *doing*? She always comes back. So far, Marge had said.

The water closed silently over Gram's head. The ripples of her passage were gone.

I ran toward the beach, hopping on one foot as I wrestled with a knotted shoelace, then hopping on the other as I stepped on something sharp and shearing. Jeans and sweater off. I dropped my watch. Into the reservoir. The floor dropped off rapidly and I was swimming. I tried to guess where I had last seen the top of Gram's head, and dived.

The water slapped me like a wet towel someone had stored in the freezer. The darkness was instant and complete. The voice in my mind kept asking what happened to that bright, sunny morning above me. I couldn't see a damn thing, just kept stroking down.

And then—

It was years ago. I remember driving across central Illinois in the early summer when almost anything I could see

*through the windshield was lush in shades of green. Then I
looked at the sky. Reversed-field images—tricks to play on
the eye: first you see something like a dark candelabrum
surrounded by white space . . . look again, and you see two
faces in profile separated by darkness.*

*I stared at the sky and no longer sat in my roommate's
blue Pontiac thrumming down the two-lane blacktop. The
clouds borrowed the swept texture of beach; the open sky
claimed the deep blue of ocean. The plane I now piloted
banked high above the crescent meeting of sea and land.
Reality had reversed. For much longer than a moment, I
didn't know which reality I should believe.*

—I lost my orientation in the cold and black. I didn't
know whether I still angled down, or if my increasingly
clumsy strokes hauled me toward the surface.

Pain ached in my lungs. Suddenly, hysterically, I blessed
stopping smoking for giving back some of my breath. The
pressure in the top of my chest demanded I spit out all the
air I held in one long silver bubble.

Light. I saw it gleam above me—or below me. I still didn't
know the referent. But I swam toward the light, a radiance
that throbbed like a beacon. It warmed me. It wasn't the
sun shining through the surface. It was more like—

Summer.

—as I burst through a subtle barrier of heat and brightness and whispering touches like wind on my skin. The sudden flower of pain blossomed in my chest and my lungs let
go their oxygen-starved load. I gulped in—air. Not water.
Air. I fell to my knees on a grassy slope and took in great
heaving gasps of air.

When my heart finally slowed to something close to nor-
mal, I saw that I was kneeling on the bank of the Trapper
River—not the great bloated worm of the reservoir, but the
river as it had once been, the river I remembered from the
hikes and picnics and raft trips. Shakily, I stood and looked
around.

The sunny morning I had left was still here. I turned from
the river bank and tried to get an orientation. I couldn't see
my car. More dramatically, the dam was gone. So were the
pumping station, construction buildings, palm trees, and all
the rest.

I turned parallel to the river and started to walk downstream toward the O'Brien house. The house sat about a hundred yards ahead of me. The frame construction with the three upstairs dormers, the picket fence and gate hanging open because the latch was broken, the immaculate white siding, all were as familiar as the lines in an old friend's face.

I hesitated. There *was* no O'Brien house. The bulldozers had splintered it to kindling. I thought I saw the house ahead of me waver. My eyes watered suddenly and I shook my head. I felt a small blade of pain twist in my chest. The image of the house solidified as I concentrated. The pain receded and I walked closer.

Again I hesitated. I was padding through the grass on bare feet. I was dressed only in panties and teeshirt. My clothing wasn't wet.

Again I slowly turned in a complete circle. No power plant loomed in the west. Only clouds climbed above Trapper Peak—no steam plume. Something else lacked. I realized I could hear no traffic hum from I-25, no snarling downshifts of trucks slowing for a coffee stop in town. I heard wind sighing off the eastern plain as it dipped toward the mountains. That was all.

I continued toward the white house. At the gate I stopped because of the throbbing ache in my foot. I balanced on one leg in a clumsy, hopping little dance and checked. The deep cut in the sole of my left foot oozed blood. I remembered I had sliced it when I was trying to get to the beach. Getting to the beach to pursue Gram O'Brien. Seeing her disappear into the reservoir with the cold water lapping over her head. Following. Diving. Finding myself—

"I do declare," said a voice from years out of my past. I let my leg straighten and looked up. Gram O'Brien, framed by the porch swing and the open screen door, stood on the porch. She smiled and motioned me to approach. "Angela?"

I smiled back at her and nodded.

"Angela, you're all grown up. You hurt your foot, dear? Come on up here and I'll take a look at it. A little tincture of merthiolate and a bandage, and you'll be right as rain. Then we'll sit in the living room and visit and I'll fix you some iced tea. There's a batch of oatmeal cookies just coming out of the oven, too."

I heard the clink of ice cubes from my childhood. The smell of fresh-baked cookies seduced my nose. I started toward her. "Gram, good morning." The smiling, robust woman radiated vigor and warmth. She was just as I remembered her.

And then, once through the gate, I crossed into the shadow of the cottonwoods. The largest of the trees had grown for more than a century along the bank of the Trapper. Gram's father had planted pine to complete the windbreak. The trees also worked as a natural air-conditioner in the summer.

Their shadows chilled me.

I stopped and looked up at the broad, strong limbs made for climbing and just right for nailing up tree houses. I *knew* those trees were dead. I had seen the boneyards of chainsawed branches lining the Interstate for a mile. Dynamite and caterpillar tractors had uprooted these giants from their home. Flatbeds and work crews had transported them to a mass grave.

"Child, you come up here!"

I heard the urgency in her voice, but couldn't concentrate on making that first step to the porch. Gram's face shivered, just as the house had wavered before. I tried to climb. My foot went right through the tread as though it weren't there.

"Angela!"

I opened my mouth to speak, to tell Gram something was wrong, but water flooded in. I coughed, choked, sucked water down my throat and into my lungs. The chill, dull ache spread all through me.

Panic came when I knew I couldn't breathe. I flailed my arms, could do nothing else, no control, could see nothing more than lights bursting in retinal darkness.

I strained to breathe, ached to scream, and then the numbing weight across my chest froze all that. There was nothing else. The lights no longer burst.

I awoke slowly with stitches of agony drumming along both sides of my ribcage. It really did hurt to breathe. But at least I was breathing.

It occurred to me finally to open my eyes. Then it occurred to me to try to focus. I saw fluorescent lights first. It was the waking-up-in-the-hospital cliché. I focused on the pointillist patterns surrounding the lights and, after what seemed a long time, felt the revelation that I must be staring at holes in the acoustical tile.

"Angie? You're awake now, aren't you?"

The holes in the ceiling truly fascinated me.

"Angie, are you alive?"

I forced myself to turn my head on the hard pillow and looked past a spray of purple flowers. Marge's expression seemed worried. Tears glossed her dark eyes. She tried to smile as she reached out to touch my hair. "Damn it, Angie, say something."

"Uh," I said, "where am I?"

"County Memorial," said Marge. She managed the smile at last. "You're drying out."

"When—"

Marge checked her watch. "It's about five. You've been here since before noon. Everybody's been wondering if you were going to wake up at all."

I noticed the tubes in my arm. "Did I drown?"

"Obviously not completely," said Marge. "Gram pulled you out of the water."

"Gram—?"

Marge nodded. "Some guys at the construction trailers saw her dragging you up onto the beach."

"My ribs hurt like hell."

"Amateur CPR," said Marge. "A two hundred twenty pound construction jock worked you over pretty good. They used a CB to raise an ambulance from town. Doc said you were real close." She began to cry in earnest. "But you made it," she said between sobs.

I reached across my body with my right hand and clumsily squeezed her arm. "I'm okay," I said, hoping I sounded more positive than I felt. "Tell me some more what happened."

Marge's eyes brimmed again and she honked into a Kleenex. "Tell *me* what happened! What were you and Gram doing out at the reservoir? Why were you in the water?" Her voice kept rising unsteadily. "What was going on, Angie?" Her fingers dug into my shoulder.

I realized each of us was grasping the other as though we both were trying to save a drowning woman. I consciously loosened my grip first. After a time, Marge did the same.

"What happened?" she said again.

"I'm still figuring it out," I said. "It was all very—odd."

Her face seemed to mirror a sad triumph. "So I was right?"

"About what?"

"To get you to help. Instead of the Hardy Boys again."

I couldn't help laughing, even if my ribs seemed to flare incandescently. "You were right, Marge."

Marge's voice tightened. "I still want to know what happened in the reservoir. You almost drowned, Angie. What did my mother have to do with that?"

I had ridden on Gram's coattails, I thought. My brain still meshed fuzzily, but something irised down into shocking clarity. "Where's Gram?" I said. "How is she?"

Marge suddenly looked like someone had slammed her across the stomach with a pole. As if on cue, machinery squeaked from beyond the open doorway in the hospital corridor. I glanced up past Marge. A nurse pushed an old woman in a wheelchair past the room. The woman was Gram O'Brien.

I looked her in the eyes for just a moment. Gram didn't see me. Her eyes were dull and drug-glazed. I stared back at Marge. "What did they *do* to her?"

Marge hesitated. Finally she said, "It's not just them. I agreed with the doctor."

"Gram's doped to the eyeballs."

Marge nodded slowly. "It's just sedation. It's only temporary."

I said evenly, "You can't keep her caged up that way."

"Just for a while. I don't want her to be hurt any more."

I ignored the platitude. "What are you so afraid of?" I put my hand back on hers. Things started to lock into place in my mind like tumblers falling in sequence.

"I'm afraid for you because of what happened. I'm afraid for Gram because of what she might do next."

I could almost see the patterns now. "To herself? To you?

The rest of the family? To others?" Marge shook her head, mute. I had the feeling that her answer should be: *to all of us.*

"If I send her back to the home," Marge said, "she'll just keep on walking away."

The fluorescents didn't vary in intensity, but the room might as well have been plunged into clear white light. "Take her home," I said. "*Your* home—not Riverview Manor." Marge didn't meet my gaze. "Do this for me. It's my advice. Believe me when I say it's more than just important. Take her home and get her off the goddamned pills." The twinges in my sides irritated me. "And while you're at it, take me home too. Call the doctor now. It doesn't matter how we do it, but I'm getting out of here." I caught Marge's eye and she slowly nodded.

I lay back against the pillow and started to gather my strength.

Sometimes I have to be reminded that clear sight doesn't necessarily need to generate from spells or potions.

Naturally it didn't turn out to be as easy to escape from County Memorial as it had been for Gram to walk out of Riverview Manor. The doctor wasn't minded to let me go all that quickly. Finally Marge mediated a compromise: I would stay in the hospital overnight for observation. If I didn't turn blue or my lungs collapse before morning, I'd be let go. Marge was, however, able to get instant custody of her mother, contingent upon repeated promises to keep the old woman quiet and unexcited. My room was in the hospital wing facing the street, and I watched as Marge and an orderly wheeled Gram out to the Ford truck like some elderly vegetable in a shopping chart.

That night I dreamed a violent dream.

I stood on the bank of the Trapper River, looking up at the power plant. Low on the horizon behind it, the sun haloed the blocky structure in a fuzz of crimson. Then it was as though the ground itself rose up and fell upon the plant with the crazy violence of a mad-man wielding a hammer. Brick separated from brick, cinder block from block, and concrete pulverized to powder, leaving twisted spaghetti works of steel reinforcing rods. What had taken years to build was devastated in a second.

The dust hurt my eyes and I rubbed them.

Gram O'Brien stood beside me atop the vast heap of rubble. Beside us both stood Marge. An aura of ghostly radiance spread like St. Elmo's fire around the three of us. Gram turned in a half-circle to survey the buckled cooling towers, the collapsed steam stacks. Then she swung back to face Marge.

Marge looked away, turned away, walked away. The radiance continued to limn her, trailing after like sparkling mist. Gram spread her hands helplessly, standing fast and watching. Marge's image diminished in the distance. Gram turned to face me and slowly shook her head.

I stood alone on the hill of broken stone and felt first grim satisfaction, and then the sadness, the grief of loss.

Marge came to collect me late in the morning. By that time, the doctor had checked my vital signs and given me a lecture concerning the dangers of cramps while swimming. When that was over, I pieced together a clean outfit from the bag Marge had brought me the day before from the motel. Dressed, I waited impatiently until I saw her park in front of the hospital.

"How's Gram?" I said in the truck.

"Pretty much out of it. She slept all night. I got her some breakfast this morning, but she was groggy. When I left, she was sleeping again." As an apparent afterthought, Marge said, "I sent Lily over to her father's." Lily was Marge's daughter. I had wanted to meet her.

"What for?" I said.

"Seems like a good idea." She shrugged slightly. "Whatever's happening, right now I don't want it to involve any more than the three of us." Her voice was firmer than I'd heard it before.

I wasn't as steady on my feet as I'd thought. Once back at the trailer, we sat and drank tea. Every ten or fifteen minutes, Marge would check her mother sleeping in the bedroom. The first time, I accompanied her. Gram looked much shorter asleep. More vulnerable. She snored peacefully.

Late in the afternoon, Marge called my name from the bedroom. I walked in and found Marge sitting at the head of the bed, and Gram stirring.

"Thank God," said Marge. "It's about time."

Gram's eyes, disconcertingly green and focused, snapped open. She looked from Marge to me and back to her daughter. "I truly do loathe hospitals," she said. "Child, you should have brought me home immediately." Marge said nothing. "You look a little peaked," Gram said to me. "How is that bum foot, Angela?"

I glanced down even though I couldn't see the bandage. "It's just fine," I said.

"Now," said Gram, "Would one of you please get me a hot cup of tea?"

Marge obeyed without a word.

The old woman and I stared at each other.

"I'm glad I could get you out of the valley," she said.

"Me too."

She exhaled deeply. "You saw."

"I know what I *think* I saw."

"It's evident that you're a woman of powers."

"I could say the same to you," I said. I heard a cup smash in the kitchen.

"I've had longer to become adept." Gram smiled. "Between my Celtic forebears and my Menomonee blood, I seem to have a feel for it."

"When I was growing up," I said, "I had no idea about you."

"Nor I about you," said Gram. "I guess early-on we all learn to be pretty self-protective."

Marge came back into the room gingerly carrying Gram's tea. The cup clattered in the saucer. She sat down and watched her mother sip.

"My daughter's self-protective," Gram said. Her voice stayed gentle, but added: "If she had her way, she'd stay deaf, dumb, and blind." Marge's face tightened. "But, then, most everybody in the family's the same these days. I've had hopes for Lily—she's still young and open."

"Shut up!" Marge's fingers whitened around the arms of her chair. She immediately looked chagrined at having snapped at her mother.

"My family." Gram looked rueful. "No one wants our legacy."

"Legacy!" said Marge. "Curse."

"Nothing sinister about it," said Gram evenly. "There's certainly nothing shameful in being what a body can be. You're my daughter. Just like Lily, down deep you have the powers too."

"Superstition," said Marge, her voice compressed.

"You know better," I said to her. "We've talked. You can't have it both ways."

"I want to leave," Marge said. "I want to walk through that door and go for good." She stood and started toward the door. Power seemed to hum, to rise. I felt like the room was awash in electricity. Marge stopped. I knew I wasn't halting her. I had the feeling that neither was it Gram. The power rose, subsided, rose again.

"It's not something you should fight," I said to Marge, "any more than you can fight having the genes for red hair and green eyes and fine cheek bones."

"I just don't want it," said Marge. She reminded me of a bundle of willows, bowed and bound by fragile twine, ready to burst apart.

"But you've got it," I answered. "Now don't walk away from it." I looked from Marge back to Gram. "Don't walk away from her." I wasn't sure which of them I meant to say it to.

No one said anything for several minutes. Then something in Marge's rigid posture seemed to melt. "Angie," she said, her voice low, "I want to talk to my mother."

I looked at them both and got up and left.

Outside the trailer, I sat on the bottom step. The Siberian husky, Roger, came up to me and tried to lick my face. I gathered him into my arms and hugged him, burying my face in his fur, until his ribs must have been every bit as sore as mine.

I sat in the shade of the tall, gnarled cottonwoods, drinking iced tea with lemon and just a little sugar. I sat in a comfortable lawn chair beside the woman of powers, the woman who knew the special sense of the land.

I was vacationing outside the world, and enjoying it.

I was living inside a ghost.

"I expect I could kill the power plant with a long-time drought," Gram said. "I could manage that. But I don't want to. I've got too many old friends still dry-land farming on the Flats. They need their wheat." She refilled my glass. Moisture beaded the outside of the pitcher. "Surely is a lovely morning, Angela."

I nodded and half-closed my eyes. Broken by branches, sunlight dappled my face with patches of heat. The patches moved as wind swayed the crowns of the trees.

"Course, I could do something directly to the plant people," Gram continued, "make all the women barren and cause the men's penises to fall off." She shook her head. "Guess I just don't have the mean streak any more. Besides, they didn't come up with the idea of killing the land. They're just trying to make a living like everyone else."

I opened my eyes and looked slowly around at the impossible serenity of this place. "How long do you figure you can go on living in the middle of the ghost of a drowned valley?" I said.

"Until I pass on." Her tone was certain. "The shade will remain long after I've gone. It will be here offering refuge to anyone who believes, anybody who's willing to see it."

"Marge?"

"Perhaps eventually. Marge, or Lily. Or you. You see now. You believe, and so the shade accepts you."

"I love it here," I said.

"It is seductive. It certainly is a place to kill time." She chuckled and got up from her chair. "Time for chocolate-chip cookies to come out of the oven." Gram moved toward the white-painted porch. "When you go back, will you tell my daughter I'm doing the only thing I can?"

I promised I would, but added, "I truly believe she'll be finding out for herself."

Gram turned back toward me from the kitchen doorway and nodded slightly. "I suspect she will." She hesitated. "You helped, Angela, and I do thank you." Then she looked at me fiercely and said, "You should leave soon and go back. You still have another life."

"Soon," I agreed, again closing my eyes and hearing the

screen door click shut. Soon. Didn't I deserve some rest? I'd always found peace for me in precious poor supply.

I started to relax. Soon I would walk away from this valley and return to the world.

That was clear sight.

Born in White Plains, New York, in 1945, Edward Bryant was raised on a cattle ranch in Wyoming and educated at the University of Wyoming. In 1978 he won a Nebula award for his short story, "Stone," and in 1979 he repeated with "giANTS" (sic.). Cinnabar (1976), about a city of the far future in which mankind can at last fulfill its final dreams, is his best-known book.

Reveling in old memories can sometimes revive things best left undisturbed.

THIRTEEN

The Attic
Billy Wolfenbarger

Brown spiders lurched drunkenly all over Ray Bowen's dreams and he had a rough time filtering them out. Tiny splotches of yellowish mold were littered across their ugly backs. But he'd begun the dream without them. The time was the present and yet it was many years ago, when he lived on Venice Beach and the great romance of voluntary poverty burned and shone in his soul as mysterious and intense as the nearer October stars. Feeble layers of darkness had come on, with only a rosy ghost-glow shuttling atop the restless Pacific. He'd tread from Ocean Front Walk, which fronted the beach, with three friends who had little to say, past Pacific Ocean Park at the edge of Venice West to Santa Monica where the bright, glary lights of the Santa Monica Pier dazzled in gaudy wonder.

The beach itself was relatively empty. All the noises emanating from the people and the 'amusements' along the pier helped populate their unmarked path, all of which was company Bowen didn't need. His friends all talked of silly, uninteresting and purely mundane things—nothing to inspire melancholy phantasmagorias or poetry. Bowen smoked a joint with them as they walked, and all shared a small can of tuna fish, which was their dinner and perhaps their breakfast as well. Then, as far as social amenities would permit, Ray Bowen stopped in his tracks and told these friends of his he was heading back to Venice. There was no problem here at all. The other three were determined to make for the Pier to pick up on chicks and wine and some more dope— with which Bowen could sympathize—but they'd blow it, they'd get too loud and rowdy, and get Bowen paranoid.

Let them go. As he trod across the darkening sands, leaving the din of the world behind, Bowen buttoned the one button of his corduroy jacket, put his hands in blue jeans pockets and watched more stars come on, walking nearer to the ocean's gossiping lip.

Darkness brought the cold. A misted fog was piling up over the ocean, and would soon enough reach Venice beach. Bowen had enough change for a hot cup of good coffee at the Venice West cafe, the best place in town. He'd have to see if he could crash someplace besides the beach tonight.

He was filled with a kind of necromantic enchantment—that is to say, stoned on the beach at night, anxious now for coffee and to fill his pocket notebook with poems and his dreams. Farther up, past where he was going and from which he would detour the beach, a jazz bongo played, primitive and real; a flute joined, as though it had always meant to be there. The music seeped into his blood. The ocean hissed, or the beach, or the oncoming fog, he couldn't be sure; and the cold came, stronger. Bowen was aware that he was very much alive. He could see them now, mere blots or blobs in the misty darkness, local musicians and oldtime Bohemians out by the rocky point, lively in the California night. Bowen snapped his fingers to the beat, and they played rhythms that got down to cellular structures. The fog came pouring upon a wave from that ancient sea to cast it among the sands and the obscure figures by the point were lost to him. Strands of infinitely thin lines shot down from an invisible sky, down which brown spiders hastily manoeuvred, scrabbling over the sands as though blind and desperate, groping, lurching, horrible and intense. They moved to him and away from him, littering the beach with their ugly bodies where tiny splotches of yellowed mold covered their backs like motes of consciousness.

With a groan of agony he awoke, shaking spiders and beach and music and California night from his head. He was on a tattered sofa in Oregon. Night brimmed darkness. A train echoed past, a quarter of a mile away. At last it disappeared into the mouth of silence. Years had passed. In October it would be sixteen years. It was the lapse of May in the country where Bowen still wrote his poetry in notebooks, transcribing them later on a typewriter he had now, both typewriter and notebooks keeping him company through the evening hours, in the night years.

The little house Ray Bowen lived in now was over ninety years old, though far from stately. It had one small bedroom upstairs, which he rarely used after living here in farmland-surrounding country quietly for five years. Adjoining it by a rude door was the attic, always dark, surrounding the remaining length of the house. He'd been inside only very rarely; he never had that much junk to store away. Once he'd used a flashlight; batteries had gone out, and he'd never bothered replacing them—candles would serve as well.

A sea of unwritten poetry swept over him as he prepared coffee, though not yet a crescendo of feelings and images, words and lines he could set to any paper. And it would be dark verse, when it finally came. He recalled his dream and tried to forget it. The poem would be about the last days of humanhood, and of a wine which runed little songs in the dark. Like infinity a wind came up, blowing words across a moonless beach, and this gave him a flickering touch of fright—a thing beyond mere unease—to be time-travelling in a lonely old country house without the compulsive inclination to do so.

Rain realmed the roof without warning, a common Northwest event, slowly, steadily, which only helped intensify the silences. Peering through green curtains, he witnessed the far distant glowing of a street light by the black-topped road, revealing nothing. Otherwise, from the background of his kitchen light, Bowen saw only the eye-glinting husk of his reflection. Standing, he sipped his coffee. Let it rain. Sometimes the rain would be a trillion tiny voices sounding as one, moving through the silence. And on a dream-haunted evening as this one, he needed their companionship. Restless, the poem far from formed in his mind, he sought some music of the spheres. This is a job for Mozart, he thought, and let the *Jupiter Symphony* retaliate his gloomings.

Bowen wanted to travel far from the dreams, which might come at any time now. He listened to his thoughts until they

bounded between the limits of his skull. It took a long while
for Mozart to seep through.

Restlessness gnawed him like an old wound, and he cir-
culated between rooms, drinking the coffee held in his large
warm hand—kitchen to dining room to living room where
music was clearest, more divine. At random he picked up
Beethoven to play next, then wandered, then sat in the living room, violins swelling in his head. Too restless for reading or writing, he'd have to simply wait it out dully or
activate himself past it.

Exhausted, Mozart ended and rain tapped at windows,
ran across the roof and Beethoven's *Fifth Symphony*
boomed out. Ray Bowen poured himself another cup of
coffee, then selected two fat white candles, lit one, flopped
the other in his jacket pocket and, holding coffee and candle, slowly walked up the fifteen wooden stairway steps with
spiderwebs long growing out of each inner corner and the
faded flowered paper on the wall grown to tender pulp. It
reminded him of so many funky beatnik apartments. With a
heartless shrug he continued, only three splintered steps
groaning near the top. Then he'd reached the tiny landing
leading to the bedroom, and strode four giant steps to face
the candlelit-flickering attic door, the old paint a color between white and grey.

Without another thought he set down coffee, opened the
door whose knob was a small, single-nailed square of wood,
then ventured the hand which held the light inside, sending
dust-moted shadows flying away from him, shuddering into
silent recesses. Stooping for his cup, Bowen wondered what
the hell he was doing. None of this had anything to do with
the as yet unwritten poem. He entered, leaving the door
half open, although it seemed more like half closed.

He had lured a stray tomcat up here not long ago, who'd
grown fat quickly on the mice. The tom had been quite
thorough. Later he'd sent the cat away, and as yet mice or
rats hadn't entered. But up here, in here now, he could in-
tangibly smell the fear, gigantic, which the rodents hadn't
lived through.

A pine footstool resided here, and Ray Bowen made a
shapeless mass of shadows die or trickily retreat—he
couldn't tell which—as he seated himself and made a can-

dle-holding wax pool atop an overturned tuna fish can. Also
nearby was a cracked blue plastic saucer, which he used for
the second candle, placing it more or less behind him and
farther away. Shadows died or ghosted into light. Illuminated with sight, only the far opposite corners remained
abysmal. It was true he didn't have much junk up here—
he'd never had much of anything anywhere. He'd always
wished he'd had a storage trunk of some sort, but no. He
did have cardboard boxes and one orange crate, lonely
and mute as vegetable children. He swallowed coffee and
looked around, listening to tattering Oregon rain and
Beethoven settling down again, though gathering for the
next sensory onslaught. Mozart had been kinder. A brave
brown spider dangled seven inches from his eyes, and
Bowen grabbed the webstrand above it, moving the thing
hastily into candleflame. He enjoyed watching it crisp. He
dug sand out of his eyes. He must be tiring after all. Tides
broke, rushing tentacled seaweed across a shoreline. He
took long deep breaths, trying to calm himself. Tree
branches, the height of the attic, washing in a wind. Ab-
sently tugging a cigarette from a fresh pack, Bowen returned to Venice without knowing why, bumming a smoke
and spare change on the beach in chilling winter, shivering
in his insubstantial jacket, wanting to be anywhere at that
moment but where he was. Groaning, he got the cigarette
lit, the tin can jittering in his hand. He set it carefully upon
the dusty floor. Hell of a note if he burned himself alive up
here. Hell of a note to be bummed up here in the first place,
he thought. Looking at his shoes, he remembered the time
he'd walked from Hollywood to Los Angeles with a kilo of
weed in a brown paper bag, errand for a friend. It had taken
all day long. His suffering feet. . . . Stabbing the cigarette
between lips, he reached outward with arms and hands and
pulled a box before his feet. Opening up the flaps, he suddenly remembered the contents and, as Bowen folded the
flaps back into place without looking, moisture formed in
each eye. He didn't *want* to remember why he'd kept these
old science fiction magazines he'd purchased when he was
sixteen and seventeen and living at his mother's house in so
long ago Missouri, before he'd taken off on the road and
found himself gazing at the wino bums dooming through

Los Angeles, and so spaced in Venice West he couldn't get any poetry written for months, when every waking moment had been concerned with the simple hassle of survival. He didn't *need* to remember when his notebooks of over eight hundred poems and his clothing in a backpack had been stolen by a spade businessman who'd stopped to give him a lift as he was hitching to Texas. Those old ghosts had no right to haunt him. They'd already haunted him for years afterwards; there'd been far enough pain already. Enough fear had washed over him to suffice twenty lifetimes. He shoved the box back with his foot.

Below, the last note dramatized the pouring rain, pelting roof and Ray Bowen's attic thoughts. He crushed the cigarette in the saucer, roaming with cup in hand. Candle-glow flickered across the shaft of chimney. Leaning a hand upon an overhanging rafter, palm and fingers pulled away years of dust. He coughed, disgusted. Underneath, his shoe crushed a vagabond pot seed. Bowen retreated, setting his cup down and picking up his saucer candle, setting it near the orange crate. It contained only a moth-eaten army blanket and a pair of moldy, toe-cracked boots he'd worn, not new even then, on his way to Miami; he'd been very grateful for the ride with the speedfreak trucker in the middle of nowhere, the highway surrounded by swampland, tired, hungry and bummed as he spied the alligator, swamplord of the highway.

Moving to a cardboard box, Bowen opened it, peering inside. Old clothing. On top was a black and white checked shirt he'd worn tripping on mescaline for the first time—two caps synthetic—with two friends, four-thirty or five Sunday morning, watching the slow seepings of tides pulling inward, the incredible wash of beach, though later to find the gross, horny gyrations of the fifty year old obese woman writhing and grovelling and pawing herself naked in sickeningly obscene gestures, making Bowen and the others want to vomit. They hurried away, away.

Another box, lidless, contained only dust—though he peered deeper, to the bottom and found phantom memories of his father (couldn't he hear him now?) as he rocked in a rocking chair, little Ray on his knee; and the outside shell of his father formed, hazily grey, his German tombstone ghostily glimmering in the space where the head would have been—buried these long absent years since World War Two. Bowen wept, the tears would never stop, and these tears hit the bottom of the box in tiny beads, the dust surrounding them rising and falling within the blink of an eye, back into the years that might as well have been centuries.

God, this was enough of all this. He moaned, pulling at his beard, roaming in the night attic in the evening years, glooming past the attic window as rain drooled down the glass. Bowen took another look outside where spiders, brown and phosphorescent, were begging desperate entry.

Bowen blew out candles and, groping through blackness, turned once fleetingly to see the decomposing ghosts of all the women he'd ever loved trying to lurch out of boxes. Scrabbling down the stairs, he shut the door and locked it, passing a window where spiders cried, lurching and tumbling down ropes of Oregon rain.

Born in Missouri in 1942, Billy Wolfenbarger worked at a variety of jobs before settling down in Oregon to write full-time. A published poet (his latest collection is The Wind Is My Brother, *1978), he has recently turned to fiction. "The Attic" was his first, and it was selected for E. E. Wagner's* Year's Best Horror Stories *(1984).*

Acknowledgements

"Harry's Ghost"—Copyright © 1973 by Talmage Powell. Reprinted by permission of the author.

"Pretty Maggie Moneyeyes"—Copyright © 1967 by Sirkay Publishing Company. Copyright reassigned to author 19 September 1967. Reprinted by arrangement with, and permission of, the author and the author's agent, Richard Curtis Associates, Inc., New York. All rights reserved.

"In the Memory Room"—Copyright © 1987 by Michael Bishop. Reprinted from *The Architecture of Fear* by permission of the author.

"Resurrection"—Copyright © 1989 by *The Chariton Review*. Reprinted by permission of the author.

"Custer's Ghost"—Copyright © 1983 by Clark Howard. First published in *Ellery Queen's Mystery Magazine*. Reprinted by permission of the author.

"The Resting Place"—Copyright © 1954 by Oliver La Farge. Copyright © renewed 1982 by John Pendaries La Farge. Reprinted by permission of Marie Rodell-Frances Collin Literary Agency.

"One of the Dead"—Copyright © 1964 by William Wood. Reprinted by permission of the author.

"The Ghosts of Steamboat Coulee"—Copyright © 1926 by *Weird Tales*. Reprinted by arrangement with Forrest J. Ackerman, 2495 Glendower Avenue, Los Angeles, CA 90027.

"That Which Hath Wings"—Copyright © 1938 by The Curtis Publishing Company; Copyright © renewed 1966 by Paul Gallico. Reprinted by permission of Harold Ober Associates Incorporated.

"In the Shade"—Copyright © 1982 by Edward Bryant. First appeared in *The Magazine of Fantasy and Science Fiction*. Reprinted by permission of the author.

"The Attic"—Copyright © 1983 by Billy Wolfenbarger. Reprinted by permission of the author.